# THE

# NOVEMBER

# MOLECULE

## S. F. RICHARDS

Book layout and interior design by Lisa Gilliam

ISBN: 979-8-9879412-0-1 (hardcover)
ISBN: 979-8-9879412-1-8 (paperback)
ISBN: 979-8-9879412-2-5 (ebook)

*For Daddy*

# PROLOGUE

*The deadliest weapon in the world is a
Marine and his rifle.*

—General John Pershing,
US Army

ONE SHOT. ONE HIT. *OORAH!*

Underneath the orange glow of a setting sun in Islamabad, Pakistan, Secretary of State Elizabeth Rhodes collapsed onto the cooling tarmac as blood trailed from her shoulder and collected into a crimson halo around her head, soaking her soft auburn hair. Her security detail ducked low to the ground and scanned the area while nearby military personnel screamed, "Everybody down! Get down! Now! Now, goddamnit, down!"

The regular airport security personnel had been replaced with Marine Corps snipers due to the perceived high threat and local unrest, a measure put in place to ensure the safety of the United States SOS, who now lay in a pool of her own blood. Commercial flights had been delayed to allow the Boeing C-32 to land without fanfare or incident. Other than the pilots and the SOS, the only people on the tarmac were Diplomatic Security special agents and highly trained special ops military personnel—there couldn't have been a more secure spot on the planet.

Based on the *crack-thump* and the angle, sniper spotter Chance Martinez looked to his right and up. On the airport rooftop, his best friend crouched low against a parapet, nevertheless visible to a trained spotter. *What the fuck? Bishop?* Martinez raised his M40 rifle and looked through the scope in time to see the muzzle flash of the second shot, which hit a nearby special agent, already down on the ground, in the back. A third shot whizzed past, barely missing him. *Fuck me.* Martinez wiped the sweat from his forehead and took aim at his friend. From the rooftop perch, USMC Scout Sniper Joey Bishop appeared to be watching the chaos unfold as he continued to fire until the return fire from a member of his own company hit him right between the eyes.

UNITED STATES ARMED SERVICES REPORT

The US Secretary of State was hit in her left shoulder—the result of friendly fire—shortly after landing in Islamabad. Military personnel responded, mortally wounding USMC Lance Corporal and Scout Sniper Joseph Bishop.

That was what the official Armed Services Committee investigative report would say. That and nothing more.

# CHAPTER 1

H E WAS PERFECT.

He was a liar. *Check.*

He was reckless. *Check.*

He needed the money. *Check. Check.*

Her computer screen glowed, cascades of files and open tabs revealing all of his secrets, his darkest moments and worst habits—some of them the kind you don't even tell your best friend about—and now all of them were laid bare, and she catalogued them with great precision. She knew everything about him. How he liked his coffee, his gym routines, his checking account balance, his favorite sex position. Everything she needed to get everything she wanted was staring back at her. This was it. She'd be a hero for this. And she'd make *General.* The word slipped through her lips. General Savarre. She suppressed a smile.

Outside her window, a Japanese maple clung to its few remaining scarlet leaves as the wind gusted ahead of a cold front. Max, her Siamese cat, had positioned himself in the window to watch the neighbor's Chihuahua run in circles. Savarre leaned back into her chair and cupped her ceramic coffee mug from Starbucks—a Christmas gift from her parents that had arrived a week late with a bag of fair-trade French roast and a stock card that read "Happy Holidays from Mom and Dad"—while she considered the situation. This was what it was like to execute flawlessly. Twenty-one years of military service and three combat tours in Afghanistan had imbued her with sharp senses and laser focus. Her decision-making skills, trademark calm under pressure, and bravery in the field had earned her a full-bird colonel in the army. Things happened because she made them happen.

Her aide, Louis Webster, hadn't been much help, but then he didn't know everything she knew. He only knew they were looking for a researcher who studied leishmaniasis. He didn't know they also needed to be vulnerable. Someone with dirty habits. Reasons to lie. Motivated by money. Louis had done the preliminary work—identifying researchers whose primary focus was the leish parasite. She'd done the rest. She'd mobilized the military intelligence corps—*in truth lies victory*. In her mind, their code was prescient. She'd assigned personnel to mine social media accounts, sift through personnel records, and dig deep into childhood details in hopes of identifying someone whose scientific reputation was strong enough to convince a Senate committee of competency but who had weaknesses that could be exploited if they didn't play ball. Will St. John was everything she needed. Narcissistic with bad habits that few knew about, a fierce appetite for research funding, and well respected in the scientific community. A softer soul might've kissed the screen. There was nothing soft about Army Colonel Susan Savarre.

Pouring a three-count Irish whiskey into her coffee, she spoke into her cell phone and waited.

She heard the line pick up. He never spoke first.

"I found someone."

"Tell me. Everything."

Savarre tapped her computer keyboard. The screen came to life with an image of an early-thirties man with broad shoulders, dark wavy hair, and teeth that were too white. He had a wide smile, and she could imagine him at the helm of a sailboat in the Nantucket Sound. She rolled her eyes.

"Will St. John, PhD in biochemistry from Harvard. Comes from a very wealthy family—grandfather owns a place in Martha's Vineyard. Attended a prep school when he was young, though you'd never know it. He's a train wreck. Not sure how he ever got his PhD, but he did. Drinks more than he should, regularly uses marijuana, and he's a troll who's racked up a few Title IX violations. Something of a rebel. Hard to contain. We can leverage that."

She paused here, and holding the phone away from her face, she inhaled deeply, counting to four, careful not to exhale into the phone.

"Go on."

"Family. He's got a real loser for a brother—a fraternal twin. His grandfather is a Harvard physician, Clemson

St. John. Dad is a plastic surgeon out in LA. His mother left when he was young, married another woman who is currently pregnant. Career. He has a few grants, some publications, a few noteworthy, cited frequently. He's up for tenure next year. Solid science in the area we need and plenty of personal problems. He's an easy mark, low-hanging fruit. He smells a rat, I'll make him eat it."

She thought she could hear him grinding his teeth. He usually did this when he disapproved of something. Something he did frequently.

"Do not underestimate him." His voice was smooth in a way that always made her uncomfortable. Did he know something she did not?

She imagined a serpent slithering and circling her, biding his time until ready to strike.

"Watch him. Listen to his conversations. Monitor his email and his cell phone activity. If he takes a piss in the middle of the night, I want to know about it. This operation is critical to our reputation as well as our bottom line, and we are running out of time, and the media is having a goddamn field day with this story. CNN has made this their personal mission. That kind of shit journalism turns my stomach. They know nothing about what we do. Keep me posted."

"Yes, sir."

"Oh. And, Susan? I'm putting the secretary of the army in charge of this operation. Rusty Carver is expecting your call."

*Shit. Rusty Carver is a loathsome slob who smells like*

*fried eggs and greasy biscuits every time I see him.* But she knew better than to say anything.

"Yes, sir."

"This could be an important career move for you."

"I understand, sir."

"Understand this: your power, your strength, depends upon his weaknesses. If you have to, exploit them. If he won't do this exactly like we need him to, find somebody who will."

"Yes, sir. And what then? What do I tell St. John?"

"If St. John isn't agreeable, I'll take care of it."

Susan held her breath. She knew how he'd *take care of it.* Same as he'd taken care of other things. Quietly. A car accident. An overdose. Or worse. She cringed. *What is so fucking important? What don't I know?*

"Yes, sir."

"Talk soon."

Susan Savarre's hand was trembling now as she hung up the phone. Not much scared her. But he did. She dialed Carver's number.

"Carver." He spoke into the phone while chewing food. *A morning pig at the trough.*

She sighed without trying to mask it. "I've found someone."

"I'll be damned. That was fast."

"Well, it wasn't easy. I had to comb through—"

"You know what to do."

The line went dead without a "well done" or a "thank you for saving our asses"…nothing.

*Asshole.*

She stared at the photo on her screen. The man in the picture was handsome. A chiseled jaw spread with a boyish grin, perfect white teeth—too white, she thought—and dark wavy hair. He was sitting on concrete stairs thick with moss and trailing with English ivy, behind him a plain brick university building circa 1970—the L.L. Charles Hall. He wore a button-down oxford with the cuffs turned over and jeans. His elbow slung over a rail while he smiled at something that was not the camera lens but something just beyond it. His body was slack and carefree. He looked nothing like the long list of accusations against him—affairs with colleagues and students, disciplinary hearings, internal audits and getting stoned before meetings. Most recently he'd been accused of using a trigger word in the classroom without alerting the students beforehand. Two days later, one student reported severe depression and suicidal ideations. He'd also failed to use the pronouns chosen by students as specified on the class roll. The only thing saving him from a delayed tenure review was his science. His science was solid, and he had the publications and accolades to prove it. She knew a bit about university politics—he wouldn't be going anywhere as long as he kept the grant dollars rolling in, no matter how bad his behavior was. She also knew that university administrators were particularly adept at making his life a special brand of bureaucratic hell if he didn't change his ways.

*And yet in his eyes a hint of naiveté*, she thought. He looked nothing like the trouble he'd caused, and if he felt threatened by anyone, you couldn't tell by looking at him. He appeared, oddly, happy.

That was about to change.

# CHAPTER 2

Will St. John rubbed his eyes and looked again. More closely this time. He chewed his coffee stirrer, his eyes unbelieving. He'd suspected it all along, and finally, he had proof. A choriomeningitis outbreak—a common virus in the animal care facility where rodents were housed—had killed all of the mice in the animal care lab but his. His mice had survived. Now, he knew why. The data was there, and data doesn't lie. Without averting his eyes from the report, he reached into his bottom drawer and pulled out his bottle of fifty-year-old Macallan, tossing the remains of his Americano in the trash. It was seven a.m., but if what he was looking at was true, he'd turn up the bottle and celebrate. This was the one thing. One. Thing. A breakthrough. Not yet tenured, he'd made the scientific discovery of a lifetime. He thought of all those who hadn't believed he could do it, those who'd stood in his way, those who wanted to destroy his reputation and, with it, his research. He punched the air with his fist. A wide grin spread across his face. *Fuck all you bitches!*

He checked his calendar. Nothing until 9:30—enough time to enjoy a drink and sober up before his first meeting. He kicked back in his chair and watched the sun rising over the campus, light splintering through the oaks in the grove and settling in shimmers on the dewy grass. He turned the bottle up and let the warmth spread down his throat and all the way to his empty belly. He could write his own ticket. He'd travel the world, telling his discovery story at all the big conferences and science meetings. He'd be asked to serve on editorial boards, the likes of which included *Science* or the *New England Journal of Medicine*, and his publications would be cited and studied by the best in the field. This discovery, *his* discovery, would not only guarantee tenure and a formal nomination to become a member of the National Academy of Sciences, this was the stuff Nobel Prizes were made of—*this* was it.

The sudden shrill sound of his phone ringing ripped a hole in his reverie. Annoyed that his moment had been cut short, he swallowed and answered.

"St. John."

"Dr. St. John. Will St. John?"

"Yes."

"Dr. St. John, this is Colonel Susan Savarre from Walter Reed Army Institute of Research. I presume you're familiar with our institute?"

"That I am. Can I help you?" *I'm celebrating here.*

"I think you can. I'd like to meet with you as soon as possible."

Will chewed on his stirrer stick, still irritated that his celebration had been interrupted.

"Ms., pardon, Colonel Savarre"—he rolled his eyes—"I'd like very much to help you with whatever it is that you think I can, but at the moment I've got quite a bit going on. It's a really busy time for me, and leaving is just not convenient. Perhaps one of my colleagues—"

"Dr. St. John, I am not interested in working with one of your colleagues. I need *your* help. Specifically *you*."

"Uh-huh." *Whack job.* "That's great. Look, I don't know who you are, and I just don't know when I can—"

"What about eleven a.m. this morning? Does that work? You've nothing on your calendar for eleven, correct?"

"How do you—?"

"I'll ask the questions. Just be ready by eleven a.m., and by *ready*, Dr. St. John, I mean sober. Dry as the Sahara." The line went dead.

<hr>

"What the fuck?" Will mumbled out loud to himself.

"What the fuck what?" Cindy Tan stood in his doorway in black joggers and a red tank. Her gray hoodie was tied around her waist like a kid who was tired of wearing it but had no place to stow it. The five-foot-eleven professor leaned against the doorframe, tall even in her running shoes. Her jet-black hair was pulled into a high ponytail, emphasizing her angular face. *Tall. Dark. Beautiful. Smart. Available.*

Will went stiff. Not a chance. She was his closest friend on a list that was quickly dwindling. She studied him with her dark eyes while she sipped her cup of coffee.

"Are you *drinking*?" She glanced at her watch and cocked a brow.

Will smirked. "That I am. Channeling my inner Jonas Salk this morning, celebrating what we in the sciences call a breakthrough—as in, I've broken through. You're looking at 'the man' of the century. I have just made the discovery of a lifetime, and after all those months of experiments and testing, what do you know? Serendipity pushed me over the finish line. It's huge, Tan, a game-changer. I was just celebrating. Join me?" Will lifted his glass.

Tan shook her head. "Man of the century, huh? I knew it had to be something. Scotch at eight a.m., and I thought maybe all the complaints to the administration and your persistent irreverence finally found your ass in a sling and you were drinking away your troubles here… but then I saw that shit-eating grin on your face. Anyway, I was just dropping by on my way over to the rec center. Thought I'd get in a few miles before work and wanted to see if you were up for a run, but I'm guessing the 'man of the century'"—she mimed air quotes in a dramatic way, rolling her eyes—"has other things to do."

"Actually, just got back from a five-miler, but thanks

for asking. I'm gonna take a moment—*this* moment—and have another shot. My adrenaline is through the fucking roof."

He poured a long shot, raised his glass and swirled the golden liquid. He felt like he might explode from the excitement.

Cindy raised her cup in response.

"To the science gods." She smiled.

"To the science gods, amen."

"All right, Mr. Man of the Century. You stay out of trouble if that's possible. I'm gonna go work out my bum. Maybe someday I'll be as pretty as you." She winked.

"Not a chance, Tan!"

She disappeared down the hall, and Will's mind returned to the call. He looked back to his phone. Who was this buzzkill Colonel Savarre, and how did she know his schedule? Had she called the lab? And what could she possibly want so badly that she was flying all the way from Walter Reed in Maryland?

Will stowed his glass in his desk, grabbed his duffel and headed to the showers on the fifth floor, hoping the hot water was working this morning.

⸺⃛⸺

USING BOTH HANDS, WILL WRENCHED THE HANDLE AS far as it would go until it was squarely pointed toward the red *H* for hot, but he already knew. A cold shower in an aging bath was a primitive experience, like showering in the Roman ruins. Cracked tiles and chipping paint and ancient fixtures. The tiled partitions shot up from the floor like Stonehenge, and decades of use had exposed the solid brass core of the fixtures. The pipes knocking sent echoes through the cavernous shower, and the deteriorating walls sounded like they might cave in. Not a hopeful sign. Will stepped onto the cool white mini-octagon tiles and braced himself for the ice-cold shock. The cold water blew out of the showerhead at unusually high pressure and stung like a motherfucker. Everything shriveled immediately, and he decided to skip the shave and rinsed the soap out of his hair as fast as humanly possible. The unpleasantness of the arctic shower did nothing to tamp down Will's excitement. In his mind, he imagined all of the things he'd need and now was in a position to ask for. If he was going to stay at the university, he would need new equipment, more space, more students and administrative staff—someone to run things while he was busy traveling to speak about his new findings that would most certainly be published in the top journals—*Nature*, *Science*, the *New England Journal of Medicine*. He toweled himself off, brushed his teeth and combed his hair with his fingers while he made a mental list of people he'd need to call.

When he got back to his office, he looked at the data again. He could hear the students laughing in the lab down the hall, and he wondered if they knew, if anyone had looked closely at the data. Just as he was about to check, Gabby appeared in his doorway. She was clad in full yoga attire, the standard uniform of most of his female students and a manner of dress for which there was no male equivalent. Her tank, if that's what you could call it, was open on the sides, revealing her sports bra and sculpted abs. Her yoga pants clung to her ass and thighs in a way that Will found distracting. Ironic given the fact that the Title IX office was up his ass about some female student he'd offended. Again. Gabby slurped her iced mocha, and the moment was lost. She leaned her head in to speak. *And here come the vocal fry tones.*

"Hey. We were just wondering if you were coming to seminar today. It's on cell-mediated response to *Schistosoma mansoni*." She sucked her drink dry and blinked.

"That sounds scintillating, but not today. I've got an interview and some woman from the army coming in this morning." *And I need to make sure what I am seeing is real.* "Take lots of notes." *And I really should set up a meeting with the Title IX office.*

"Okay."

Will listened to the steady hum of conversation and instruments that vibrated and rattled, which formed the perfect two-part harmony. The printers, centrifuges and the rattle of the minus-eighty freezer complemented the din of students' morning chatter about the latest trivia games, who had the best pizza in town, and who'd left the sink full of dirty glassware.

Will could've never guessed that his work on leishmaniasis would have led him to this. For as long as he could remember, he'd been fascinated by the immune response people have when they're infected with parasites. And while diseases like malaria and Ebola got the lion's share of media attention, it was leishmaniasis that had intrigued him—one of nature's great ironies. A parasite that makes its home in the very cells meant to destroy it—the human immune cells. It begins when a sandfly, tiny and silent, takes its blood meal from a human host, trading its dinner for a parasite. The parasite then enters the bloodstream, multiplies and spreads, sometimes to the organs, causing death. In other infections, it travels to the mucous membranes—the nose, mouth and lips—causing the person to suffer enormous lesions as the parasites destroy any mucus-producing tissue. Fascinating and gross at the same time. And now this tiny parasite, thriving and visible in the macrophages, had given him the gift of a lifetime—a secret that only *he* knew. *That's right. Fuck all you bitches.*

He studied the graphs, and his heart raced. He wanted desperately to share his news, but for now, it would remain confidential. He wanted one more test to confirm. A knock at his door interrupted his train of thought.

"What is it now?" he practically hissed, without looking up. There was shuffling movement in the doorway but no audible reply.

He looked up from the report. In his doorway stood a young woman, her entire body pulled in tightly like an Olympian in the luge, arms snug against her sides and legs pressed together. Her platinum hair pulled into a loose bun, large pale eyes that examined him, and generous lips that she pressed into a modest smile. Her waist was small, but her hips were full, and her thin wool sweater stretched nicely across her chest. At first glance, she appeared matronly in her gray pants, dark blue sweater and pearl studs, but close examination found her stunning in her soft round curves and large blue eyes. One of those second-look beauties, the type that catch most people off guard until the big party when all heads are turning. Will drank her in while mentally he sized her up. *She must be lost.*

Will, anxious to return to his data, said, "If you're looking for French and Italian, they're located on the east side of campus, near the student dining hall."

"Actually, I'm looking for Dr. St. John. Will St. John."

"I'm Will St. John." Will grimaced at the clock on his computer screen. "Are you my eleven o'clock? I was expecting a uniform and, quite frankly, someone a little more…stalwart and manly. You hardly seem like the person I spoke with earlier."

"I'm Eve Konisken. Your 9:30 interview." She stepped in and extended her hand.

*This morning is full of surprises—most of them extremely pleasant.* Will shook her hand, surprised by such a firm grip from such a delicate hand.

"Oh, that's right, Eve—from Paschal's lab, right? Have a seat."

Eve nodded and took a seat.

Will studied her countenance. She sat erect, elbows at ninety degrees, arms by her side, feet uncrossed and flat on the floor as though she were sitting in an executioner's chair waiting for the first surge of electricity to pass through her. Momentarily, he imagined what an awesome librarian she might've been, shushing young students who talked or giggled and collecting cell phones from those not following the rules. Or maybe she'd give a good go in the Title IX office. Her vitae had been near perfect, but now that she was sitting here in front of him, he felt differently. She was pretty, but clearly type A—a rule follower. No accidental f-bombs or trigger words. No nips at lunch or before meetings. He suppressed a sigh. He could imagine her as a clock watcher, policing the lab on weekends for anyone working alone without backup, or worse, reporting him for cussing. *Fuck* was a critical part of his vernacular—hell, his life.

Evidently, he'd offended some undergraduate student with his language; his go-to expletive was somebody's trigger word. *Well fuck that.* He'd have to refrain from telling the Title IX office what a crock of shit these accusations were. Nanobiotechnology wasn't for pussies, last he checked. He chewed on a coffee stirrer until it was a gnarled piece of pink-and-white plastic. A bad habit—one of many, some would say. Eve looked as though his very existence offended her—she'd never fit. But here she sat. *Now, what to do about it?* A slight smirk turned the corners of his mouth. He tossed his coffee stirrer and ran a hand through his thick, dark waves. *Go ahead. Size her up.*

Will spoke. "Comfortable?"

"Yes, thank you."

"'Cause you don't look it."

"I beg your pardon?"

"Let me guess. You store your shoes in their original boxes arranged according to color and style, and your clothes are hung according to color and sleeve-length; you rarely eat out, and when you do, it's strictly vegan-organic-gluten-free-farm-raised-local-dairy-free food, you finished your PhD two years ahead of your colleagues, who already disliked you and in the end hated you for it. You never tell people where you're from—stop me if I'm wrong—some hillbilly town you escaped when you realized you had half a brain, you've never had a best friend; you're five foot four, 140 pounds, size ten, no gym membership 'cause you're too cheap for that so you stream NPR podcasts on the unique abilities of *Drosophila* cells to take up gold nanoparticles while you run, ahem, jog, what, a nine-minute mile? People see you as uptight, but you consider yourself shy, reserved, perhaps even misunderstood."

Eve's entire body went heavy, and her throat felt constricted. She could feel the heat flushing her chest and neck, and her left eye started to twitch. She'd heard about him and his ability to "read" people. It was legend around campus, and while she hated to admit it, he was as good as she'd heard. And while most of what he'd said—not all, most—was true, and the truth stung, she'd done her homework, too. She hated assholes like him. *Arrogant know-it-all prick.* And she'd learned a thing or two working in academia, not the least of which was how to deal with assholes head-on. Like the ancient Greeks used to say, call a fig a fig, a trough a trough. *Give it your best shot.*

"Mmm. Wow. You think you know a lot about women,

but you don't, and a smart woman wouldn't touch you with a ten-foot pole, so you're still hooking up like a high-schooler and still with your one-night stands at your age which, let's be honest, is a joke. Your students only work for you because of your success—personally, they are disgusted by you. You've had three Title IX violations that the university dropped because of your success, you're a spoiled rich boy from Harvard trying to prove something, but it's not working, so you drink and smoke dope to feel better about yourself, you spent last Christmas Eve here, by yourself—stop me if I'm wrong—the only redeeming factor about you is your scientific prowess, which is undermined by the fact that you have no decorum despite your country-club background. You've never mowed a lawn, made a bed, or eaten a PB & J. You've no religion, but you worship yourself. You need your own awareness day. You have a horse but no friends, and now, you don't have a post-doc either." *Prick*.

Eve smoothed her pants, still stiff with starch from the morning iron. Her eye no longer twitched. An uncomfortable silence passed between them, neither able to read the other.

"What makes you think I was here on Christmas Eve?" Will was grinning at her now.

*Fuck*. She'd been so proud of her rejoinder, she'd given herself away.

"You were here too. I get it. You're hired. I'll get the paperwork started effective, what, say, November 1 if Paschal's okay with that."

"Oh, and I'm a size six. Okay? And I run a seven-minute mile. And okay."

The truth was she had no other choices. This was it, and it was only for a year. She could survive anything temporarily. And she worked hard to keep her weight in check. *Size ten, my ass.*

# CHAPTER 3

WILL STOOD AND STRETCHED. SHE'D DO. MAYBE even better than he'd thought. Feisty *and* pretty. It was a gold-medal morning. He looked at Eve, who still looked petrified despite her clever reply. Will smiled, and this time, he was not mocking but genuine.

"Okay, Eve whose last name I can't pronounce, let's introduce you around so the students don't think you just wandered into the lab on your way to find the humanities building."

They walked a short distance down a hallway, past large academic posters of the life cycle of leishmaniasis parasites coupled with closeup photos of the horrible lesions they cause and minus-eighty freezers full of cryogenically stored parasites—extraordinary for a biochemistry department—but then Will had always been an outsider. Some might say a biochemist who studies parasitology and other infectious disease was a rule-breaker working outside their area of expertise, but

Will enjoyed his space at the edge. The edge was where he thrived.

Inside the lab smelled of solvents and various chemicals. There was a wall of hoods and rows of long benches punctuated with tall shelves stacked with boxes of supplies including latex gloves, pipettes, custom glassware and a million tiny bottles, all labeled with their contents. All around, lab equipment clicked and hummed and sighed in a way that gave the space a life of its own. The high frequency sound of the HPLC pumps, the hum of refrigerators, the chugging of vacuum pumps on the rotovaps, shaker tables shaking, centrifuges and microfuges whirring, water gurgling through circulation baths and cooling jackets and hoods sucking the chemical gases and smells from reactions that would eventually make their way up the air shafts and out of the building via the large stacks on the roof—all this combined with the air exchange that kept the air from being noxious resulted in a symphony of sound, each distinctive in the way it contributed to the special brand of white noise that was a working science lab. Overhead, rows of fluorescent tubes buzzed, adding to the din of voices. Large windows overlooked the campus quad, and near the center of the room, students were hovered over Amy's laptop. She'd been the one to run the last set of assays on the mice and was probably just realizing she'd run a TH2 kit by mistake. A glorious mistake, but nonetheless an error. A gift from the science gods.

Five pairs of doe eyes looked up from the computer.

"Everyone, this is Eve whose last name I cannot pronounce." Will gestured toward Eve. "She's our new post-doc beginning November 1. Eve, this is Amy, Gabby, Devon, Shea and Sanjay. Amy's been running assays on immune responses to leish infection in mice. Most of our equipment is in here, but we do have an instrument or two down the hall in our instrumentation room."

A collective voice of hellos and welcomes came from the group as they eyed Eve carefully. Will imagined what they must be thinking. Even in the absence of makeup or yoga pants, Eve was a standout. Not the usual fare around these parts, but then neither was Will. Will had never relied on his looks to open doors, and he didn't have to. He had all the talent and experience he needed, but more importantly, he had the drive to go after what he wanted, and he wasn't afraid to take risks or speak truth to power. He also knew that people generally found him attractive, and that gave him an edge—an edge he couldn't deny existed, however unfair it might be.

Will talked while Eve followed him back down the hall and into his office.

"So the students generally show up anywhere between eight and nine. I'm an early riser, and I stay late. I teach Tuesdays through Thursdays at 9:25. Your schedule is flexible, but I expect results, and if you run into problems, I need to know as soon as possible. If there's a problem with equipment, or orders are sitting in the queue too long before getting approved, if parasites aren't thriving or the mice seem sad, you know, the usual day-to-day stuff. There's a break room down the hall with a fridge and microwave, and other than that, I guess I'll see you on the first."

"Sounds good. Should I just take any bay in the lab or—"

"I think the spot in the corner is open. We can go check."

Will stopped. Something was wrong. The hallway, normally filled with chatter, had gone silent. The only perceptible noise was the minus-eighty freezer, a reassuring sound given the number of infected mouse livers it housed. As he was about to show Eve back down to the lab to check out her new operations hub, two figures appeared in his doorway, one standing, one in a wheelchair.

"Dr. St. John. We've just been through your lab." A tall, thin woman in a uniform made a dismissive motion with her hand. "It's quaint, and the equipment seems a bit…vintage, but I think it'll do." Just then, she stepped on a small roach crossing the hall and scraped the juice remains off the bottom of her shoe with the edge of a manila folder, tapping them off into a nearby recycle bin. "We'll just head down to the conference room for our eleven o'clock."

As quickly as they'd materialized, they disappeared down the hall. Will tried to mask his surprise.

"Two rights and then a left." Will hollered after them, but they were gone. Will glanced at his Omega Speedmaster.

"They look important," Eve said.

"My eleven o'clock. Guess they're right on time. Not really sure why they're here. Why don't you come down and join us…find out what all the mystery's about."

"Sure." Eve followed Will down another short hallway, this one flanked with large, matted nature photos of the trees and flowers that grew on the campus. The sleek frames were a modern touch in an otherwise dated building. They walked down the hallway into another and another until they reached a tiny conference room barely large enough to seat eight people. Seated at the head of the table was a woman in uniform, a full-bird colonel. Her strawberry-blonde hair was pulled back into a tight low bun not unlike Eve's. Her dark eyes scanned her surroundings in a manner that set Will on edge, and her presence filled the room in a way that made everyone else seem small, insignificant. Also, she seemed to be aware of this. Next to her sat her assistant, a younger thirty-something man in a wheelchair. He had an innocent face, handsome enough, with gelled-back blond hair and a muscular upper body that caused his blazer to stretch taut against his chest. He drummed his fingers lightly on the table until full-bird shot him a look that said "Stop or I'll break them." Will was amused by this unusual entourage. He couldn't wait to hear what it was they thought he could do for them, and more importantly, how she'd known his schedule *and that he'd taken an early morning swig.*

"You must be Colonel Savarre. Will St. John. My new post-doc, Eve whose last name I cannot pronounce." He nodded his head toward Eve and extended his hand for the colonel to shake, but she ignored it.

"This is my associate, First Lieutenant Louis Webster, retired, civilian. I don't have much time, so I'll get to the point. Our therapeutics program for leishmaniasis at Walter Reed has hit something of a snag. We're confident that the drug we currently administer to our military in the field, Larmentin, is both safe and effective, but a few of our men on the front line are experiencing some adverse psychotic events, albeit rare and minor. Some members of Congress want to blame the drug, and they're like a dog on a goddamned bone. I need you, Dr. St. John, to screen for neurotoxicity and identify biomarkers that would suggest sensitivity to the drug. Prove Larmentin is safe. Louis will provide you with de-identified samples from our lab, and I want you to run the assays. Report back to me any evidence of a correlation between reported psychosis and blood tests for biomarkers that might indicate whether the drug is an issue. Louis will be your technical point of contact. You will submit your findings directly to him. The email address and phone are on the contract."

She slid the plain manila folder across the table.

"Okay then, thank you. And I think we can do the work but—"

"Five million dollars."

"Excuse me?"

Will's heart skipped a beat, and his throat went dry. He didn't blink and couldn't swallow, but his face gave nothing away. He'd dealt with the likes of her before.

He'd been raised by her XY equivalent. He could navigate this blindfolded.

"Five million dollars, Dr. St. John. The money is in place with your university and ready for immediate spending. With that kind of money, you can purchase some new equipment to replace some of those old clunkers you've got now. Get yourself an honest-to-god mass spectrometer. I did a quick pass through, and it's like I'd time traveled back to the days of the Manhattan Project. Things look grim."

She had the empty stare of a psychopath as she spoke. Her blinks came in rapid pairs.

"I honestly don't understand how research thrives in an environment such as this. I had better at the Point, and that was two full decades ago. Nevertheless, you seem to have a stable operation here."

"Thanks, I think. Glad it meets with your approval, shortcomings notwithstanding. Five million dollars is a lot of money." Will cleared his throat. "And I am very tempted, but I must ask—"

"I ask the questions, Dr. St. John."

"Seems to me, correct me if I'm wrong, Colonel, that *you* need *me*, not the other way around, and I have some questions of my own. Who exactly is funding this project? What's your timeline? How do you know my schedule? And what do you know about my"—Will cleared his throat again—"habits?"

Will's face settled onto its bone and brow with no sign of tension; it was the perfect poker face. Colonel Savarre returned his poker face with her own expressionless stare,

Louis seemed bemused, and Eve's face flushed red. However intimidating she might be, Will had been training all of his life for this moment. He wasn't stupid. He knew enough not to let her get to him. He glared right back at her, his eyes equally as empty and unrevealing as hers. Neither blinked. *It's on.* Will counted two full minutes in his mind before she spoke through her steepled fingers.

"Four weeks. Five million dollars. It's a quick turnaround, but then you're the type who does his best work under pressure. As to the other, you're a creature of habit, habits that are the stuff of legend, and you *are* legend here. I've heard you prefer afternoon meetings if you must meet at all, you have a certain lascivious reputation, and while you would've been an utter failure as a member of our armed services, you seem to thrive in this environment, same as your parasites and whatnot." Savarre made circles in the air with her hands. "Like bacteria in a warm, moist enclosed space. This grant could be precisely what you need to get early tenure, which means a nice salary increase and the lab you've always dreamed of. Take the money. Do the work. Do we have a deal?"

Will's instincts flickered. Something didn't feel quite right, but then five million dollars certainly put to rest any concerns he had. His world-changing discovery could use some financial props, and he had an obligation—a moral obligation—to share his news with the world. Lives depended on it. And she was right about tenure. He studied her face. Her large nose split her perfectly symmetrical face in two. Her dark eyes had no perceptible pupils, and they were wide-set, just like a great white. And while she hadn't opened her mouth wide enough, he could imagine if she did, she would have exposed the fact that she had fifteen rows of teeth. She was tall and thin, flat chested in her uniform and brutish in her manner. It was no wonder she'd made full-bird colonel.

"We can do it. I'll have our sponsored research office—"

"Louis spoke with them early this morning. The contract is in place, fully executed with all of the signatures except yours, which we will have immediately following this meeting. We have a deadline, Dr. St. John, and I never miss a deadline. Four weeks. We'll be in touch. Make me a believer, Dr. St. John." She turned to walk out and at the last minute turned her head. "Oh, and Dr. St. John," she said, her eyes like an accusation, "make that meeting with the Title IX office soon. I can't have you suspended until after my project is completed."

Will, fuming, started to speak to this, but she'd already left without even waiting for Louis, who struggled to back his wheelchair out of the cramped meeting space.

"It was nice meeting you both." Louis half smiled.

Will began to speak. "Let me guess." Eve shot him a look and shook her head slowly. "You love dogs, Halloween and fast cars—not NASCAR, Formula One. You're not a fan of football or basketball, but you do love baseball—the Washington Nationals. You like chips, especially Doritos, and had a fantastic score on your MCATS but decided against med school. You're a collector—autographed baseball memorabilia. You get regular manicures, sleep in a single bed and can bake a mean chocolate lava cake. You were about to cross the street when you saw some elderly woman about to get hit and ran out in front of her, pushing her out of harm's way but putting yourself in front of a car, and voila, the chair."

Louis's eyes grew big. He looked amazed and, shaking his head, he spoke. "Wow. That's incredible. All mostly true, but not how I ended up in a wheelchair—that was combat. Afghanistan." He slapped his legs. "Sucks except at the Nationals games. I have great seats just behind home plate. Anyway, again, it was nice meeting you both. Good luck with the project."

"Nice meeting you also." Eve nodded in agreement. "Do you need help?"

"No, I can manage, thanks."

After a few careful maneuvers, Louis exited the room. Down the hall, the buzz was back as if the colonel had swallowed the noise and spit it back out as she was leaving.

Will wondered about people like her. People who think they're above it all—that the rules do not apply to them. Of course, there were those on campus who would've said the same about him—that he thought he was above it all, could say and do as he pleased. His last Title IX violation had threatened to push back his tenure review and forced him into sensitivity counseling, the closest thing to a medically induced coma he'd ever experienced. Even more preposterous was the reason he'd had to go. A female undergrad had accused him of inappropriateness in a meeting—a meeting she'd set up and one in which she'd worn a short skirt and no underwear. Not even a thong. Of course he'd noticed. Who could've missed it? He'd been sure it was intentional, but the council had found in her favor. He'd looked. And she had wanted him too. Cindy told him he was just too pretty and that he'd need to be extra cautious.

"You can't expect to walk around looking all Josh Hartnett–like and nobody's gonna notice. In the sciences? Baa-baa black sheep, baby. And don't pretend for a minute ya don't know what I'm talking about. Ya do."

The colonel must've been immune to his charms, because she'd walked in like she owned the place and without much resistance from anyone managed to get her way in the end. Of course, it was five million dollars. And five million dollars was a lot of fucking money. He'd be crazy to turn it down, and he knew it. This sealed the deal. He would have tenure, and he'd get to write his own ticket. Still, the way she'd asked—demanded—he didn't like it. He felt threatened, and he didn't know why.

He looked over at Eve, now covered in red splotches, who was pulling a nearly rotten banana from her bag.

"What'd you think of her?"

"She seemed direct. Businesslike. I like that in a person."

*Mmm. I bet you do.* "She didn't seem pushy to you? Is it businesslike to just waltz into a place with few hours' notice, shut it all down and sit at the head of the table like Attila the Hun?"

"I agree, she's not subtle. But she did just give you five million dollars. That's something. Most researchers I know would take the money and run. Plus, I think five mill makes it okay for her to call the shots. Besides, it's only four weeks—that's 1.25 million per week. You hit the research lottery. Don't look a gift horse in the mouth."

"Hmm. I guess I'm not convinced. There was something…something in her face that wasn't quite right." Something that betrayed her. She seemed uncomfortable beneath her tough talk. *Maybe she's not calling the shots. That would rattle someone like her.* "I learned a long time ago, everyone has an agenda—their *own* agenda. I'd like to know what hers is." He ran his hands through his thick hair, still damp from the shower. "Grab a cup of coffee before you head back to your lab?"

Eve glanced at her watch. *A clock watcher.* Maybe he'd make her the safety officer for the lab. She was certainly cut out for that kind of work.

"Sure, I have a few minutes."

They walked back down the tangle of hallways and took the elevator down to the coffee shop. Will grabbed an Americano for himself, a black coffee and banana for Eve. They made their way over to an empty table, quiet except for the sound of people clicking away on their laptops.

Will watched as Eve pulled back the skin of her banana so that each peel was pulled only halfway down and each to precisely the same spot. Using a plastic spoon, she scooped a tiny brown spot out. Type A. He wouldn't be able to depend on her to generate new project ideas, but she'd be perfect for running rote tests in the lab.

"Do you think people pound away on their keyboards because they're frustrated? Full of angst? Or do you think they have no idea they're doing it? Or do you think that it's some sort of weird unannounced competition to see whose work is most urgent based on how hard they're hitting their keys?"

"Beats me." Eve lopped off the top of her banana. "Why do you do that thing? I'd heard about it. Around, people talking. It's like this thing you're known for. Well, *one* thing you're known for." Eve smirked.

"What thing?"

"That profiling thing. It's insulting." Eve took a bite of her banana.

"You heard Louis. I'm good at it. I like to be amused, and I find it amusing. At first, I did it to impress people, but these days I do it because it helps people come out of their shells. I like to know the people I'm around—like to know what I'm dealing with, what I'm up against and how to channel talent and steer the wayward back on track. It's how I stay on top. You said that was one thing I'm known for. There are others?"

"Yes."

"What are they."

"You know—stuff."

"Don't play shy now. You just told me off to get a job. Spill it."

"Your nickname."

"My nickname. Do tell."

"William the Conqueror."

"William the Conqueror? The first Norman king, who kicked ass in the Battle of Hastings in 1066, William the Conqueror? That's fucking awesome."

"I don't think it's meant to be awesome."

"But it is."

"If you're so awesome, how come you didn't profile the colonel? How come you didn't say"—Eve mocked a male voice—"'Let me guess, as a child you were never bullied—not ever. In fact, you *were* the bully. You had your own little shit gang. You used to beat the hell out of boys 'cause you liked to hear 'em squeal for their mamas. When you weren't beating them, you were taunting them. You've been eating the same thing every day since you were seven. You attended West Point, top of your class, and in the field, you had a record number of kills for a female warfighter. Men fear you, and you like it—you don't love it 'cause you can't love anything but the army. You like pit bull terriers, despise yogurt of any kind, and you've never enjoyed a cup of tea. You don't own a TV, and you still use a flip phone. You're a luddite. A luddite and a bully. There is not an emoji for you—you're just not that emotionally complex."

Will guffawed. "Eve. Damn. Not bad—not sure I sound like a Neanderthal, but that was pretty good. I would've pegged her for a cat person, though. Somebody who likes animals known for their unrequited love and kill for sport. Probably has a cat with a Russian name like Stalin."

Eve only half smiled. *I have a cat. Boris.*

"I'm not proud of my behavior, you know. I stooped to your level. I let your little thing you do get to me."

"That little thing is a gift. I've done it all of my life, as long as I can remember. It's a special talent I have. One of many." Will winked.

"Mmm, well. I should get back to my lab now. See you on the first." She didn't smile, but Will thought maybe her face had softened just a little when she was in the midst of her profiling monologue. She'd loosen up.

"You're immune to my charms. That hurts right here." Will patted his chest.

"See you on the first."

Will watched her disappear behind the double doors that led to the bioscience building. *That ass.* He hoped she was as good as Paschal said. Paschal was out of money and sorry to see her go but had to cut her loose. The funding just wasn't there. *If I could keep her forever, I would. She's that good.* Paschal had genuine regret, and Will was hopeful. His lab was full of first- and second-year students, and it'd be nice to have some experience for a change—an adult he could talk to, bounce ideas off of.

# CHAPTER 4

Back in his office, Will studied the contents of the envelope. The contract was in a manila folder, and he wondered at the significance of it. These days, research contracts, even those from top agencies and foundations, were delivered via email with electronic signatures and confidentiality statements at the bottom. The use of the manila folder seemed antiquated. Great. So he was dealing with a Luddite who couldn't possibly understand the requirements of contemporary science. Good research, thorough examination and analysis take time. She hadn't given him time. He scanned the pages for something that might tip him off—anything out of the ordinary that would point to what she was after. Congress might be like a dog on a bone, but then, so was she. The first pages were the standard collaborative research agreement he'd seen in the past. And just as the colonel stated, all of the signatures had been obtained without so much as a phone call to Will despite the fact that he would be the lead investigator and without explanation of exactly what he would be investigating. He flipped to the statement of work.

APPENDIX A
STATEMENT OF WORK

TITLE: Sensitivity Screening for Leishmaniasis Infection for Identification of Biomarkers for Safe Prescription

Background: Leishmaniasis poses a serious threat to deployed armed forces in endemic regions. Tropical diseases such as leishmaniasis, malaria and schistosomiasis receive little funding. Walter Reed Army Institute of Research (WRAIR) via the Military Infectious Disease Program is the primary agency for research and development of drugs for diseases with military relevance.

Research objectives include A) screening of Larmentin as provided by WRAIR using brain-on-a-chip technology for human neurotoxicity B) screening of de-identified whole blood samples as provided by WRAIR.

He'd need to contact the Institutional Review Board office to clear the path for human subjects' research, and they would have to contact the army. He'd also contact his colleague for access to the brain-on-a-chip technology they'd developed expressly for the purpose of research on neurotoxicity in humans.

The brain-on-a-chip technology was exactly what it sounded like. It was quite literally a fully functioning miniature brain-on-a-chip. At the center of the apparatus, a thin plastic film formed the blood-brain barrier, known to those who worked in the field as the "BBB"—the membrane that protected the brain from toxins, including blood. Endothelial cells—the same cells found on the inside of blood vessels—were attached to the blood side of the barrier. Brain cells, which included neurons, astrocytes, and pericytes, were applied to the brain side. And voila, a miniature replica of a brain and a way to test drugs and toxins without killing animals. Drugs, such as Larmentin, could then be introduced or perfused into the vascular blood side and run through the device to test for toxicity. The blood-brain barrier is unique in that the endothelial cells are so tightly packed, only certain drugs and molecules are able to get through—aspirin and alcohol are two examples of drugs that can pass through the BBB.

Will was familiar with most of the medications for leishmaniasis, including Amphocin and Pentamidine and Larmentin. He was also aware that there were associated side effects, but then all drugs have side effects. He stared blankly out the window of his office. Something just didn't add up. What was he missing? What was the big deal? So people were having a few bad dreams and some dizziness. Was that worth five million dollars? For this? Why not go to the pharmaceutical company directly? Why wasn't WRAIR conducting the research using their own labs? Will knew they often leveraged the use of academia for access to trained personnel and equipment, but like Colonel Savarre had said, his lab was "quaint." Why him? It felt strange, but then, peculiar wasn't a feeling *five million dollars couldn't fix. Right?* He smiled. Nothing quaint about a seven-color flow cytometer—the *Mercedes* of flow cytometers and easily a million-dollar purchase, but the real prize would be the mass spectrometer. Very few labs boasted their own.

Will picked up the phone and called the IRB office.

"IRB. Can you hold please?"

"Sure." Will listened to the classical music play for several minutes. It was long enough that he relaxed a little at the violin and was tempted to pour himself a scotch when a high-pitched voice cut in.

"IRB. This is Brittany. How can I help you?"

"This is Will St. John calling from biochemistry. I need to speak with Director James Dodson, please."

"One moment, Dr. St. John. I'll connect you."

The phone beeped over with no music this time, and a deep, raspy voice came on the line.

"Mornin', Dr. St. John."

Dodson sounded like someone who might've been working at a tackle shop off a remote highway near a favorite fishing hole. Friendly enough, but rural. Chevy trucks and night crawlers, catfish and PBR. Will could hear Merle Haggard on the radio in the background.

"Good morning. I'm calling in reference to—"

"I'll save you some time, Dr. St. John. A one Colonel Savarre contacted me regarding the research you'll be doing on the anti-leish drug Larmentin. Nasty disease, that leishmaniasis." Through his words, Will could hear him chewing gum. "Not a very friendly gal, either." Dodson chortled and went into a coughing fit. "Reminds me of my mama. Rough around the edges. But we got our marching orders—no pun intended."

More chortling led to more coughing, and Will was beginning to get pissed off about the way this entire thing had been handled.

"Then you have a copy of the CRADA"—a cooperative research and development agreement is an agreement between a government agency and a private company or university to work together on research and development—"and the instructions, yes?"

"Yes, sir, we do."

"And what about the approval from the Army Human Research Protections Office?"

"Well, seems Colonel Savarre took care of that also."

*Of course she did*, Will thought.

"I have the authorization I need from the Army Human Research Protections Office."

"Okay, well, great. So the schedule calls for weekly data. Would it be possible for you to forward that to us each Friday for reporting the following Monday?"

"That'll work."

"Thanks. We'll be in touch."

"Thank you, Dr. St. John. You have a nice day."

Will hung up the phone. His day couldn't get any nicer or any weirder. He'd seen some weird things in research, but never had he seen a research agreement set up like this. Someone just swooping in, handing you millions of dollars and a signed agreement, with instructions and approvals and prescribed protocols already set up. He thought about Eve's words—don't look a gift horse in the mouth—and decided he'd leave it alone for now.

# CHAPTER 5

Down the hall, Will could hear Amy cussing in the lab. The centrifuge must have been down again.

"Piece of shit! I need this done! Who in here is letting the Bernstein lab use our centrifuge? They busted theirs, and now ours is busted, too. Damnit!"

Mumbles and denials filled the air.

"I think I can help with that." Will walked into the lab.

"Everybody, listen up." Will waited until everyone had gathered 'round. "I've just been awarded a five-million-dollar grant to run neurotoxicity screens on a drug. As a matter of fact, I'll be calling Bernstein for some supplies. I need her brain-on-a-chip technology. Those are worth some money. Maybe she can spot us some since her students broke my centrifuge. In the meantime, you can order a new seven-color flow cytometer, a new centrifuge, *and* a mass spec."

"Whoa. Are you fuck…sorry, are you serious?"

"I am. Here's the specs and the quote on the cytometer

and mass spec. Go for it. Oh, and expedite the shipping and arrange for priority installation. We've only got four weeks on this one."

Amy's mouth spilled into a huge smile. "Awesome. Thank you, thank you, thank you!"

"No problem. And, Amy, we need to meet later around say four? Should last about twenty minutes."

"Sure." Amy grinned.

*Just wait, Amy. If you think this is good news, just you wait. The really big news is coming.*

Will walked slowly back down to his office. He'd chewed his stirrer straw into a mangled ball of plastic, a sure sign he needed a drink and a smoke. On his bookshelf, he glanced at a photo of himself and Clemson taken at his graduation. He'd done something great without his grandfather writing a check or arranging a meeting with important people who had big ideas for his future. *He* was paving the way—his *own* way. Pity he couldn't share it just yet. He needed to check and double-check and triple-check. Before he could convince anyone else, he needed to convince himself. He needed to put eyes on his mice… *confirm they're alive.*

He thought about how this discovery, if he was right, would represent the pinnacle of his career but was also the very essence of what had driven him to science in the first place. He'd wanted to know a thing inside and out, study something so deeply and for so long that it was a part of him. He wanted to uncover something, one of nature's biggest secrets, and in this case, one of her best-kept secrets. Long before college, he'd decided medicine wasn't for him. He recalled a blistering argument between his father and grandfather at his high school graduation when they disagreed on Will's future plans. His father had asked Will to consider medical school.

"So he can spend his days doing jelly breast implants and Brazilian butt lifts? You're out of your goddamned mind!" His grandfather pounded the cherry dining table with his fists so that the wine goblets shook and the sterling forks rattled in their linen napkins.

"I make a fine living in California, son. The people are nice, and the weather is even better. And despite what your grandfather thinks, I change people's lives. I give people happiness. The confidence imbued in them is astounding, and it's humbling."

Before he had a chance to even exhale, Will's grandfather, a professor of neurosurgery who also had appointments in neurology and mathematics, interjected. "You know what imbues people with confidence? That moment the light bulb comes on and they realize they understand how to solve linear ordinary differential equations using an integrating factor. Do you think the Kardashians can do that? It's no wonder to me why children these days have no analytical or critical thinking skills. Your profession is a disgrace. Your ex-wife is a disgrace. I will not allow you to add Will to the list!"

There'd been no mention of his fraternal twin, George. Unlike Will, George had attended public schools and taken the first train out of town immediately following his final exams—final exams that were probably never taken. His high school years had been riddled with problems. Problems with teachers (he'd had sex with two of them), fights, bad grades, bad attitude and three car wrecks. His excess drinking hadn't helped matters. George was a "lost cause" according to their grandfather, and so Clemson had focused exclusively on Will. Will had been sent to the best schools as soon as it was clear George was not and would never be college material, let alone Harvard material.

As an adult, Will realized that both his father and his grandfather were arguing about the same thing—appearances.

He'd chosen a different path. He wanted the chance to study problems, invent and discover. To take a crack at the root of a problem, the cause of a disease and the opportunity to set the balance in favor of life. He was doing just that.

In fact, his morning had started with the discovery of a lifetime followed by a check for five million dollars. It was surreal. One minute he thought he must be living right; the next minute his mind was filled with doubt. His skin still vibrated with excitement, and he felt very alive…and at the same time, very alone. It felt like a dream. Things had just fallen into place. He was still in shock, and he needed another pair of eyes on it to be sure he was looking at the truth. The truth of his future.

———— ∞ ————

EVE KONISKEN WAS WAITING FOR CHARLIE PASCHAL when she got back from lunch.

"Eve! Hello! How'd it go? Tell me everything." Charlie pulled her silver hair into a messy bun and stuck it with a pencil, and shoving books and papers to clear a path, she leaned forward in her chair with clasped hands, a large turquoise-and-silver ring on her finger—the only jewelry she ever wore—and around her shoulders a large colorful shawl from a trip to New Mexico, where she'd communed with a shaman. She was too optimistic for her own good.

"I'm not sure I can do this, Charlie. That guy's a tool." Eve shout-whispered despite the fact that they were alone. "He's arrogant and obnoxious and unprofessional and insulting and a whole bunch of other things I can't even think of right now. Oh, and a troll. He's a troll. And I'm pretty sure he called me fat. Fat, Charlie! Can you believe that? He tried to guess my weight. Who does that, Charlie? Who does that?" Eve rolled her eyes and shook her head. "Why'd you send me to that guy? I need a job, but I'm not sure I'm that desperate. Can't you figure out something where I can stay? What about your NIH grant that got scored? Maybe that'll come through. I just don't think I can do this." Eve slumped in her chair.

Charlie Paschal bit her bottom lip.

"Are you smiling? Are you about to laugh? This isn't funny, Charlie—that guy's a prick, and I need a job."

Now, Charlie was grinning. "Okay, okay—Eve, calm down for just a second. First, if I thought that NIH grant was going to actually materialize, I wouldn't have suggested you talk to Will, but Congress is cutting re-search funds, and I don't think I'll make the pay line even if I have a great score. On the other hand, I just heard Will got handed millions of dollars. He's not one to let the grass grow under his feet. Second, this is *academia*. You know how people are here. They're hardly polished professionals, and most don't even have decent social skills. If you're looking for sophisticated colleagues, you're in the wrong business. Nobody, not even *you*, Eve, nobody here is that refined. Believe it or not, Will is actually pretty good at that mannerly stuff when he needs to be. He's cotillion stock. He comes from money. Lots of it." Charlie rubbed her fingers to indicate. "And despite the fact that his grandfather is a renowned neurosurgeon and professor of neurology at Harvard Medical Center, Will St. John has built what he has *alone* with zero favors. That's something in this world. Most would have capitalized on the type of connections he has, exploited every avenue to get where they wanted to be. Not Will. He did it on his own. And yes, he's brazen at times, but I think the fact that he looks like the cover of a men's magazine makes navigating this environment tricky for him. The female students think he's hot as hell, and he gets more than his share of offers. I've even heard female faculty fantasizing about him and at least one or two males. But all that aside," she said, shaking her head, "Will's science is as solid as anyone's, and further, it's cutting-edge stuff." Charlie ticked off the accolades. "He's well funded, he publishes a dozen papers a year in top-tier journals—*Lancet*, *Nature*, *JAMA*—and his students are the best. He is wicked smart. Don't underestimate Will St. John just because he's full of himself—and he is, don't get me wrong. But he has high standards, and everyone knows it. It'll be a great move for you and may even help when you go looking for other jobs—especially in your dream town of Boston. That's Will's old stomping ground, so chin up. It'll be okay, I promise. I wouldn't send you to just anybody, Eve. Despite his reputation, Will is one of the best. *You* are one of the best. And you're just gonna have to trust me on this one."

Eve sat up a little.

Charlie sighed. "Look, Eve. People are binary. They've got their good side, and they've got their bad side. *Their ugly side.* If you only focus on the negative, you won't be able to avail yourself of all the positive aspects of working in that lab. This is the kind of experience that could really help you on your career path. Try to focus on Will's good side and take advantage of your time in his lab—use it to build expertise in different areas."

Eve thought about this. It made sense, she guessed. Will did have the money, and even if the circumstances were unusual, she still needed to make rent and eat.

"Okay, but promise if the NIH comes through, you'll let me know? I like it here."

"I promise. Why don't you help Sara finish up her poster and call it a day?"

"I'm fine. I may hit the gym at lunch. That always helps." Eve rolled her neck around in an effort to loosen up the tension steadily building in it.

"All right, suit yourself." Charlie waved and turned back to her computer.

Eve went down to the lab, checked on Sara and grabbed her gym bag from her desk.

Outside, the day was beautiful, and Eve took deep breaths of the crisp fall air. The sun popped in and out from behind a few clouds, and the breeze carried maple leaves in a full spectrum of autumn colors. All around campus, foliage wowed in shades of red and gold and plum against a clear blue sky and the promise of another season. Eve grabbed her phone to snap a few photos as she walked across campus. *Five missed calls from my dad.* She hadn't even felt her phone vibrate. She could guess what this was about. Her mother crying that she needed Eve to come home and help around the house, and why was Eve working in a job where she made no money, and people with as much schooling as she had should be making real money. But mostly she wanted Eve to come home and mop floors or dust and cook while she drank vodka all day. Eve decided she'd call back later. Right now, she wanted to run out the steadily growing ball of angst she had in her gut.

⁕

SHE WALKED THROUGH THE DOORS TO THE GYM COVERED with advertisements about beating the bulge over the holidays. She noted her favorite treadmill was empty, and so she changed quickly into her running shorts and sports bra. Leaving the locker room, she took the stairs two at a time to get the machine on the end, but as she topped the stairs, she could see someone was already running on it. Instead, she hopped on a machine two spots down and put in her earbuds, but then something caught her attention. She glanced up at the news scrolling across the TV mounted from the ceiling. Secretary of State Elizabeth Rhodes was in critical condition after a near-fatal shooting accident in Islamabad. Film footage of the SOS being loaded from a helicopter and transferred to Walter Reed Medical Hospital played in a loop. The news ticker at the bottom included speculation about her prognosis, which looked bleak. But that wasn't what interested Eve. It had been a friendly fire incident—the shooter, a Marine sniper, high on cocaine. Then, in subtext so obscure it was almost invisible, another story: a fellow Marine blaming the incident on the drugs they were given for various diseases—drugs mandated by the military. Eve strained her eyes to read the tiny scrolling messages, but her focus was cut short in a boorish manner. Will St. John slapped Eve on the arm to get her attention.

She plucked her earbuds out with such ferocity that she lost the rubber cover to one, only to hear the explicit lyrics blaring from Will's iPhone.

"Oops." Will smiled.

"Hi." She was intentionally bitchy and curt. He needed to respect her break time, especially since she would be working for him. "This is my running break. Did you need something?" She glanced at him briefly, but then her eyes went right back to the TV screen. In her peripheral, she noted that her favorite spot was empty and snatched her water bottle to move. But when she stepped on, she noted the machine had only been paused. She looked around.

"That's mine." Will grinned. "I always get on that one. Pardon me." He stepped in front of Eve.

Eve's insides began to sizzle. "Fine." She waved him off and stepped back over to her original spot while she tried to figure out how to tune in to the news station so she could listen. The accused sniper's family was on TV claiming he'd been a gentle soul, a kind person. His mother wiped her tears while she cradled a family photo. What they were reporting, according to his family, was a lie. "They are saying he was high on something. Joey was a good boy who'd never used drugs in his life. The only drug he took," said his mother, "is the drug they gave him. They made him take it. They did this to my baby… my sweet baby." Joey Bishop's mother broke down.

Eve wondered if the fellow Marine would be interviewed. She knew that military personnel took a lot of medications, and depending on where they served, they might take meds for malaria, yellow fever or leishmaniasis. Eve's mind went back to the meeting with the colonel. *What was the name of that drug?*

"Your banana not sitting well?" Will was still smiling.

And just like that, Eve's train of thought derailed.

"Do you need something, Dr. St. John?" *Or are you just trying to be an annoying asshole?* How was she going to work for this guy? "Look, I've had kind of a bad day, and I come here to wind down, get in a few miles, and I'm just not really in the mood…" Her voice trailed off, nearly cracking toward the end.

"Well, my day has been splendid, to say the least. Maybe if I talk about mine to you, I can cheer you up."

"I don't think that will work. You see, I began my day with you, and you began your day with me. See the problem here?"

"Maybe I can shed a different light on our circumstances. When your friends can help you change your paradigm, isn't that helpful?"

"You're not my friend."

"Okay, then boss." Will grinned.

*Does this guy ever stop grinning?* "You're not my boss, *yet.*" Eve turned her eyes back to the television. She watched with great interest and now wondered if their meeting with the colonel to screen this drug was related to this story. *What had it been called?*

"Details. Technicalities." He waved his hands in the air like an orangutan. "I like technical people with that kind of attention to detail. It plays well in my lab. You'll be happy to know that we are spiffing things up for you."

"Shhhhhhhh! Do you mind? I'm busy."

At this Will shout-whispered, "Sorry. We have a new centrifuge on the way and a new seven-color flow cytometer *and* a mass spectrometer. It's a fucking beast—you'll love it."

"Mmm. A beast, huh. Well, that's great news. Speaking of news, I'm trying to watch it." Eve pointed to the screen. For a second, they'd flashed up a list of drugs given to military personnel, and then it was gone. She'd missed it. Now she was completely frustrated.

Will ignored this.

"I thought you'd be happy." Somehow Will was running but also looking at right at Eve.

"Geez, do you ever stop talking?" *I just missed an important story!* "Happy for you. Right now, I'd love to run. Need to run off some of this size-ten weight."

At this, Will fell out. He laughed so hard he doubled over, and the girl at the desk came over to check on him.

"Dr. St. John! Are you okay?" Her eyes were big, and her cheeks flushed just asking.

Eve was thoroughly disgusted.

When Will finally caught his breath, he reassured the student-worker. "I'm fine, thanks. My colleague here is funny as hell is all. Sorry to have startled you."

"No problem. Just wanted to be sure you were all right." She trilled. She was trilling. Singsonging. Bouncing all the way back to her post, dramatically swinging her long ponytail.

Eve thought she might dry heave right there but was certain she would never get the kind of attention he'd just received. She glanced over at him. His Nike shirt was clinging to his biceps, and his pecs were indeed impressive. His dark wavy hair hung loosely around his eyes which, while narrow, twinkled continually. He was smiling even when he wasn't. *Gross.*

"Must be nice to be in a constant state of amusement."

"Who, me? I got life by the short hairs. That's the way I like it." All of his teeth back to his molars showed when he smiled.

"How…charming." Eve sighed through her words and put her earbuds back in, one without the rubber cover so that it was poking the inside of her ear. Perfect. She turned on her music and began to run. Will went back to her favorite machine, gone for now, and Eve was thankful.

Eve turned up the speed on the treadmill, returned to her music, and thought about the news. And that was when it popped into her head. *Larmentin. That's it. The drug we're screening is called Larmentin. It's prescribed by the military for leishmaniasis.*

# CHAPTER 6

WILL WOLFED DOWN A CHEESEBURGER FROM the student union while he waited on Amy. His mouth was full of organic angus beef when she appeared in his doorway. He motioned her in, swallowed and wiped his mouth. She sat down in the chair, pulling her legs up underneath her like a human pretzel, easy enough in her yoga pants and long flowy sweater that fell off one shoulder. Her dark hair was pulled into a large knot on top. *Namaste.*

"Missed some," she said.

"What's that?"

"You have mustard on your face." She pointed to her own face, indicating an approximate location on his.

"Thanks." Will wiped again. "I've been looking at your data, and something seems off and at the same time pretty awesome."

"Yeah, I accidentally ran a TH2 kit. Pulled it from the right stack but didn't check the label."

"Looks like you ran a few."

"Yeah, uh, I was gonna mention that…" She glanced at the floor, then at the ceiling, and then her eyes seemed to trace the room, as if making eye contact was an admission of guilt.

Will toyed with the corner of his calendar, waiting.

"Guess I got sidetracked by broken equipment and then distracted by ordering all the new. Sorry, I'll run them again using the right kits."

"Not so fast. Remember that choriomeningitis outbreak that killed all of the mice in the animal care unit? All of them except ours?"

"Yeah. That was so weird. We got lucky."

"I thought so too, at first. But then, I've had my suspicions for a while. Turns out, luck had nothing to do with it. Look closely." He turned the report so she could see.

"That's odd. The flow cytometry shows immune function."

"Yes. And…?"

"The kit detected proteins…specifically, cytokines… the molecules that signal the immune system." Amy touched the report gently so as not to disturb the results.

"Yes…"

"Our immune-deficient mice…have an *immune system*? I don't get it."

Will drummed his fingers on his desk and began to snap his fingers. He started to sing in his head. *Start spreading the news…* Not only did they appear to have an immune system where there hadn't been an immune system, but it was a *kick-ass* immune system.

Amy didn't budge. She was used to his singing and the fact that he had zero inhibitions.

She squinted at the data. "I don't understand. How? Are you sure?"

"I'm more than sure. Run a kit—any kit, TH1 or TH2—to look for immune function in an immune-deficient mouse, and you should get nothing. Zip. Zero. Nada." He snapped his fingers, still humming between words. "That, and our mice should have died like all the others. Check the data. Our mice are flourishing, yes?"

"Umm, yeah, no signs of aggression. They're eating… no rumpled fur. They seem good. Happy as clams."

"Happy as clams with?"

"A fully functioning immune system?"

Will clapped his hands and pointed at her. "Bingo!"

"I don't understand…how? Our mice were BALB/c nude mice… They had no immune system."

"I think I might know. Are you familiar with the hygiene hypothesis?"

Amy shook her head no. "I've heard the term used but can't say exactly what it is."

Will hopped up from his chair.

"In medicine, the hygiene hypothesis is this idea that when kids aren't exposed to

infectious diseases, bacteria, parasites, the natural development of the immune system is somehow suppressed. We have altered our risk of infections—of transmitting disease such as the flu, the common cold, and stomach bugs. But some scientists believe what we have really done is made a swap."

Will tapped his computer, and a slide showing a world map appeared on the wall.

"This is a world map of the occurrence of autoimmune disease, and it's a long list—rheumatoid arthritis, diabetes, thyroid disease, lupus, Celiac's disease, Crohn's disease, multiple sclerosis, and the list goes on and on."

Amy nodded. "Okay…autoimmune diseases occur when our immune system attacks our own tissues inside our body instead of fighting off colds and other diseases."

"Exactly!" Will's excitement was obvious now. He clicked to bring up the next slide, a world map with certain countries shaded in various colors representing the incidence of autoimmune diseases.

"Notice anything about this world map?"

"Ummm…yeah…it looks like autoimmune diseases only occur in the US, Canada, Europe and Australia."

*For now. I've just made a breakthrough that will forever change this map.*

Will clapped his hands together. He was beginning to sweat and had slipped off his loafers and now paced the floor in his bare feet.

"That's right. Autoimmune diseases occur almost exclusively in the developed world where we have access to antibacterial and antimicrobial products, antibiotics, antifungal and antiviral medicines…" Will ticked off the count on his fingers. "Now, let's look at another map. Notice anything different about this one?"

Amy answered without hesitation. "The only shaded areas are in Africa, South America and Asia."

"That's right! So, in developing nations where the

usage of antimicrobial and antibiotics is lower, and the risk of infectious disease is much higher, the occurrence of autoimmune disease is lower—much, nearly nonexistent. Anything else that we know about these countries with regard to diseases?"

"Yeah. They get different diseases."

"Like?" Will wiggled his fingers anxiously.

"Well, like they have malaria, and we don't have that here. And Ebola."

Will pointed at her. "Yes, Amy! Good! Now, let's overlay the two maps."

Will clicked again to reveal a map using two colors that highlighted the fact that there was little or no overlap between the countries with and without autoimmune disease.

"Here, we can see clearly there is almost no overlap between developed countries and autoimmune disease, and the developing world and their lack of autoimmune diseases. In fact, what we notice is an inverse correlation between countries with autoimmune disease and those without. But there's something else—something else that they have quite a bit of that we do not, and that is parasites and helminths such as pinworms and hookworms. And what they've noticed in these countries where there are large populations of people infected with parasites and at risk for infections with helminths is that when they are treated with antihelminthic drugs, the patients develop guess what? *Allergies!*"

Will was practically yelling, and Amy reared back in her seat.

"And what else have scientists and researchers noticed? These worms are doing something! They are changing their host's immune system—tempering it, such that the immune response isn't too strong or too weak. Too much, and the body attacks itself! Not enough punch, and you could get very sick and die! Some scientists believe that helminths and hookworms are the key to understanding this map. Helminths produce a molecule that prevents the population of people in these regions from ever developing an autoimmune disease. Researchers are even looking at treating diabetes with helminths, and in laboratory mice, the outcomes have been very promising. Same with multiple sclerosis. Let's run kits on all the mice and find out what's going on. Confirm they all have immune function and—"

A group of curious students had gathered just outside Will's office.

"And then figure out *why*."

One student began to clap, and others soon followed.

Will took a bow. "And that, folks, is your impromptu lecture on the hygiene hypothesis! Thank you for your time and attention!"

This was followed by more clapping and a piercing whistle. Will felt electric.

*A new molecule is at work, and it is rebooting the immune system in the mice. Thank you, dear leish parasite.*

"I'll get right on it. What about the other project? The new one from the army?"

"Don't worry about that. I'm putting Eve on it. I need you to focus on the mice. See what we find, and we'll go from there. Let me know as soon as you've got something. Call or text me."

"Will do."

"Thanks!"

"Sure thing." She sauntered off down the hallway. Just two years into her graduate work, and one of his best students was not completely aware of what she'd stumbled upon. This changed *everything*.

Will felt like a drink, or two, or five.

———⊗———

THE NEXT DAY, THE BLOOD ARRIVED AT THE LAB. Five hundred de-identified samples of whole blood collected from military personnel who had taken Larmentin in the field. The colonel had taken care of everything just as she'd said she would. She'd ensured they got the brain-on-a-chip units from Dr. Bernstein and that Cindy Tan was ready to go with the analysis—the only thing Will had to do was get to work. Projects like this were often months in the making—this one had taken only two days. Will had to admit, it was pretty fucking amazing.

He chewed his coffee stirrer while he stared again at the cytometry data. It was surreal. In his mind, he couldn't fathom a bigger discovery in his lifetime. His parents' lifetimes. Clemson's lifetime. Clemson. His grandfather wasn't easily impressed, but Will couldn't imagine that this wouldn't somehow meet the bar, no matter how high. Amy would run the kits again, but this time, she'd run them on his new equipment, thanks to Colonel Savarre. He was pondering the data when Cindy appeared in his doorway.

"What's up, SJ? And who's this skank you got callin' all the shots around here. She's basic as hell. And I had a tiger mama."

Will guffawed. "Fucking hell, she *called* you? Well, if you enjoyed that conversation, you should meet her. I think her uniform's too tight around the neck. It's cutting off her circulation to her frontal lobes, if she's even got any. That *skank*—she's a full-bird colonel."

"Full bird as in vulture?"

"If you mean will she be circling us until something dies, the answer is yes. However, this project came with a substantial payday. Five mill."

Cindy's face looked incredulous. "I'm sorry." She fisted her chest and coughed. "Could you repeat that?"

"Five million dollars. That's what she's paying us to screen an anti-leish drug, Larmentin. They want to know whether it's tied to some psychological disturbances the military in the field are experiencing."

"Mmm. Larmentin. I think I've heard about this one. Wasn't that the one in the news…I don't know, I can't remember."

Will shrugged, unable to concentrate on anything other than his own discovery.

"Anyway, I guess I can help with the software to run the analysis…for a small price." She winked. "Sounds like a quick turnaround. She said four weeks. Can you really get it done in four weeks?"

"Well, the samples are here. All five hundred

de-identified samples of blood. We've got a new flow cytometer coming today, and Bernstein is providing me with the brain-on-a-chip technology…so yeah, I'd say we can hit the ground running."

"Shit. Gotta admit I'm jealous of the efficiency. God knows we could use some of that around here. I guess the government can make anything happen. What's the rush?"

"Don't know. She just said they hit a snag. Didn't elaborate, and for five million dollars, don't guess I'll ask. This is rudimentary science and not worth what she's paying, but I guess she didn't have the personnel to do it. Not our first rodeo with the military, but first-ever grant to be dropped in my lap like this."

"Hmm. She must've read about your work. You've got quite the rep in your field. Top dog."

"Thanks, but leishmaniasis is not a particularly huge field. Big fish in a small pond. Not sure I can carry my field on a single vector and its parasite. On the upside, I can thank those parasites for the discovery I've made… and if my next set of experiments go well, it's going to be big. Just need to get through this project for the colonel."

"Well, I'm on cue. Let me know as soon as you've got something."

"Will do. Thanks, Cin."

Cindy disappeared down the hall, and Will looked out his window at the tangles of bare limbs, some with a few autumn leaves still hanging on. Something about it, the way the leaves hung on, made him want to blow through this work with the army. Just as the seasons were changing, he felt like he was ready for a change—ready for something new—and his discovery was that new thing. Something big. Exciting. He needed this. He needed this success and all its trimmings—tenure, publications, invited lectures, AAAS nomination and maybe something bigger. He looked at a large nest in the top branch, now visible. He wanted to be that nest—he wanted to be visible. Not for his jokes or his looks or his family's money. He wanted his *science* to be out there. He wanted to blaze a new trail. He wanted to tell the world about his scientific breakthrough. He wanted a cover feature for *Time* magazine.

The phone rang.

"St. John."

"Dr. St. John, Colonel Savarre. Just checking to be sure you received our samples, all five hundred of them, and that your team is ready and everything is in order."

"Yes, thank you. I understand that you contacted my colleagues regarding their roles on the project. Thanks for that, but I would appreciate it if you let me do my job."

"Stepping on your toes, am I?" *You will not like it if he "takes care of it," so you'd better shut up and listen.* "If you don't like to be micromanaged, you'll need to get over it. I just gave you five million dollars and a very short list of things to do over a four-week period. A grant large enough to catapult you through the tenure hoops and enough money to purchase several of the high-end instruments you need. And we both know that's how you measure your dicks in the world of academic science. Yours is a foot long with a five-inch diameter, so cut the bullshit and start the experiments. I will be checking in frequently." The line went dead.

Again. *Bitch!*

---

COLONEL SUSAN SAVARRE HUNG UP THE PHONE. *Who the fuck does he think he is? I just gave him five fucking million dollars. If St. John makes this difficult, I won't be able to save him—not from what's coming.* She had congressional leaders breathing down her neck, CID wanting answers, but she had her orders. Make this disappear or your command here is done. She shouted down the hall for Louis just as her phone rang.

"Savarre here."

"Savarre, Rusty Carver. Where do we stand with getting this drug tested and this shit storm cleared up?" He sounded like he was about to explode.

"I'm working on it. They have the samples, and everything is in place. These things take time, Rusty. Four weeks and you'll have your answers."

"Four weeks, my ass. You'd better make it two. This story is blowing up. The media has already turned it into a three-ring circus, and the phones are ringing off their goddamned hooks. If this gets out, Larmentin and the billions of dollars it brings to us and some very important shareholders will vanish into thin fucking air. I've got senators threatening my job, members of Congress who don't know what to say to their constituents with elections right around the corner, not to mention the family members of that Bishop kid. This is out of control. The Secretary of State is lying in the hospital barely hanging on. If she dies…"

"That's right, Rusty. The Secretary of State got shot by one of ours. I'm not a fucking miracle worker. I'm handling it like I said I would." *Like I told* him *I would.*

"Look, you know the pressure is coming down from the top. He is not a patient man, and he's making my life hell right now. Sooner or later, someone is going to put this all together. That soldier, that drug. Then what? Respect, Susan. These guys deserve respect. They're putting it all on the line. If people find out they're wandering off post in a goddamn daze, acting like clowns at a rodeo and going postal, we're in the shitter."

"You don't think I know that? My entire family was military. Mother, father, grandfather. You know what the army means to me, so don't lecture me about respect." *You dumb son of a bitch.* "If you knew this drug was causing psychosis, why didn't you switch it? Wait. Don't answer. Let me answer for you. You *like* your crazies in the field, and the crazier the better. You like them on the front lines. You like them charging out into the line of fire while they scream maniacally and taunt the enemy. You like them getting drunk, starting fights and getting locked up just long enough that when they get out and back in the game, they're primed to kill. You like them hopped up on adrenaline, spooked whatever. That's on you, Rusty." And *him*. "Let me do my job." Louis was sitting in the doorway. Savarre held up a finger for him to wait a minute.

"Nice speech. You're lucky I like you." Rusty was chewing food while he spoke, and her misophonia filled her with rage. "He called. He's changing the timeline. Two weeks instead of four."

*Two? Is he out of his fucking mind?* Savarre thought her head would pop off.

"Get it done. And, Savarre, watch your tone. I'll be in touch."

The colonel hung up and looked at Louis.

"I need you to stay on top of St. John and his associates. Also, send me the names of the people working with him. I want to know who he's got on this. We've just had our timeline cut in half."

"Yes, ma'am. Right away."

"Oh, and, Louis?"

"Ma'am?"

"You need to keep whatever you overheard to yourself."

"Yes, ma'am."

Louis wheeled away, and the colonel wondered if he'd been sitting there long. He didn't know *anything* about what they were doing, and that was the way it needed to stay. She'd have to call Will St. John back and cut the timeline. There would be no way they could run five hundred samples in ten days. She'd either have to up the time or reduce the sample group. She sighed heavily. This whole thing was a farce. She'd already suspected

Larmentin was dangerous. She didn't need St. John to tell her that. What she needed was for him to cover it up.

———❧———

Will walked out of his office just as his phone rang. The very sound of it made him angry. Why couldn't it just vibrate like his cell? Whatever it was would have to wait. He exited the building and swapped the musty atmosphere for fresh air and clear skies. There was a snap in the air, and squirrels everywhere nibbled on acorns and wrangled their way in and out of garbage cans. He thought about the mice that didn't die and how much of what he did was hard work and how much was just dumb luck. That the mice had survived was a serendipitous mistake that had led them to the discovery of a lifetime. A discovery that would change not only his life but had the potential to change the lives of all who suffered from autoimmune diseases.

# CHAPTER 8

WILL'S PHONE HAD VIBRATED A FEW TIMES during his meeting with Amy, but he'd waited until it ended to look. His dad had called—and he rarely called.

Will returned his call on his walk back to his office.

"Dad, hey, it's Will. Returning your call."

"Will, hi. How's things at the university?"

"Well, you know, busy making big discoveries. Same old, same old."

"Well, speaking of old, Clemson called."

Even though Will had called his grandfather Clemson all of his life, it was still strange to hear his own father refer to *his* dad by first name.

"Clemson called *you*? What'd he want?"

"Seems you have not RSVP'd to the reception and ball honoring his fifty years of service to Harvard University Medical Center. And of course, this has become *my* problem. Could you just please call and RSVP?"

"Shit. Sorry, Dad. When is it?" Will watched a large flock of blackbirds circling, diving and dipping, some lighting on branches and digging at their wings with their beaks. Momentarily he was distracted by their large numbers while his dad buzzed on about Clemson's party, what to wear, and reviewed the names of those people who were important enough that Will needed background. Will stared down at his third-season Armani loafers and smiled. He'd need new shoes.

"Next Saturday. November 6. Oh, and it'd be nice if you could bring a date. Clemson's concerned at your lack of interest in developing a permanent and acceptable relationship with a woman. Secretly, I think he's concerned that you'll end up gay like your mother. By the way, her girlfriend's baby is due soon, too. Don't forget to send something. I don't know where your brother is shacked up these days, but if you hear from him, you'll let me know? Oh, and your mother decided she'd like breast implants, and she wants me to perform the surgery. D cups after all this time. I missed the boat on that. Tell you what, kid, you've been missing out on all the good family gossip."

*That suits me just fine.* "Sounds like it. I guess I can fly up for the party, but *only* for the party. Things here are blowing up—I've got a military project on a breakneck deadline with Attila the Hun in charge, and it'd be hard to get away any longer than that." *And I've just made the breakthrough of a lifetime.*

"I understand. You know Clemson can always send down his plane."

Will rolled his eyes at this. "That's not necessary. Look, Dad, do I really need to be there? Is this really all that important? Why can't I just take a pass this time? I can send him a pen or something. I've got priorities here." *I have my discovery. Then there's the military project on an impossible deadline. Oh, and let's not forget the Title IX office is up my asshole.*

"Clemson won't go for it, but I think you know that. This is a big deal. Half of Congress and all of Harvard will be attending. You know the drill. Just take the plane. Fly up for a day and right back home. Oh, before I forget. He's also asked that you stay with him."

"No way. Not doing that. Things here are just too busy for me to get away even for just a night. Sorry you had to deal with this. I'll call him." He'd have to come up with an excuse. He just couldn't leave this breakthrough hanging in the wind while he was away partying.

"I kinda wish he'd called you, myself. He's always liked you better anyway." They laughed.

"Maybe you'll get lucky and his assistant will answer. He lunches at noon every day. You could call at 12:10." They laughed again.

"Thanks, Dad, but you know Clemson. He won't be avoided. I'll call, I promise." *Not today, though.*

Will hung up. He'd call Clemson tomorrow. He walked slowly now, kicking up the leaves and wondering where his twin brother might be hanging out. They'd grown up differently. Where Will had excelled, George fell short. Will had the looks of a Hollywood star *and* brains, and George was all personality—an average student and fun-loving but irresponsible and, as he got older, reckless. Will had been something of a rebel, but he'd kept his grades in check, and his college placement exams put him in a position to choose among the best, and he had. The night of their graduation party, Will from a top boarding school and George from a local public school, George had disappeared. They didn't see him for six months, and when they finally did, some girl they'd never met showed up with him at Thanksgiving dinner. It was a bad scene. George got drunk and broke a crystal decanter that had been in the family for generations. Thick crystal shards covered the hardwood floors, leaving their marks behind. Clemson had damn near ripped his head off. "You're a waste. Always were." That was what he'd said.

The memory made Will flinch. When Will tried going after him, Clemson started in on Will for trying to apologize and begging George to stay. But George didn't. He left again, drunk and broke. A few months later, he'd called Will for money, and Will had given it to him. He loved George despite everything. George had a spark, still. True, it had dimmed through the years, but Will still saw it sometimes. In the early morning hours, when George was sober enough, he'd race Will to the kitchen for waffles or fart in his face. Despite everything, something still thrummed alive on the inside. A flash of something that refused to be tucked away—like a present that is rarely used but cannot be tossed out with the trash either. Will lived for the moments he saw the flicker. George always disappeared, but Will knew his brother. He'd show up again close to the holidays—around Thanksgiving, when he needed money, and then he'd be gone again on New Year's Eve.

These days he struggled with drug addiction, which had alienated him from nearly everyone, including their parents. He could be frightening when he was high on something—no one ever knew exactly what—and Will was the only one who seemed to be able to get through to him, talk him down. They'd been each other's best friend when his mother left, but George was never really the same after that.

---

As he walked back toward his office, Will made a mental note to call George soon. Maybe he could fly up for a long weekend or George could come down, maybe see the university and make fun of his brother, the professor. Neither would ever have guessed Will would be leading a top research effort at a top university.

As if the universe had an ear to Will's musings, he nearly ran into Amy, who spun on her toes like a ballerina on point and looked back.

"Hey, I'm running those kits. I will let you know as soon as I have some data. Fingers crossed!"

"Great. If I'm not around, call or text my cell."

"Will do."

"And, Amy, no flip-flops." Will looked at her feet. "The admin downstairs sees that, and she'll report you for wearing improper clothing, and you know she will. She loves that kind of shit. She's always looking for someone to break the rules—makes her feel alive. Besides, it's almost November. Aren't flip-flops summer attire?"

"Flip-flops are a year-round staple, but okay." Amy rolled her eyes.

Will walked back into his office, sat down in his chair and kicked his feet up. His computer beeped. An incoming Skype alert blinked at him. Walter Reed. He rubbed his eyes and palmed his mouth. Damn. Had it even been eight hours? He clicked to answer.

"St. John."

"Dr. St. John. Hope you are well and things have started humming along. I spoke with my superior, and they'd like to expedite these tests. They'd like the results in two weeks rather than four."

"Are you fu—" Will cleared his throat. "Are you serious?"

"Two weeks, Dr. St. John. Make it happen."

"Is your uniform coat cutting off the circulation to your brain? Two weeks is impossible. Four was a stretch. We will need twice as many personnel on this and access to the mass spec core facilities. I can't do this with my people alone, and we've only got one mass spec. You want this done in two weeks' time, I'll need more funding to cover the additional personnel and access to instruments outside of my own lab."

"How much?"

"One and a quarter million."

"That's rich, Dr. St. John. Perhaps something is cutting off circulation to *your* brain."

"That's my price." He was not about to halt work on

his discovery—a discovery that could change the world—
to run drug tox screens on a drug that had already been
approved by the fucking FDA. Not on his life, and if he
had to slow his own discovery down, it came with a price.

"I'll have to check with my superiors on this. In the
meantime, get started."

"May I be so bold as to ask what the rush is on this?"

"No. You may not."

"Fine. We'll *see* what we can do."

"*See* that you get it done."

She clicked off. Jesus, what a *bitch*. He flipped off
the monitor with both middles and called Cindy Tan to
give her a heads-up, but she was in meetings, and quite
possibly Attila the Hun had already called her, too. He
pulled open his drawer and poured himself a shot of
whiskey. Next, he went to find Eve.

She was sitting in her bay in the corner, watering a
plant that was too large for the area. In fact, there were
numerous plants, including an orchid in full bloom and
a bonsai tree with a healing crystal and a few shiny stones
scattered around on the soil. Next to the arrangement
of plants was an angel fish in a modest-sized bowl with
blue pebbles on the bottom and a green plastic plant
in the center of it. The fish seemed annoyed by Will's
presence and darted in and around the plastic plants.

"Looks like a rainforest over here."

Eve looked up. "Not sure a few plants and a fish
constitute a rainforest."

"Maybe not, but that's quite the jungle…plants with

stones, crystals and a fish." Will waved his hands around all of the plants—especially a large-ish palm that threatened to poke him in the eye, and the solitary fish still darting in and out of the plastic plant. "Looks like you're settling in just in time to hit the ground running. I need you to start on this project for Walter Reed."

"Okay. I was about to as—"

"Like now—as in the indoor landscaping project will have to wait, now." Will eyed the plants.

"Oh. Okay. I can do that." Eve leaned over a wastebasket and dusted some potting soil off of her hands.

"We're gonna have to double-time it."

"Double-time it?"

"The colonel called. They cut us. We've got two weeks instead of the agreed-upon four."

"Two weeks? That's impossible."

"That's what I said. Glad to see we agree on something. Two weeks."

Eve sighed and looked around.

"Okay, well, seeing as I have zero social life, I can be here pretty much all day and night, I guess."

"Can't work in the lab alone. There needs to be someone else here. One of my students or me, doesn't really matter who. We have a nazi admin who's always checking to be sure the rules are being followed. If one of my students can't be here with you, I'll stay. We'll get as much done as we can. I don't expect you to get this done all by yourself. I'll put as many people on this as I can—you'll have lots of help."

"Okay, well, I'll get on it."

"Great. Amy can show you where we keep the supplies. Devon picked up the brain-on-a-chip units, and the Larmentin samples are in the locked cabinet next to the printer. The code is 1234. We like our security. Start with the Larmentin. Run it through—start with three units and sample at zero, six, and twenty-four hours. Then we'll start on the whole blood samples they sent." *Five hundred fucking samples. Two fucking weeks. Fucking crazy-ass bitch.* "See what comes back and let me know asap."

"All right. Setup will take me a little while. I can probably start by three p.m. today…samples for baseline at zero hours and again at six hours…so nine p.m. and again tomorrow afternoon, twenty-four hours post-exposure."

"Sounds like a plan. I'll check on you later. Break a leg."

Eve half smiled and gave a thumbs-up. Her nearly platinum hair was pulled back into a low bun, and her long gray sweater clung to her body in an almost desperate way. Her pale eyes, nearly the same color as her sweater, were glassy and piercing. Will found her striking. A thought passed in his mind as he walked toward the door. He turned back but said nothing.

The other students were in seminar. He'd round everybody up to help with the other components as soon as they returned. Everyone would have to pitch in and help if they were going to get this done. Still, he couldn't wrap his mind around why this had to be done in under two weeks. Something wasn't right, but he didn't have time for that right now. He needed Amy to finish up on the mice. He was sure he already knew what she would find.

⸺ ✢ ⸺

Susan Savarre sat at her desk alone, concerned. Will St. John was asking too many questions, and if he wanted to…*live*…he needed to shut up and run the tests. It was noon. The break room was full of people eating red velvet birthday cake. Susan didn't like cake. She didn't much care for people either, and so, like most days, she ate lunch at her desk. She pushed a lump of day-old extra-spicy guacamole around on a plastic plate with a tortilla chip. She was staring at a large bolus of raw data sent to her from military intelligence. The computer screen filled with his latest emails and phone call logs. William Jefferson St. John didn't have much of an online presence and ran close to being off the grid. Much to her disappointment, he barely existed in the universe of social media, making a deep dive near impossible. He had a LinkedIn account and a defunct Facebook account on which the only posts had been about scientific discoveries or an occasional photo. He had a soft spot for string theory and dark matter. Deep. *"Do not underestimate him."* The words came back as she scrolled through pics of him funneling a beer at a party. *Don't you worry, pecker-head. I'd never underestimate anything with a Y chromosome.* Eye roll. She nibbled the edge of her Tostito while she read an old Facebook post about the acidification of oceans and blah blah blah. One post about global warming had led to an eighty-something back-and-forth-comments rant about whether or not global warming was caused by humans or a naturally occurring cycle. Will had fought until it digressed into a shit-match.

His phone calls were almost exclusively family, his graduate students or Uber Eats takeout. His schedule consisted of work, an exercise routine, and weekly visits downtown to a cigar club. At this, she smirked to herself. Really? PhD from Columbia who hangs out at a cigar shop? Truth *really* is stranger than fiction. She chewed her food slowly as she watched snips of a nearby security camera catch him dancing with a scantily clad salsa instructor. Another eyeroll. She read emails from various university administrators and colleagues, none of which were useful. There were a few snapshots of him stumbling out of the cigar shop, but that was it. Initially, she'd stumbled upon an email of interest, only to find out it was a student propositioning him, not the other way around.

Dr. St. John,

I'll be at the Red Bar on 8th at around 7...if you're interested. I am.

xxoo
Delana

Not exactly what she'd hoped for.

She continued scanning emails and eventually moved on to his cell phone logs. Seemed his father had called him numerous times, and he hadn't returned any of the calls. Trouble in paradise? Something she should know? She looked back through the photo log and found pics of him with his family, dad, mother, and a pic of him with his grandfather—a Harvard physician and professor of neurosurgery—Clemson St. John—and twin brother, George. Clemson had his arm around Will, but George barely made the frame. Any farther away and he'd have been out of the picture. Unaware of herself, she frowned. Curiosity dug its claw in, though, and she began digging.

Like her, both had attended a boarding school until George was kicked out. For nearly an hour, she found herself clicking through the records for George, searching for his story like some precious object she'd lost between the sofa cushions. *Why do I even care?* Oddly, his file had been heavily redacted, and the reason for the expulsion was a mystery. She flipped through everything she could find but came up empty-handed. George had been forgotten entirely. She looked again at the photo of him with Will and the grandfather. Here was the story. A single photo. A grandfather who was grooming one brother and clearly very proud, protective even, of Will and would prefer to disappear the other. He had the file redacted to save his own ass. No one was going to besmirch the family reputation. She wondered if he knew about the favorite son's antics at his own university.

After his expulsion, George attended public school. He spent most of his time using drugs, dealing drugs, getting arrested for truancy and DUIs, and as far as she could tell, had no permanent living address. *A grandfather with a place in Martha's Vineyard has a homeless grandson. What kind of person are you, Clemson St. John?* But she knew. He was the kind with no loyalty to his own. The kind she would never understand. In her life, loyalty meant something. It meant the difference between life and death. She had no use for anyone who had no loyalty. And while George had floated between cities homelessly, Will had learned what it meant to wear an Italian suit, drink the finest wines and make small talk with million-aires and senators at the kind of parties where the dresses women wore were discarded the next day and the guests left with gift bags that rivaled those given at the Oscar after-parties in Hollywood. Will had graduated at the top of his class, attended Harvard, where he graduated summa cum laude, and moved on to finish a PhD in biochemistry at Columbia University.

She leaned back in her chair, her hands steepled. She thought of her own years in boarding school. Her parents had called once a week when they weren't traveling or serving abroad, and when they were, she got post-cards and an occasional souvenir—never anything nice but the kind the tourist traps sell in bulk, all made in China no matter which country they'd traveled to. Hol-idays were spent near the school. Her parents would rent a nice hotel room and take her to dinner. She liked steak, but they rarely obliged, opting mostly for seafood restaurants where you ordered, took a number, and a minimum-wage employee delivered your foam platter with plasticware to your Formica-top table. To this day, she never ate fish. Ever.

She wondered where George had gone wrong and Will had gone right. If she needed another reason to dislike Will, she had it. Because somewhere deep inside her, right or wrong, she blamed him for George's fate. Their parents had checked out—same as hers—and when they did, Will had looked out only for himself. He could have fought for George, taken George under his wing, included him or refused to be a part of Clemson's life otherwise. Instead, he'd made other choices. Choices that didn't involve loyalty to his brother, and the rest was history. George had been left alone to find his own way. She scribbled a note on her pad to request data on Clemson St. John. Not because it had anything to do with the operation but because now she was curious.

She'd scanned a small batch of information on the post-doc. There was very little information. *This is it? These people barely exist outside their science.* The girl she'd met that day, Eve Konisken, had just been hired that morning. Like Will, she had no social media presence, but she did have a Spotify account full of lousy music. No Stones. No Beatles. No Queen. Her mouth went dry just reading the emails, which tended toward the abrupt. After sifting through the voicemails and call logs—she never called anyone except her vet and her parents back home in Mississippi—Susan decided that Eve led a boring life. *Almost* as boring as her own. Eve lived alone with her cat, Boris, a tabby, and wore entirely too much plaid. She studied the photos. Eve's hair was the color of straw, and she had a distinctive dark rim around her pale blue irises. Her light skin set upon her high cheek-bones gave her an exotic flair, and she might've been were it not for the head-to-toe tartan and abundance of gray clothing. She was average height and build with round hips and generous breasts. She enjoyed reading—something Susan knew only from routine posts on her Goodreads account. Her reading consisted of mostly historical fiction and romance, though she'd had no boyfriends, which might've made things easier as well. Susan would need to dig deeper on Eve as well.

Her phone rang. She glanced at the caller ID. Rusty. *Cocksucker.* She let it go to voicemail.

# CHAPTER 9

VE STEPPED INTO THE TINY ROOM ACROSS THE HALL
from the main lab. Live human cells meant her
work would have to be done in a biosafety level
two room, and for now, she would work alone, which
suited her. She didn't like to be micromanaged, and the
last thing she wanted right now was to be annoyed, and
Will St. John was just that. It pained her to think this
was where she had to work, but she had rent. And a cat.
And a career she was trying to build.

Carefully, she removed the brain-on-a-chip units from
their cabinet and lifted them into an incubator. She
looked at them closely. They were simply amazing. Each
unit had taken twenty-one days to grow. A thin piece of
porous plastic separated the endothelial side, or vascular
side, from the brain side. 100 mcg/ml of Larmentin
would be introduced via a small pump outside the incubator. The drug would be pumped into the vascular
side, and the blood would pass through the blood-brain
barrier and carry Larmentin to the brain side. Eve would

sample fluid from both sides at zero hours before adding Larmentin to get a baseline reading, again six hours post-exposure and twenty-four hours post-exposure. Those samples would be run through the mass spec to look for any anomalies, and next she would stain the miniature brain-on-a-chip to look for cell death after one day of exposure to the drug.

Dealing with things this small yet powerful always thrilled Eve. That this tiny apparatus, with all of the components of a live human brain, could answer her question in a relatively short period of time was nothing short of a miracle. This technology saved lives. She went about her work in a circumspect manner, with all the attention of a gifted surgeon, as if she held a tiny life in her hand. Meticulously, she dropped the Larmentin into the blood after taking her baseline samples. She closed and sealed the incubator, checked the temperature and gas mixture and listened. Her dad said you can hear success if you listen closely enough. The steady hum of the incubator confirmed this.

Now, she waited.

She texted Will.

Eve: Just put the Larmentin on the first 3 units.

She slumped into the chair and pulled out her Agatha Christie.

⁘

IT WAS DINNERTIME, AND WILL GRABBED A TURKEY SAND-wich at the student union. His phoned vibrated.

Eve: Just put the Larmentin on the first 3 units.

He responded.

Will: Excellent news. Keep me in the loop.

He now walked toward his car without knowing why and without a destination in mind. He sat in his car, eating small bites of his turkey on rye, his mind a blank. Why had he come here? The colonel had gotten under his skin, and he didn't know how. Nothing really bothered him much, but this was different. And he was suspicious. This was *his* research, *his* experiments, *his* fucking lab. Who did she think she was to walk in and start barking orders. *His* name, *his* reputation. It was as if she had dropped in and taken over. But she was not in charge. Not of *his* operation. He could not afford to let this discovery wait because she needed lousy tox screens on a drug that was already approved by the FDA. He was sure of two things—something was not right, and his discovery would not be waitlisted or put on the back burner for her bullshit experiments. She was a bulldozer just like Clemson. His brain now twisted up into something that couldn't think straight, and his heart raced. He needed to settle down, or he'd be all over the place with his thoughts and ideas, and that wasn't good for his science. He knew what could happen if he went too long like this.

He needed his mind to go blank. He needed to lose the thinking part of himself. Smoke. Drink. Sex. He decided the easiest option was weed.

Minutes later, he pulled up outside a plain two-story brick building and finished the last of his tasteless turkey on rye. He stepped inside the door, heavier today than usual, or maybe it was him. The multi-use building contained an Indian restaurant at one end, and upstairs there were all manner of spaces. Will walked past a small group of three women on rubber mats all contorted in various ways, a tattoo parlor where a young girl put on the finishing touches of a full-sleeve tattoo, an art studio where a class worked simultaneously painting the same aspect on canvas while sipping wine, and a dog groomer where a small black poodle shivered nervously under a pair of shears. At the end of the hall was a cigar shop. A reedy woman with large green eyes and long dark braids buzzed him in.

"Well, look what the cat drug in! Will St. John. Haven't seen you in a while. How've you been?"

"Never better, Georgia." *Well, maybe after I smoke a joint. Maybe as soon as I'm stoned out of my goddamned mind.* "Yourself?"

"You know me. Roll with it. Life's been good. Speaking of, got some good stuff." She talked while she emptied boxes of Cuban's finest. Montecristos and Cohibas. "Unless you're looking for a cigar." She laughed.

"You might throw in a Cohiba or two today…along with the usual, of course."

She pulled a plain paper bag from under the counter, slid it wordlessly across the counter, and plucked two Cohibas from a box.

"May I?" Will motioned toward the bag.

"But of course. Drink?"

"Whiskey, neat." Will pulled the contents from the bag, and before Georgia returned from the back, he'd settled into a tufted leather chair and was smoking from a small glass pipe. The afternoon sun sent bars of light across the room, and Will watched the smoke tendrils rising through the light, mesmerized and completely relaxed after one hit. "Thanks." He took the whisky tumbler and turned it up.

"Easy there, tiger. That's some fine Columbian, but you've probably already figured that out. One hit is enough to get you where you're going."

"Yes, ma'am." Will grinned. "Where I'm going now is work."

"Stoned? Hope it's nothing important. Nothing to do with your nasty diseases."

At this they guffawed.

"I don't work with anything else."

"Well, don't be letting your nasty diseases out of the freezer just because you're stoned. You hear me, Will St. John? If you unleash a plague, I will tell the police everything I know about you."

They laughed again until their bloodshot eyes were full of tears.

"I promise not to let anything harmful out." He stood to leave and kissed her forehead.

She waved him off like she was dismissing him. He walked down the hall, and something about the yoga now struck him as funny. He watched as a few toppled over during their sun salutation, and he laughed all the way back to the car.

The drive back to campus was intentionally slow. Whiskey breath and marijuana would do nothing for his already tarnished rep. He'd already racked up a few Title IX violations this year. And sooner rather than later, they'd be calling him. "Fuck. Fuck. Fuck," he said to himself as he pulled in to the parking garage. "And fuck." He chewed on a mint, but that wouldn't keep his head from spinning.

The lab was quiet. He found Eve at her bay, reading while she watched a timer. She nearly came out of her skin when he walked in.

"Didn't mean to startle you. Are you alone?"

"No. Sanjay is here. He's in the restroom."

"Ah."

"You smell like…pot…and…" She crinkled her nose and sniffed at the air. "Mint whiskey. Are you stoned?"

Will tried hard to suppress a laugh, but the harder he tried, the worse it got.

"Where have you been? Did you leave?" Her eyes narrowed with disapproval as Will's grin grew wide. "You reek of pot, you know? And cheap whiskey."

"Cheap? You can smell cheap whiskey?"

"Yes."

"Oooh. A secret talent. I like it." Will stumbled and caught himself on the bench.

"It's not a secret and hardly a talent." She glowered at him. "You've been somewhere, and you're stoned and drunk and in the lab. And you wonder about the rumors that circulate? You wonder where people get their ideas about you? How? Why?"

Will looked at her face, part anger, part concern. It was almost maternal. But he couldn't answer. Not right now. His smile was aching, and before he knew it, he was howling with laughter, which rolled forward, undulating, and every time he tried to stop, he'd laugh that much harder, sucking in a breath and clutching his stomach, and now he dabbed his eyes. He was crying. If only that bitch colonel could see him now. Oh, how he wished she would call right now, right this very second. Oh, the things he could think to say, the golden shit that would come out of his mouth. The very idea, scintillating his every nerve ending.

Will cleared his throat. "I…I was with a friend." Will tried hard to compose himself.

"Oh, I see. A friend. Well, friends don't let friends drive drunk, you know."

"I didn't drive very far, Eeeeeeve." He sung out her name in a very annoying manner. Why was everyone trying to tell him what to do? "I came back to check and see if you needed anything…like a good boss on your first day."

"I'm fine, thanks. I think I can get by without help from a…compromised individual."

"Compromised individual?"

"Yes."

"What does that mean?"

"You know."

"Say it."

"I already did."

"Say it again."

"Why?"

"Just humor me."

"Fine. I don't need help extracting effluent from the brain-on-a-chip units from someone who is drunk and stoned."

Will laughed again, harder. Eve was rolling her eyes, shaking her head.

"Okay. Okay. I'll let you get back to your Agatha Christie mystery book."

"Thanks. I think that's best."

"I won't bother you anymore."

"Okay, great."

"I think you're pretty."

Eve stared at him without a word. She didn't blush. She didn't breathe. She didn't even blink. Her eyes were especially blue in the natural light from the window, and he found them haunting. He suspected she didn't know what to say. And this was clearly Title IX territory-ish behavior.

Will grinned. "See you tomorrow."

"See you then." Eve's eyes never left his, and he couldn't get a read on her at all. She'd make a hell of a poker player.

# CHAPTER 10

Colonel Savarre walked down the hall to see if Louis was around—he needed to be checking on the Larmentin project regularly. She found him at his desk halfway through a bag of Doritos.

"Louis."

"Colonel." He always saluted her despite the fact that he was now a civilian, retired.

"Do you ever eat anything healthy?"

"You mean like meatloaf and mashed potatoes?"

"No, Louis, I mean like kale or brussels sprouts with spinach on top."

"No, ma'am, I don't. Where I come from, that's not food. It's compost."

"Well, you're never getting out of that chair on a diet of Cheetos and Pepsi."

"Doritos. Don't think I'm getting out anyway."

"Okay, cut the crap. I need you to check on St. John and his colleagues. Make sure they are getting shit done. Can you do that in between chips? Thanks."

She walked back to her office in a huff. Rusty Carver could go fuck himself. This Secretary of State shit was not her personal problem. All of this was way above her pay grade. She didn't have time for this or for dealing with the CID chumps and their questions about how they ran their research labs. This was her goddamn program, and the fact that they couldn't properly command their guys in the field was not her issue. And as if she'd sent a subliminal message to the universe, Rusty Carver stood in her doorway. She got up from her desk.

"Have a seat, Susan."

"Sir. What are you doing here?"

"Well, Susan, I am here to make sure you're doing your job. I want to know these clowns you've got working on this Larmentin project are moving along. Swimmingly."

The colonel swallowed. She was not going to let this bastard get to her.

"Sir, yes. They're on it. I'm on Louis, and Louis is on them. We can handle this, sir."

"Well, just so you know, I'm gonna stick around until this is handled."

"Sir?"

"I'll be putzing around WRAIR, your labs and your office for the next fourteen days until this is handled. The army is not going to suffer a chink in their respectable military honor because some joker got anxiety and tried to blow the Secretary of State's goddamned brains out. This is bigger than that. More important. It is paramount. This is all riding on you and your team. Get it?"

"Got it." The colonel was still standing, imagining a

nice red laser spot between his eyes, a gun in her hand, large caliber anything.

"Something wrong?"

"No, sir. We'll take care of this, sir."

"Good. Oh, and Susan, Smithson's sixty-second birthday is a few months from now. He'll be retiring. Nominations for his replacement have already been discussed, your name among them. You know what you need to do. I'll be back tomorrow."

"Fine, sir." *Son of a bitch cocksucker.*

On her screen, a message blinked. Something new on Will St. John from her friends in military intel.

Louis appeared in her doorway. "I've been checking St. John's activity online, scanning his Google searches, looking at cookies, etc. I came across something odd you might be interested in."

She sighed into her coffee cup, her dark eyes registering just above the rim. "Well, don't just sit there. Spit it out."

"Someone else is watching Will St. John. Listening to his phone calls, reading his emails."

"Who?"

"That's just it. I don't know. I'm having a hard time tracing the IP address. I'm a programmer, not a hacker."

She clicked her message from the military intelligence division. They had a name. A name she recognized. *Clemson St. John.*

# CHAPTER 11

T HE NEXT MORNING, BEFORE HIS SHOWER BUT AFTER three cups of black coffee, Will called Clemson. His personal assistant, Adrienne, answered.

"Good morning, Adrienne. It's Will." *Damn lucky she answered!*

"Will! Oh my gosh, hello! How are you?" Adrienne lived in Boston but originally hailed from Charleston, and her accent was unmistakably not Boston. "Will you be joining us for Clemson's fiftieth anniversary celebration?"

"Well, that's what I'm calling about. Can I just RSVP with you?"

"Now, Will, you know your grandfather would never allow that. He'd tan my hide if he knew you called and didn't speak to him. Can you hold just a second? I think he's just sat down to his breakfast."

"Sure." Will imagined Clemson over his omelette, his pinky finger in the center to test for warmth; cold eggs meant somebody's ass in a sling. He was feared by nearly all who knew him, though Adrienne had been with him since the beginning—for as long as Will could remember. The hold music played as Will's anxiety slowly ramped up.

"William. Good morning." His grandfather had a sort of flat affect and an abrupt manner of speaking that always put Will on edge. He could never tell if his grandfather was pleased or something else—only his words gave him away. He could see him already in his Italian suit and silk tie over one shoulder while he read the *Wall Street Journal* over breakfast after the *New York Times* and before the *Washington Post*.

"You are coming to my celebration. Adrienne says you've RSVP'd in the affirmative."

"Yes. I'll be there. Wouldn't miss it."

"Excellent. We have you down for two." It was a statement, not a question.

"Two?"

"Yes, Will. Two. You plus one. I'll send Bill down with the plane."

"No, that won't be necessary. I can get there."

"Flying commercial in coach? Dear God, boy. I won't hear of it."

"Fine, but I've got to get back to my lab here. We're in the middle of two very important projects, and I cannot be away for long."

"Understood. We will see you and your significant other on Saturday at six p.m. sharp."

"See you then."

Will hung up. Significant other? He didn't have an "other," let alone a *significant* other. He ran his fingers through his hair while he ran down the possibilities. Colleagues. Friends. Grad students. He had to show up with somebody classy. Sophisticated, and clever enough to navigate Clemson. *Eve.* Will grinned. Eve was perfect.

He swished down the last of his coffee and decided to go for a run. The weather outside looked breezy and bright. He got dressed and stepped out into the brisk morning ready to face all the day would send his direction. Just like the colonel, he'd trained for this. He ran two miles from his midtown condo to a French bakery, grabbed a dozen cream puffs for the lab and an espresso for himself. He walked back. His watch flashed with messages and missed calls. Walter Reed. They were an hour ahead, but this was ridiculous.

*What could you possibly want already?* He'd have his say today. This micromanaging shit was going to stop. Today.

By the time he reached the lab, everyone was already in, working like fiends, prepping, extracting, getting the live-dead assay kits on board for the post-twenty-four-hours staining. First things first. He wanted to talk to Amy. He found her in the breakroom at the Keurig machine, waiting on a coffee to brew.

"You run the kits on the rest of our survivors?"

"Yeah. Should have something back midmorning." The Keurig sputtered out a pumpkin spice coffee, and Amy reached for a lid. "I'll find you. Don't worry."

"Okay. If we get immune function, we need to talk about next steps."

"Next steps…like what would happen if we exposed them to other diseases?"

"That's one idea. I'm thinking something bigger."

"Ebola?"

"Actually, I'm thinking autoimmune disease. I have a hypothesis swirling around in my mind. Your boyfriend still working with those diabetic mice?"

"Yeah, I think so. I'll check and let you know."

"Perfect. I'll be around."

⸙

AT HOME IN HER APARTMENT, EVE SEARCHED FOR HER peacoat and scarf and found her cat, Boris, nestled snugly on top. "Boris, c'mon, big guy." Boris weighed twenty-one pounds and change. "I need to go, and you're holding up progress, buddy. I'm going to be late. C'mon. The sofa's all yours, look. See? Choose any cushion you like."

Boris moved with all the urgency of a child being sent to bed. He stretched, plucking at the wool coat with his claws, licked his paws a few times and eventually moved. Luckily, Eve didn't have a tough commute. She could almost see her campus building from her apartment and, if she'd had binoculars, might possibly be able to see the lab she now worked in.

Her dad had called several times now, but she didn't have the fight in her. She wasn't coming home to babysit two sixty-something-year-old people, *one* an alcoholic. Her parents had moved to Mississippi from Finland; her mother longed for a warmer climate and a more prosperous life, but after only a year, she'd grown home-sick and become severely depressed. She'd always been a hefty social drinker, vodka rocks, twist of lime; now she drank all the time, and her organs were failing. She smoked all day and read magazines while her father worked at a local Toyota factory. But Eve wanted to be part of something bigger. She wanted a faculty position at a big university, preferably in the northeast. She wanted her own projects, her own students, and someday, she was determined to have it.

For now, she was running experiments for Will St. John. Paschal hadn't exaggerated. Will was sharp. Eve had checked his publications on PubMed and read his last four papers. He had several grants—NIH, NSF and DOD. And while she found him obnoxious, in academia, obnoxious often doubled for friendly. His reputation with the women on campus was dismal. He was a player. But even she had to admit he was handsome—well built with a great smile and thick, wavy hair. His laugh was infectious, and the twinkle in his eyes ever-present. *And* he'd told her he thought *she* was pretty. But of course, he'd been stoned and even a little drunk. Maybe? Hard to say. She felt a blush come in her cheeks despite herself.

Boris had found himself a nice comfy spot on the bridge of the sofa. Eve stepped out to lock the door, but something jammed. Great. She tried several times to lock the dead bolt, but it wouldn't turn. She finally reached around and turned the lock on the center of the inside doorknob and pulled the door shut. She'd call the building manager later. Her watch already had her sprinting to campus. She slipped on her pack, and that's exactly what she did.

She walked toward the lab quickly while she pulled her hair into a ponytail. She ran her chapstick around and over her lips once while sloughing off her bag and shimmying out of her coat and scarf like she was a puzzle she disassembled every morning. She walked across the hall and checked the incubator. The timer read six hours, fifty-nine minutes and counting. Soon, she'd have the first batch of post-twenty-four-hours exposure, and they could begin staining with the live-dead staining kits. Green meant live brain cells. Red meant dead brain cells.

She sat down with a cup of hot tea and inhaled the spicy amber liquid while the steam warmed her face. The sound of the phone ringing in the lab pierced the morning tranquility. Sanjay answered it and called out to Eve, "Telephone. St. John."

Eve took the phone. "This is Eve."

"You don't answer your texts?" He sounded displeased.

"I beg your pardon?"

"Your phone. *Look* at your phone. I've texted you twice this morning already."

"Oh, sorry. It was in my pack and I—well, I just checked the incubator. Six hours, fifty-nine minutes and counting."

"Great. Thanks. I need to see you in my office."

"Be right there." Eve pulled her phone from her bag and walked down the hall to Will's office.

She stood in the doorway stiff as a board, and Will thought for a minute about suggesting that yoga might help loosen her up. *Or some weed.* Her ponytail looked a little disheveled. Even in a plain black tunic and white leggings, she was the picture of class and beauty. Just what he needed.

"Please come in and have a seat."

"Look, if this is about running late, my door was jammed, and I couldn't lock it, and Boris was on my jacket, and I did run here if that counts for anything—and I did just check the incubator before making my morning tea, and I was here until almost ten o'clock last night, so if this is about that, then I've done exemplary work, and I'm as good as anybody you could get…so… if you're thinking about yelling at me or jumping down my throat, well, then, you're wrong. I am good at what I do. Paschal wouldn't have recommended me if I wasn't, and so okay? I—"

"Whoa, whoa, whoa." Will put up his hands, a mangled stirrer straw in one. "Jesus Christ, Eve, calm down already. Don't be so defensive. I didn't call you in here to 'jump down your throat.' It has nothing to do with work, actually." *A cat with a Russian name.* Will smiled.

Eve's countenance relaxed a little as she slid down into the chair. She was staring without blinking now. He guessed this was a thing she did. Her wheels were turning, and he could tell she was wondering and nervous. Her cheeks became instantly rosy, and her neck was now covered in red blotches.

"I think you got yourself worked up."

Eve unconsciously touched her neck.

"I need a favor." He chewed on what remained of his

third stirrer straw. The crumpled remains of countless others lay on his desk. It was a nasty habit, but it beat the hell out of chewed-up pens and pencils—that was nasty.

"Favor?"

"Yes. It's a big favor, I'm not gonna lie. But if you say yes, I promise to personally help with the rest of the experiments so that you're not here too late."

"Okay…what do you need?"

Will sat up in his chair, leaning in while he chewed feverishly and considered how to phrase this in favor of a yes answer.

"I have this event coming up, and I need a—to bring somebody with me. I need you to come with me to Clemson's fiftieth anniversary gala. He's a professor of neurosurgery at Harvard Medical School and kind of a big deal there. He is also very wealthy and domineering, controlling, sophomoric, you know—all the good stuff."

Eve's face revealed nothing. She was good at this poker-face thing.

"I need a date *and…*" Here he paused to evaluate his word choice, and in the end decided on "thing" rather than "girlfriend" or "fiancée." "I need it to seem as though we're a *thing*…you know, in it for the long haul like a forever thing maybe. We'll fly up on Clemson's private jet just long enough for the big party and fly back home as soon as it is done. It's a black-tie affair at Martha's Vineyard, probably around five hundred people, colleagues to Washington insiders, he's well connected." He was practically mumbling through the elitist details.

"I will provide you with a dress, shoes, jewelry…whatever you need, just…I really need this."

Will watched Eve's face subtly twitch and contort as if she were suppressing a sneeze. *This was good sign, no?* She pressed her lips firmly together, then pursed them into a kiss, then to the left, then to the right. It seemed she was having an honest-to-god emotional reaction, but for some unknown reason, she was trying hard to subdue any outward signs. She was processing. Will lowered his head and watched her face relax into a smile, and then she slapped her hand over her mouth, but it didn't work. She began to laugh maniacally. Now it was Will who sat stone-faced. It took an inordinate amount of time for her to collect herself, and she attempted an insincere apology between clearing her throat and catching her breath.

"Are you done?"

"Yes, I'm sorry. You just—that's a ridiculous story, and you seem so serious." Eve straightened in her chair and adjusted her ponytail, more crooked than before. She looked borderline goofy.

"Well, I can assure you I am quite serious, Eve." Will grabbed a fresh coffee stirrer.

"This is real?"

"Yes."

"Okay…look, I don't know you that well, but I know your reputation. I heard about how you stood up to the Title IX council when they thought they had you backed into a corner about that student who accused you of sexual harassment, and when you were written up for dropping an f-bomb in the classroom and ordering a microscope from Awesome Fucking Science Instruments or whatever they were called, and I saw you in action with that brute from WRAIR. She could scare the pants off Satan himself, and she didn't even *faze* you. You didn't even blink. So who is this Clemson guy, and why shouldn't *I* be intimidated by him if you're such a scaredy-cat?"

"Fair enough. Clemson is my grandfather, and here's a little St. John family history. We must all, including my father, refer to him as Clemson. He has ultra-high standards for everyone in my family. I am the only one who has not failed him in some way. Not yet. My father shamed him by choosing to become a plastic surgeon out in Hollywood. Clemson often refers to him as a boob. My mother left my father when I was young for another woman—nearly twenty-five years younger—who is, as we speak, pregnant. My fraternal twin, George, is an addict who roams the country only to return for money. Then there is me. The only remaining respectable hope according to Clemson. Clemson himself is a renowned neurosurgeon and Harvard Medical's biggest rainmaker. People come from around the world for his hands. In his office, he's got a map with a pin in every country where people have come from, and he is a crown jewel in the Harvard family of faculty and physicians. He has a home in West Tisbury on the cape near Boston. He has a flat in the city, but he's semi-retired and spends more and more time on the cape. He sails and rows, and he sent me to cotillion, and in his mind, now is about the time for me to begin searching for a suitable spouse. Someone who will produce acceptable offspring. He's a tour de force, but I think *you'll* do fine. You know, like you did in your interview kind of fine."

Will grinned with his entire face. He had beautiful, perfectly white teeth, all of which showed when he smiled, and gathered in all of his expression into such great lines. His look was ruggedly handsome when he hadn't shaved, and his dark hair hung in a wavy frame around his face when he wasn't running his hands through it. He could've been a model for Ralph Lauren if he hadn't become a scientist.

"And your grandmother?"

He hadn't counted on this. *She left when my father was an infant. I never knew her. I've never even seen a photo. She left no evidence of her existence behind other than my father. And no one—not one person I've ever met in the family—will speak of her or what happened.* Will was sure that even his father knew little or nothing about her.

"I never knew her. She died when my father was young. Cancer, I think."

"Oh. I'm sorry to hear. Okay… When is this celebration happening? I have all those experiments running, and we've got that ridiculous timeline from the colonel."

"I think I can have a word with your boss on that, but to answer your question, this Saturday. We can fly up and be there at six, and fly back home immediately following the celebration."

"All right. I'll go." She looked right at him when she

said it. Some women might have turned down such an offer or agreed sheepishly or with fear or reluctance, but not her. She'd walk through fire. Eve was just what he needed. Clemson would no doubt be pleased.

Will pulled the coffee stirrer from his mouth.

"Thank you. You have no idea." *My only other choice was a student, and that would not have gone over very well.*

"I'm gonna get back to the lab now. I'll let you know as soon as the twenty-four hours is up. I'm going to show Sanjay how to use the live-dead staining kit. Also, we should have the mass spec data back on the effluent I extracted earlier in a few hours."

"Great."

Amy busted through his door. "They've all got functioning immune systems! We have cytokines!" She looked from Will to Eve and back to Will. "Oops, I am so sorry! Am I interrupting anything?"

"We were just finishing up, actually."

Eve smiled and mouthed "See you later" as she walked out.

"Sorry! I just can't believe it. I ran the kits on all of our mice—it appears they all have functioning immune systems!"

"Okay." Will motioned for her to calm down with his hands. Her body was already twisted up into a pretzel in the chair, waiting for ideas, instructions, hypotheses.

"Let me think." Will sat quietly for not more than a minute, chewing on his stirrer. "I think we ask your boyfriend for some of those diabetic mice."

Amy's enthusiasm was replaced with a look of uneasiness.

"You want me to ask Joe for some of his mice?"

Will could now see the idea wasn't sitting so well with Amy. This was important, and the mice were there, already sick with an autoimmune disease. And he'd replace the mice as soon as he could.

"Yes."

"Is that okay…? I mean, he's been working with those mice for months…" Her voice trailed off into a whisper.

Will took a breath. "I'll replace them as soon as possible. His research won't even skip a beat, I promise. It's just a few mice. He's got what? Fifty? And this is huge. We are talking about a medical breakthrough—a cure, for fuck's sake. C-U-R-E." Will spelled it out. "How many people can say they've discovered a cure for something? This is about diabetes. Multiple sclerosis. Arthritis. Lupus. Fibromyalgia. Thyroid disease. Even AIDS. Borrowing a few mice in the quest to cure autoimmune diseases is nothing, trust me. You gotta look at the bigger picture, Amy. Think big science. Think breakthrough. Think. Cure." He watched Amy's face relax a little. "It's not a big deal. It's a few mice, and I am gonna put them right back."

Amy looked at the ceiling and then at Will.

"Okay. I'll do it."

"Good. And then you know what to do, right?"

"I think so. I'll take a blood draw from our mice, inject it into the mice sick with diabetes…"

"Exactly."

"You think the parasites are producing a molecule that is resetting the immune system."

"Yes. It's like a stem cell transplant, only the parasites are doing all the work. And the kicker? No downtime. We just need to be sure."

But he already was. Nothing could possibly happen now that would bring him down.

"Wow."

"Wow is a place to start. This will change the course of disease. If we can cure these mice… But first, the mice." The implications were infinite.

Amy's enthusiasm was back. She hopped out of her pretzel in one smooth motion.

"I'm going to find Joe now!"

"Excellent."

"I'll be back!" She left, and Will had no doubt that if anyone could make it happen, it was Amy. She was driven, and nothing would get in the way of her discovering the truth. A truth Will was certain he already knew.

# CHAPTER 12

From his desk, Louis could hear the secretary of the army and Colonel Savarre arguing. Louis stopped crunching his Kettle Salt & Pepper chips and listened.

"We are working on it." Savarre was steaming, but she knew to tread lightly with Rusty.

"This is day three." He held up three sausage-like fingers to indicate three as if she were a preschooler. It was this very kind of patronizing shit that really got under her skin. "I've got a dead soldier, half a dozen witnesses with CID up their asses, and Secretary of State Elizabeth Rhodes hanging on to life by a thread. The conspiracy theories are through the fucking roof on this thing. You need to make this Larmentin problem go away—every man and woman we have in the field is popping that crap. I'm talking with my guy at the *Post* on Friday. This is going to be a case of homesick-and-depressed-soldier-goes-postal-after-getting-high and nothing more. They're printing on Sunday. You'd better be ready for it."

*Or what?* It was a veiled threat, but he wasn't the one who scared her anyway. She bit back. She stood up and leaned over her desk.

"This whole thing might've been avoided if you didn't actually *like* what Larmentin does. You've never cared much for those subdued garrison types. Truth is, you like 'em a little hopped up. You like somebody's who's gonna charge out into a firefight guns blazing. The ones who drop to their knees in the middle of a street in a war-torn enemy village, screaming obscenities about Allah until their purple faces pop every vein in their foreheads and eyes like some overly drawn dramatic scene out of a goddamned Hollywood war movie. You don't fool me, Rusty. This isn't about Larmentin or that dead soldier or the army's reputation. This is about your dirty little secret—the crazy ones make the best warfighters."

Rusty leaned into her space, his fried chicken breath heavy against her face.

"Now you listen to me and listen carefully. There is more at stake here. We"—he pointed at himself and her simultaneously with his thumb and pinky—"you and I—the army—invented this drug, and *that* drug is responsible for billions of dollars in revenue, revenue that comes back to the army, and while the military's budget is always on the chopping block these days, I'd say that is money we cannot afford to lose. So you're gonna back me up on this whether you like it or not, whether or not you agree. This story's gonna break on Sunday. The soldier was depressed, and he lost his goddamned mind under the pressure of serving on the battlefield. And this pet project of yours is going to be done whether you like it or not. I gave you 6.25 million dollars. You better see that it does."

He huffed out of her office and past Louis, who returned to his grazing.

In her mind, she thought about how many people were watching Will St. John at this very moment. About the fact that she wasn't the only one. There were others. His grandfather, Clemson. But *why*?

In the reflection of his monitor, Louis could see Colonel Savarre walking toward him.

"Louis!" She always shouted when she was agitated, which was nearly all the time, even though he was sitting only two feet away. He looked up with a mouthful of chips.

"Yes, ma'am."

"Louis, I need you to check and see if those clowns are making any progress on the Larmentin project."

"Yes, ma'am." Louis swallowed and licked his lips, nodding.

"*Now*, Louis." She eyed his bag of Doritos, and he thought for a minute she might slap them off his desk or throw them in the trash. But she did not. She just stomped away.

Louis had never taken Larmentin, but he'd had plenty of friends who did. They'd all talked about the psychological side effects—hallucinations, bad dreams, paranoia, memory loss. They even made jokes about the day they took it. Wacky Wednesday and Psycho Sunday. The mood alterations were so pronounced, they had nicknames for the day they took their dose. The list of side effects was so exhaustive and so well-known, Louis couldn't see how the colonel possibly expected to clear Larmentin as safe. Maybe she knew something he didn't. He picked up the phone and called Will St. John.

⁑

"St. John."

"Dr. St. John, this is Louis Webster calling from WRAIR."

"Good morning, Louis. How are you? And how's my favorite gorilla today? She busy beating her chest and standing her ground against the other silverbacks?"

There was no audible laughter, but he could hear Louis smiling, and his voice was light.

"I'm good, sir, thanks. Just calling to see if you've any preliminary results on the Larmentin."

"Well, Louis, you're in luck. We've got about two more hours, and we'll know something. So far, the mass spec looks clean on the effluent. I'll let you know what our testing turns up. Call you back in say two and a half hours?"

"Two and a half hours sounds good. Thank you."

Will checked his watch. He had one meeting with the Title IX office between now and the time Eve would be wrapping up.

# CHAPTER 13

WILL ORDERED AN AMERICANO WHILE THE barista batted her long, false eyelashes. Will smirked, pocketed his change, grabbed his coffee and made his way to the administrative building. Minutes later, he stepped into the decadent corridor and mused at how this atmosphere reminded him of Clemson. The luxurious brocade draperies with large silk tassels, the oversized equestrian-themed oil paintings, the Victorian-era furnishings and tufted leather chairs, the polished brass handles that clung to enormous glass doors were reminiscent of Clemson's flat in the city. The rooms were cavernous and paneled with dark woods oiled to a sheen. Bronze statuary filled every corner, and leather settees were carefully placed for optimal viewing. Will found the decadence nauseating and the pompous blowhards that often visited even more so. The people here were as pretentious and hollow as the rooms they occupied. University administrators who enforced policies only as often as it suited their needs and who had no idea what integrity meant. They were politicians first, academicians second, and liars *always*.

He checked in with the Title IX office receptionist with whom he was now on a first-name basis. Hers was Mary, though her faux walnut name placard read "Ms. Pembroke" in a  sans serif font. Appropriately, she sat very erect, this fact made more pronounced by the fact that she was five eleven with spindle-like limbs and twigs for fingers. Around her long, pale neck a choker of pearls, that might've been a bracelet for a larger woman, was the only horizontal interruption to her plain navy head-to-toe ensemble. And what might've been an otherwise classic look on a softer frame looked austere on her, consistent with the air about the place. She was on a phone call, which from all accounts appeared to be going poorly. They had to be the only office less popular than internal audit. With a wave of her skeletal hand, she directed him into the conference room. An image of the grim reaper came into his mind, and he suppressed an ironic smile.

The Title IX office looked as much like a corporate office as anything he'd seen, with a larger staff than the average academic department and growing, thank you, feds. Here, one felt like they were in the belly of the beast, or perhaps Room 101 like in Orwell's *1984*. Only he was not here to be broken as much as to do the breaking. Will found the government and their influence in the academic world unsettling. In a place he had hoped celebrated freedom of expression and outrageous ideas, and one that understood the positive correlation between high risk and high reward, he felt more and more that academia was on the verge of returning to the days of banned books. Weren't trigger words the gateway to censorship? Today, he'd get one more chance to explain himself and risked having his tenure clock set back a year—or worse, *suspended*. He couldn't afford that right now with all that was going on—his breakthrough discovery and this project needed to continue.

In the back of his mind, he wondered what would happen when they found out he'd made the discovery of a lifetime. That he may have in fact found a way to reset the immune system, making diseases like diabetes obsolete. No doubt this sexual harassment claim would vanish, but that was beside the point. True, he liked women, he liked sex—he'd slept with a colleague or two, or ten maybe; he'd watched porn before, and he liked getting high, but he wasn't abusive—he was *not* the person this student said he was. And while his personal reputation had taken on a life of its own, growing arms and legs and walking circles around him, his scientific reputation was sterling. The idea of no cussing and trigger warnings in the classroom cramped his style, and that offended *him*. His students cussed all the time. He couldn't have guessed that an f-bomb would offend anyone. But this particular meeting, one of many, was about a female student who'd accused him of sexual harassment; he made her feel uncomfortable when he noticed she was not wearing underwear, something he was certain had been intentional, and that it was not his interest but rather his *lack* of interest that had gotten him into trouble. He drummed his fingers on the table while he waited. The longer he sat, the angrier he got, and then he stopped himself. *Remember your breakthrough.* He gathered himself internally. Any signs of anger would only mean defensiveness and a guilty conscience, and he was not. He sat up straight in his chair as the council members filed in. One white woman, one black woman and an older Indian gentleman.

The man spoke first, his accent thick.

"Dr. St. John, good afternoon."

"That remains to be seen." *Damnit, Will, shut your fucking mouth.*

The man looked over his glasses at Will while he opened a file folder. A manila file folder. The second over the past several days. A sign of what he was dealing with.

"I think we all know the circumstances under which you are here, so I'll get right to the point. The university needs to make this right for the student who has issued the complaint, unless there is some reason why we should believe that she has been untruthful."

"Untruthful?"

"Yes, Dr. St. John. Is she lying about your behavior on the day in question."

"What day is that exactly?"

He cleared his throat. "The day…" He looked down at the file. "She claims you ogled her in her mini skirt, that you had clear sexual intentions, and that made her extremely uncomfortable. That is the day and the incident we are here to discuss. She cannot transfer out, and there are no other sections of this particular course being offered. She needs this class to graduate in spring."

He could tell both women had already made up their minds. He looked at them, both in their modest-length tweed skirts, with white cotton blouses buttoned up to their necks, blazers and pearls, and likely wearing flesh-toned bras underneath. They would've thrived during the Puritan era.

He looked at them both and spoke.

"Are you ladies wearing underwear today?"

"I beg your pardon, Dr. St. John!" The Black woman clutched her throat and leaned backward in her chair.

"Answer the question. Are you wearing panties?" He looked from one to the other. Their eyes were anything but dull now. Good. He had their attention.

"Dr. St. John!" The Indian man tried to speak but was interrupted.

The white woman spoke. "Not that it is any of your business, Dr. St. John, I think it is safe to assume that we are."

"And if you were not wearing underwear—if you happened to pop into this meeting commando—I wouldn't know, would I? Your skirts are too long. May I ask if you intentionally dressed that way this morning?"

"We ask the questions, Dr. St. John. You are here only to provide answers." Dr. India sounded stressed. He turned back to the women.

"Just humor me, please. Why aren't your skirts shorter?"

"This is work, Dr. St. John. We dress appropriately for our careers—our positions."

"The thing is this: you're both wearing underwear, and if you were not, I wouldn't know because your skirts are long enough that even while seated, it is not discernable. When that student came to my office, she sat in a chair with no table or desk, and no long skirt to hide the fact that she wasn't wearing underwear. She sat, legs spread, short skirt and no panties. So, yes, I noticed. Did I stare? No, I did not. I don't think that was what she wanted. In fact, that we are all here is proof that she desired a different outcome. I am certain there are girls—women—on this campus who are sexually assaulted and harassed on a daily basis, but I am not one of those guys. So if this is about whether or not I noticed, yes, I noticed. You all would've noticed, too. But that is all. If the fact that I *noticed* makes me guilty, well then. But harassment? I harassed no one. If anything should concern you, it is that her complaint, and any like it, undermine every female on this campus who has a legitimate grievance."

The council sat silently while Will continued. He watched the women as he spoke, from arms crossed to hands folded, they listened intently and jotted down occasional notes. He hoped they understood.

"I know it is your job to protect. But I can also assure you there is no reason to ever protect anyone from me."

"Dr. St. John, you've made your point in a most unorthodox manner. However, I feel strongly about the mission of this institution and the responsibility we have to our students. And while this student's behavior indicates poor judgment and a lack of self-awareness, we expect these things from our young students. Your behavior, on the other hand, Dr. St. John, is reflective of a pattern that has resulted in a total of nine complaints. This isn't your first rodeo. One is inexcusable; nine is another matter entirely. This meeting was a formality, Dr. St. John, a courtesy so that we could speak with you in person. That said, we are suspending you with pay, pending a full investigation to determine your tenure and future with this university. We all want the same thing, a safe environment for our students to thrive and prosper."

Will was incensed. Courtesy! They'd no idea what they were doing suspending someone who'd just made a discovery that would change the world.

"Self-awareness? Are you out of your goddamned minds? She knew exactly what she was doing. She was fully aware!" Will was shouting now and leaning across the table while each of the council members leaned back farther in their chairs. "She knew exactly what she was doing, but you know who does not? You! You've no idea what you've just done!"

Will stood without shaking hands, left the room and slammed the door. He would not be stopped over some bullshit accusation. His focus was a singular thing now. His discovery, if they wanted him off campus, out of his lab, they could come find him and throw him out, but until then, his work would continue uninterrupted.

He walked out and headed back toward his building. Outside, the sun was shining, but the air was much colder than when he'd walked over only a short time earlier. He walked briskly and braced against the raw wind.

With gloved hands, he grabbed another espresso at the campus coffee shop and kicked up the last of autumn's leaves restlessly as he walked. He didn't have time to worry about being suspended by the Title IX office right now with everything else that was going on. Sooner or later, they'd come for him, but first, he needed to find out whether Amy had spoken with her boyfriend about the diabetic mice, and second, whether Eve had started the staining process. He was so close to an answer on both fronts. He couldn't let this shit with Title IX cloud his thinking. He had real work to do. Science. After he tracked down Eve, he'd call Cindy about the analysis for the mass spec. He hoped he could call Louis Webster at WRAIR and put this Larmentin thing to bed. Lots of balls in the air made his skin vibrate. He emptied his lungs and took a deep breath of November air. He was upon it. Something big was about to happen. He could feel it in his bones.

⸎

BACK AT THE LAB, EVE AND SANJAY HAD BEGUN THE staining process. Eve opened the staining kit and went through the protocols with Sanjay, showing him each step and how to properly apply the stain. Once applied, it took only twenty minutes to see results. Next, they put the brain-on-a-chip under the microscope. Sanjay looked first, then Eve. No red cells. No cell death meant no neurotoxicity. Eve spotted Will coming down the hall toward the lab. She waved him over. "We're done staining. Take a look."

Will leaned over the microscope. The cells were all green.

"Hmm. All green. I suppose that's good news. The colonel should be pleased. Shall we take a look at the others?"

Eve pulled the other units, performed the stain protocol and checked each under the microscope. Will stood by intermittently checking. The results confirmed it. Larmentin wasn't killing brain cells.

"Eve, Sanjay, thank you both. I'm going to go call the colonel—actually, I think I'll call Louis and skip the gorilla. I'll let you know about next steps."

Will made it to his office quickly, sat down and Skyped Louis, whose face appeared after the first ring.

"Louie, hello! How's things there?"

"Uhh…never better, Dr. St. John."

"Please, call me Will. So we're done with the initial screening, and the Larmentin has shown no signs of neurotoxicity. How do you want me to proceed? Do you want me to send these results and start on the de-identified samples or—"

In the computer screen's periphery, there appeared a large pair of pale hands, knuckles laced with bulging blue veins—they might've belonged to a wide receiver in the NFL—on the handles of Louis's wheelchair. Will watched as Louis disappeared wordlessly, wheeled to the side of the screen, and suddenly *her* face filled the screen. *Jesus.* Will feigned being frightened, but she ignored him. Her nose looked especially pointed and large, and her black eyes darted and shifted, her reddish-blonde hair pulled into a severe bun. Scary AF.

"Just what in the hell do you think you're doing sitting there in your office like nothing has happened?"

"I don't kn—"

"You're suspended, Dr. St. John. The council suspended you less than an hour ago." *And if he finds out, I can't save you.* "I need those results, and that means I need you to hold up your end of our agreement, and I hardly see how you can follow through with any of this if you are not there."

"I won't ask how you know that. I don't even want to know. I don't care." *Beat your chest, silverback.* "As I was saying to Louis before I was so rudely interrupted and before you wheeled him to the side, my team is done with the preliminary Larmentin screening. No signs of neurotoxicity. Not yet."

"Great. Send the reports to me. Thank you and your team for your efforts."

"About the de-identified samples—"

"You may discard those, Dr. St. John. Then I suggest packing up your things and laying low for a while."

"Yeah, I can't do that. See, we need—"

"I said discard them, Dr. St. John. You're done."

"All we've done is run the control experiment. We ran the drug through the brain units, but not the samples you sent. There's a possibility—"

"Discard them."

"But we—"

"All five hundred."

"Fine. But just so you know, I'm telling you that all we've done is run the Larmentin through. Sometimes the drug itself is not toxic, but once the body has processed the drug—metabolized it in the liver—a drug can become toxic. It's possible we may have missed something really important." *But hey, no big deal, to hell with scientific accuracy and integrity.* "But we'll send the reports we have to you directly." Laying low was not a part of his plan either. He had BALB/c nude mice who began with zero immune function now with fully functioning immune systems, and he only needed to confirm what he already knew. He wasn't going anywhere. And even if he did, they'd be begging him to come back.

The Skype call had ended with her image frozen on his screen. He looked at her face until the screen saver took over. Never mind that she knew his every move—that he was suspended—something wasn't right. Will sat for a long time thinking about how she'd been breathing down his neck over the last week, how she'd cut the timeline in half, and now she didn't even want him to run the blood samples she'd sent. This was not the way he did science. In point of fact, this was the precise kind of shit that ruins the reputation of scientists and deteriorates public trust in science. There are entire industries being formed around the ability to reproduce experiments, companies that *guarantee* your experiments can be reproduced by other labs. That is the current state of science, and it was situations like this that contributed to the problem. She had paid him millions of dollars to find the truth and was now asking him to quit before he had the full answer. It just didn't make sense. Any other time, he might've dug a bit more, but he had bigger things in the works, like finding a cure for autoimmune diseases. Plus, he was sure Eve would be pleased that the pressure on her to get it all done in two weeks was over.

Will found Eve hunched over an ivy plant, trimming and plucking spent leaves, watering and cooing while her fish circled the tank anxiously under the watchful eye of a raven who sat on the sill. She was beautiful. He would have to choose something special for her to wear. He had a student, Taylor, who had a crush and was always hinting at him to come by the boutique where she worked. Have a glass of champagne, maybe pick out something pretty for your girlfriend or your mom, she'd winked. Time to cash in on her offer. He could use the help.

She stood to empty a handful of brown foliage and noticed Will standing there.

"Oh, hi. Didn't realize you were standing there."

"Were you cooing at your plants?"

Eve shrugged. "Humming. I hum sometimes, I guess."

"Well, I can give you something to sing about. You're done with the Larmentin project." *Now the real work begins. You can help Amy identify the molecule I think is resetting the immune systems of my leish-infected mice.*

"What? Done? How?" Eve couldn't believe it.

"I called Colonel Savarre with the neurotoxicity screens, and she was perfectly satisfied."

"But the blood samples. What about the de-identified samples they sent? We haven't tested those yet."

"She said we can toss them."

"Toss them? Toss five hundred samples of blood taken

from the same population of people experiencing the side effects?"

"That's right. That's what she said."

"That just doesn't seem right to me. There could be metabolites produced by the liver that—"

"Look, I think she was in a hurry, and we didn't see any cell death. No dead brain cells, no neurotoxicity."

"But—"

"But what, Eve? What do you think you're going to find? We screened the Larmentin. We both looked at the brain cells under the microscope. You saw what I saw."

Eve shook her head. "There could be other issues. It's possible the body is breaking down the drug into a dangerous metabolite. Something harmful or even fatal to humans. We *both* know that. It is possible for a drug to be perfectly safe in the lab setting *outside* of the human body, but when it's ingested, and the human body breaks it down, it changes, sometimes into something very toxic. It's not the drug, it's the way we break it down…*the metabolite*. You know this."

"That is true, but that is not what she asked for, and we got 6.25 million dollars to do what we were asked, and that's what we did. We fulfilled our part of the contract. Her lack of judgment is not my problem." *I can't worry about her lack of judgment. I have a cure for autoimmune illness. A cure. And now I'm not sure how much time I have to confirm my hypothesis.*

Eve's voice got louder.

"Really? You can't be serious. You don't think 6.25 million dollars was a ridiculous amount of money to pay for a week's worth of lab experiments? You don't think it was odd that she rushed us, that she was calling every day breathing down our necks? This woman just shows up out of the blue, hands us a bazillion dollars and then tells us we can throw out five hundred samples. I smell a rat."

Will agreed. She was right, but he really, really did not have time for this.

"I agree with you. It is odd, and I've mulled it over in my own mind. But that isn't the issue here. We weren't hired to assess her business practices. So she has deep pockets, so she's in a hurry…so the fuck what?"

"I don't know what." She shot him a look. "But I won't just stand around while you turn a blind eye to whatever it is she is doing!" Eve protested. *I will find out the truth with or without your help.*

Will looked around the lab. Thankfully the students all had their earbuds in, and so no one had heard Eve raise her voice. He turned back to Eve, shout-whispering.

"Look, you have no idea—*none*—what, if anything, she is doing. This tirade of yours is all based on some pretty large assumptions you've made with zero evidence of wrongdoing. And now you are acting as if I have done something wrong. Well I haven't!"

Eve started to interrupt but sucked her words back in.

"This entire lab and the work we were doing came to a complete and total standstill because of this Larmentin project, when we have much bigger, much more impor-tant, and dare I say world-changing research things that we need to accomplish. I pay *you*, Eve. Not the other way around. And you will follow my instructions on this. The research sponsor has asked that we suspend our research and toss the blood samples, and that is what we are going to do. Am I clear?"

"But—"

"Am I clear?" Will's voice thundered.

"Yes." Her eyes met his directly as she said it. *And by yes, I mean over my dead fucking body. I will not stand by while you help the military cover up whatever they are covering up. People deserve to know the truth, and that is exactly what I plan to find out. And when I do, you'll all be sorry.*

"Honestly, I thought you'd be happier than this. I really thought you might enjoy yourself more on Saturday night without this project hanging over your head."

"I guess." *Hanging over my head? Like a pack of lies?*

"Okay, well, I need to meet with you and Amy on another project, one so much bigger and more important than this it'll blow you away. Trust me on this. I'll come get you later or text you a time."

"Okay." Eve returned to her pruning. She didn't care what the colonel said. Or Will either. She was not going to throw out five hundred samples. She was going to test them…a few anyway.

# CHAPTER 14

EVE FINISHED UP AT HER DESK AND FED HER FISH. She stepped into the hallway, stood and listened. Down the hall, she could hear Will laughing, but there were no students around, nobody in the hallway. She scurried across to the biosafety lab, where the blood samples were stored. She began by randomly choosing three of the samples the colonel had sent. She took three of the brain-on-a-chip-units, and instead of perfusing Larmentin, she introduced the blood from the samples into the port. The blood sample would run through the miniature brain, and soon she would know whether or not something in the blood samples was toxic to the human brain. She didn't understand Will's attitude at all. Didn't he want to know the truth? Hadn't he admitted something about this entire project didn't pass the sniff test? Was it the money? His reputation as a scientist was sterling, and yet he was willing to throw out the key to this whole project—five hundred samples of blood taken from soldiers in the field. That wasn't good enough for her. She wanted to know the truth—for herself, but more importantly for the people taking the drug. She set the timer for six hours and looked at her watch. She set the alarm on her phone. She'd need to be back at six o'clock to make her extractions at precisely six hours post-exposure and again at six p.m. the next day. Even though she was new to this lab, she felt pretty good about breaking the rules to get to the truth. It was the right thing to do, and deep down inside, Will St. John knew it, too. She would never understand why he had walked away simply because the colonel had cut him loose. It was precisely these types of half measures that gave scientists a bad rap. Shoddy research and incomplete data would lead to erroneous results that propagate the lies fed to those outside their community, including popular media outlets and eventually into the tributaries of society. The pursuit of undeniable, objective truth was the hallmark of great science. Eve would be tenacious, or she would not be anything at all. And now that she had everything set in place, she realized she was starving.

She grabbed her coat and scarf and walked over to the student union for a garden salad and some soup. Thick colorless clouds had replaced the bright sunshine, and the air outside was damp. Eve wrapped her scarf around her neck and over her head and back down around her face. Across the stone path, the wind whipped the autumn leaves into miniature whirlwinds, and her eyes watered. The large pin oaks that lined the sidewalk were mostly brown with thinning leaves, and the cityscape of downtown, once hidden by thick canopies, was now visible. Concrete spires rose in assorted heights, dotted with windows, and the yellow-orange promise of warmth inside contrasted against the cold ash of the November sky. Eve loved being in the city during the fall and winter. She imagined sitting in an office on the tenth floor of an academic building with a cup of hot oolong tea, looking down on the campus full of old buildings covered in English ivy and moss, and watching students and faculty scurry between buildings.

Inside the student union, she grabbed a ready-made salad and a vegan-friendly tomato soup. She ate by herself at a table in the corner while she checked emails and listened to voicemails. Her father had called again, and she really needed to call him back even though in her mind she could recite the conversation they would have verbatim.

*"Hi, dad it's me.*

*D: Eve, can you come home soon?*

*Not really, I'm busy here with deadlines and, you know, stuff.*

*D: Your mom is struggling—really struggling, and I know seeing you makes her feel so much better. She's always so much better when you're here, after you've visited with us.*

*I know, Dad, and I'm sorry—I'll try to get home over the holidays, okay?*

*D: Okay. Proud of you, Evie. You're working so hard. Love you.*

*Love you too, Dad."*

Eve thought about her dad, his job and how it was

*just* a job. He was a critical thinker who was as good at analyzing complex problems as he was at understanding the most complicated people. He was thoughtful and astute. He might've been a great attorney or physician, but someone had to babysit her mother, and that was the life he'd chosen. Occasionally, Eve would catch him reading Tolstoy or Emerson in his spare time, and she had seen copies of Milton and Homer on his bedside table. Inside him was a genius. She knew it. And all the time, he used to say to her, "In you, I see a thousand suns. Someday, Evie, I hope you show the world the bright light that's inside you." *Touché, Dad.*

She now walked with a sense of purpose back toward her building. She was anxious to check on her project and make sure no one had been around the incubator or asking about the items inside. If Will caught her using more of the brain-on-a-chip units, she'd be in big trouble, and she needed this job for now. She was sure that if she found something, anything at all, that might point to a problem with Larmentin, she could convince him after the fact that running the blood samples from WRAIR was the right thing to do. Until then, she'd have to keep what she was doing a secret. She couldn't let him or any of the other students see her walking in and out of the BSL2 lab, especially since the Larmentin screening was complete. She'd have no reason to be in there now. She already had a plan. If she found something, she'd tell Will *first*. Then she'd call Louis at WRAIR. He seemed like a reasonable enough person. She'd run it by him first and ask for advice about going to the colonel with it.

Once they knew the drug was poisonous, they'd want to take action, she was sure. Pull the drug from the shelves and go with something different. Something that was not neurotoxic—something that was *safe*.

Back at her desk, she sank down into her chair, which dropped suddenly and unexpectedly six inches further, jarring her spine. She cursed and spent the next fifteen minutes trying to adjust the chair height to something appropriate before giving up and settling on an eye-level view of the edge of her desk. She felt like an adult seated in a chair intended for a toddler. Otto eyed her suspiciously as he swam in and out of his plants. In another lab she'd worked in, one of the chairs was duct-taped together, and in another, acid had eaten through most of the cover and good portion of the foam on the inside. This would do. She began scrolling through the literature on Larmentin, but she just didn't find much. However, when she googled it and selected the *News* tab, she couldn't believe her eyes. Pages and pages of stories—stories of homicidal rampages, split personalities, paranoia, permanent psychosis, and mental breakdowns. Stories of lawsuits against government agencies and defense ministries. She read countless stories, and just when she thought she'd read the worst possible story, there was another. The BBC reported one mother came back from serving in Iraq and mutilated her entire family. It was later discovered that she'd been on medical leave twice due to mental issues and psychosis—psychosis that the psychiatrist suggested was related to the drug she'd been taking—*Larmentin*. A story on Al Jazeera detailed a soldier who continued to suffer from depression and anxiety with occasional stints of feeling homicidal even though it had been more than ten years since his last dose. An Irish newspaper reported a soldier who'd hung himself shortly after serving his final combat tour.

On one site, a still image of a young woman crying, her head lying on a casket draped with the American flag as the tears poured out. Her suffering was unimaginable. Beside her, two little girls, their faces blotchy and red, their daddy gone forever. Eve couldn't think of losing her own dad. She choked on her breath as she reached out and touched the screen. She clicked to play a video. The voiceover of a journalist narrated the story of a man who'd been a loving father and husband. Neighbors talked about his generosity. Family spoke to his integrity and humor. One elderly woman described how he'd gone out in the middle of a tornado to bring her cat inside. Then he suddenly snapped. He butchered his military dog, Roscoe, the shepherd who'd been by his side on all of his tours, before turning a gun on himself. A quote from the wife said, "He didn't kill himself. He wasn't himself. The life he took wasn't the man I married. The life he took, that was somebody else." CNN. Fox. BBC. Al Jazeera. MSNBC. ABC. CBS. Every network, every newspaper, every magazine and periodical. This stuff was dangerous. Poisonous. And it was everywhere. Inside half an hour, she'd only just scratched the surface. This drug had a long history of adverse side effects. The last article she read mentioned a soldier, Joey Bishop, who'd fired on Secretary of State Elizabeth Rhodes. Some sources reported that he'd struggled on the anti-leish medication.

Boom.

There it was.

Eve sat stunned. The drug was bad, and they'd known from the beginning. *They knew, and they did not care.* Her heart pounded at the thought. Had she unwittingly become part of some scheme to cover this up? The heat rose in her cheeks. The money. The rush. The whole dump-the-samples. They had what they needed. Data that put Larmentin in the clear.

Next, Eve checked the revenue streams at the pharmaceutical company. Their reported earnings for the last four quarters confirmed Larmentin was a huge payday in a we-can't-afford-to-lose-it kind of way. It was worth billions to the army. Billions. Eve let it sink in. What was 6.25 million to make sure a drug worth billions of dollars remained on the shelf? A drop. Nothing. She could hear Will laughing in the hallway outside the lab. He was talking with Cindy Tan, who'd written the software for the mass spec analysis. Cindy would need that software before this was all over, but for now, Eve decided it was best not to say anything. She'd accompany Will on the trip to his grandfather's retirement party and play her role. Maybe she'd even score some brownie points and build some good will to soften the blow when she revealed what she'd been doing. Maybe. He didn't seem the type to blow up, but then she didn't know him that well. Besides his infamous reputation around campus, all she knew was what Paschal had told her.

She stared at her screen. One by one, one story at a time, the search results she'd pored over disappeared in front of her. The screen was now a blank Google search. She punched her Enter button and restarted her browser. She searched again. Nothing. Gone. The only remaining search results were a handful of scholarly articles. Everything she'd just read had disappeared right before her eyes. *What just happened?*

"What the hell just happened?" Her fish, Otto, watched her as if he knew what she was up to. She shot him a look. "What are you looking at? How about I give you some food and you keep your mouth shut?" She tapped some beta flakes into his water and watched him snatch them from the water's surface.

"Keep your mouth shut? Are you talking to your fish?"

Eve turned around to see Amy looming over her. Maybe the corner was a poor choice of bay. She suddenly felt boxed in, trapped, and her secret made the small corner feel crowded. She slammed her laptop shut.

"Oh, Amy, hi. Did you need something?"

"Hi, I didn't mean to interrupt something if you were working. I was just dropping by to let you know Will would like to meet with us at 5:30 in his office. Why are you sitting so close to the ground? You look like you're ready for hibachi."

"Chair's broken…5:30…let me think…" She was still processing what she'd just read and the disappearing stories and now trying to process the meeting time and her experiment running and felt like she was short-circuiting her brain.

"Yes, does that work for you? I mean, I can check with him if you need a different time."

"No, no, 5:30's good for me." Her experiment would need attention at six. She'd need to take samples from the neuro-units. Maybe they'd be done by then, and if not, she'd just excuse herself to the restroom.

"See you then."

Amy walked away slowly, her face illuminated by the blue display light on her phone.

Eve opened her laptop and returned to the remaining crumbs of her search results. Maybe the wireless internet had reset something. She decided to reboot and begin her search over again. Otto floated near the side of his bowl, watching. "Watch it, Otto. Or I'll take you back home to Boris. That didn't work out so well for the last guy."

She searched the news tab again, but there were "no results found." Maybe she needed to refine her search somehow. She decided she'd search what happened to the secretary of state, hoping that might yield something useful. About the time her eyes began to burn from the computer screen, it was time to head down to Will's office. She grabbed her notepad and pen and headed over there.

The inside of Will's office was oddly neat, and even though she'd seen it a few times, it still took her by surprise. Books were shelved neatly; manuscripts were in a tamped stack on his desk, and other than a few random items, likely gifts rather than personal purchases, his office gave nothing away about his personality, hobbies, likes or dislikes, whether or not he skied the black diamond runs or took island vacations. There were no photos of him in front of the Trevi fountain or hiking in the mountains of Colorado or the canyons in Arizona. The only photo was of him with two other men, one older, one younger, who she presumed were family. She tried not to stare at it. His hair was longer then, and he was tan and in good shape. All three men wore white linen shirts with blazers of varying shades of blue. Will looked like a Hollywood star in his aquamarine, and it was easy to see why he was so popular with women. The older man had his hand on Will's shoulder, and both men bore a strong resemblance to Will. The third man looked as though he was laughing, his cheeks tanned from summer weather and a glimmer in his eye just like Will had. Father and brother maybe? She looked more closely at Will's face. His smile was different. There was an uneasiness in it, unlike what she'd already come to expect—the easy, genuine grin that he wore nearly all the time. In this photo, he'd clearly forced a smile, and she wondered why. She wondered what he thought of her fish and plants—her rainforest as he'd referred to it—but she liked caring for things like her fish and plants, and she also liked a personal touch in her workspace. By comparison, her apartment was fairly sterile and lacking in personal touches. She'd always had a habit of making her workspace homey and her home less so. She didn't know why.

The lack of personal items in his office made her nervous for some reason, and she thought that was how people hid who they really were. She sat down and sipped her water, waiting for Amy and Will, neither of whom had arrived yet. After a few minutes, she began to wonder, but then a group text appeared. Will was running late and would be there by 5:45. *Shit! Shit. Shit.* She'd have to fake a bathroom break. How else would she be able to check her experiments? She had to know if there was something in the blood samples—something they hadn't seen with the drug alone. She would simply excuse herself, was all. What else could she do?

A second later, Amy walked in eating an apple while still talking to the biohazard guy in the hall. She was instructing him to empty the containers in the BSL2 lab. Eve sighed. At least it was the trash pickup and not some nosey student going in there and noticing her experiment…the one she wasn't supposed to do…the one that was costing a few thousand dollars.

Amy sat down next to her, crunching, and Eve tried not to let the sound of someone else eating send her into a rage.

"So is that your real hair color?" Now she was talking with her mouth full of food, and Eve wished she'd just kept with the crunching.

"Pardon?"

"You know, your hair. It's, like, practically white. Is it real? Or do you bleach it?"

"It's real." Eve tried to disguise her irritation at the question. People asked all the time, but it still annoyed her.

"Wow. It looks fake. Not in a bad way, but lots of

girls pay for that platinum hair. Did you see that movie *Legally Blonde?*"

"No." Lie. She had seen it. "Hair care's not really in my budget. I'd have to give up my pricey espressos." Eve managed a weak smile. Eve owed her platinum tresses to her Scandinavian background, but she got the blonde jokes all the time. What she wanted to tell Amy was that blondes had higher IQs on average than brunettes, redheads, and people with black hair and that her IQ fell in the gifted range despite her appearance to the contrary. And that she'd graduated summa cum laude and her GRE was in the 94th percentile.

"Soooooo, how do you like it here so far?"

"So far, it's great. Everyone seems nice, and Dr. St. John seems very nice. My old boss spoke very highly of him, and so far, it's worked out pretty great. He seems understanding, you know, like a fair guy." Eve wondered how fair he'd be when he found out what she was doing behind his back.

"Fair?" Amy popped off a laugh. Most of her apple fell out of her mouth and into her lap. She scooped it up and back into her mouth in time to speak. "I mean, I guess he's fair. He's fair until somebody makes a mistake, or worse, does something he instructed them not to do."

Eve swallowed hard. And as Amy finished her sentence, Will entered the office.

"You do something, Amy?"

"Nope! Not today!" Amy spoke with a mouthful of Red Delicious.

"Eve, you do something?"

"What? Me? No. I mean. No."

"You sure? You sound a little confused."

"No. I mean, yes, yes, I am sure." She plucked nervously at the seam in her jeans and scratched her neck until she knew it was streaked with red marks.

"Okay, well then, do you itch?"

"No." Eve folded her hands on her notepad and clicked her pen on and off before she realized she was making a scene.

"Well, let's get on with it, shall we? Eve, are you familiar with the hygiene hypothesis?"

"The hygiene hypothesis? The idea that washing hands with antibacterial soaps has led to super bacteria? That we could be making ourselves sicker as a result?"

"Well, that is part of the formula, yes." Will turned his computer monitor around. Pictured on the screen was a world map.

"On this map, the countries in red represent those countries where autoimmune diseases occur. And as you can see, autoimmune diseases occur almost exclusively in the developed world regions—the United States, Europe, the United Kingdom and Australia. Conversely, autoimmune diseases are almost nonexistent in developing nations. If we look below, a second map shows in blue, those countries where parasitic and helminthic diseases are endemic—mostly in developing nations, none here or in other developed countries. There exists for reasons we still do not fully understand an inverse relationship between countries with helminthic and parasitic infections and those with autoimmune disease. Some researchers have suggested that the worms, or parasites, produce something that stabilizes the immune system—keeps it in a state of equilibrium so that it is not hyper, as it is in autoimmune disease. I concur. I believe there is a molecule produced by the parasites and helminths that keeps the immune system from attacking the human tissues and organs. Keeping that in mind, about two months ago, there was an outbreak in the animal care unit where our leish mice are kept. Choriomeningitis."

"I heard about that. Wiped everything out. All of the mice died in that outbreak. That was horrible."

"Yes, well, not all of the mice died. Our mice survived."

"Survived?"

"Yes."

Eve blinked and sat very still, thinking. Amy was grinning ear to ear.

"How?"

"Well, we have an idea. Amy here accidentally ran a TH2 kit on our mice. What she found were cytokines. Our mice, who are supposed to have *no* immune system, showed signs of a functioning immune system. And not just immune function, but a kick-ass system. What we believe now is that the leish parasites who live in macrophages—aka immune cells—are creating something that is rebooting the immune system. A molecule. And we hypothesize this molecule can do much, much more. What we think is that this molecule could be a gateway cure. Our plan is to see whether the blood from our leish mice, when injected into diabetic mice, presents a new immune system—one that kills diabetes."

"Kills it? *Kills* diabetes? As in cures it?"

"That's right. And possibly other diseases. I'm thinking that it might be a cure for autoimmune diseases of all types. And I want you and Amy to take the lead on this one. Amy is going to sweet talk her boyfriend, Joe, and see whether we can borrow some mice, and then we run the tests."

"That would be amazing." Eve glanced at her watch. "I'll be right back! I've just got to run to the restroom! Be right back! That sounds so exciting!"

Eve sprinted down the hall at her fastest pace toward the BSL2 lab. She took the neuro-units from the incubator, slid the syringe into the ports and made her extractions. She checked her watch. Eleven minutes. *Shit!* She transferred the extractions to a tube and ran down the hall to the mass spec machine. Here she took out another syringe, sucked the samples back out of the tubes and shot it on to the mass spec. She'd been gone sixteen minutes. She ran back down the hall and into Will's office, where he was talking to Amy about experiment protocols.

Breathless, Eve plopped back into her chair.

"Everything okay?"

"Yes, I just…bathroom was busy."

"Long line…?"

"Uh, yeah, long line."

"Well, glad you made it back. We were about to send out a search party."

"I'm so sorry! I should have gone to another restroom when I saw how busy it was in there."

Will's eyes narrowed on her, and she could feel her lies floating out of her mouth into his ears and back out again.

"I am very excited about this project. So much better than that Larmentin stuff."

"Yeah, glad that's done." Here, Will paused and looked over at Eve, who shifted in her seat. His eyes rested on her as she picked at a hole in the cushion. Without diverting them, he continued.

"Anyway, Amy, if you'll talk to Joe, that would be great. See if he can help us out. The project is, as I said, confidential, so try not to divulge many details to him when you're asking about the mice. I don't want this getting out. You know how this place is, and if we get a result, I'll need to notify the university's patent office of our discovery." *And we need it before the Title IX office figures out I'm still around.*

"Got it. I'll go find Joe right now." Amy untangled her legs from her yoga pretzel and sprinted out the door.

Will turned to Eve. She'd lied about the bathroom line. He knew there were only two stalls in each of the restrooms, and he also knew there were not many people on the floor. The bathrooms were almost always empty. Eve, his Goody Two-shoes librarian who dressed like she was an eleven-year-old leaving for vacation bible school had lied about going to the restroom. *Why?*

His eyes narrowed as he studied her for a moment. He couldn't imagine what she looked like underneath her head-to-toe schoolgirl wool and tartan. God knows he'd tried. He smiled to himself. Her cheeks were rosy enough, her hair fair enough and her eyes blue enough that she might've carried off black like a red-carpet champion, but owing to her reserved manner and classic, borderline-matronly wardrobe, he'd opted for an off-white creamy silk. That afternoon, the flirty student from the boutique near campus had helped him with the selection of a dress, shoes and jewelry. He wanted something elegant, not flashy, something Eve would feel comfortable wearing. He wanted her to feel confident—she'd need it with Clemson. He glanced briefly at her figure and hoped he'd gotten the size right. It was a sleeveless gown with a deep V-neck and a beaded bodice with a high-split leg. She shoes were four inches high in an off-white satin. He'd gotten a pearl choker and some pearl-drop earrings. He hoped she'd like it.

"I have something for you. It's in my car. I got you a dress and some shoes to wear to the party on Saturday. I hope that's okay."

Eve smiled. "Thank you. Not sure my wool pants and turtleneck sweater would've worked for Clemson. He sounds like a tough customer."

"Indeed, he is. But I think you'll do just fine. We can chat on the plane about details. I'll bring the dress and shoes with me. You can change on the plane—there's a separate room."

He searched her face for something to register—excitement, nerves, regret—hopefully not the latter. But it was impossible to tell what she was thinking, if anything. She was nothing if not mercurial, he thought. One minute she was sassy, the next quiet and pensive. And in the back of his mind, he thought about the lie. He wouldn't have picked her for a liar. Nevertheless, she had. But liars had a way of showing themselves, and sooner or later, whatever she was hiding would reveal itself.

"I've only flown a few times in my life. Never on a private jet."

"You're in for a treat, then. I'll pick you up at your place around three o'clock, and we'll leave for the airport. If you want to see the dress or anything beforehand, I can show you."

"Normally, I'd take you up on that offer, but since this entire plan is kind of spontaneous, I'll wait."

"All right, then. We have a plan, and I'll see you soon."

Will smiled, and Eve thought she felt something light on her insides, the soft flutter of a thing she quickly dismissed and later in the day denied altogether. True enough, he was handsome, but he knew it, and she'd heard things even though she wasn't anywhere near the inner circle of university gossip. How far did news have to travel before it reached her? A helluva long way. He was a player. Most important, he was her boss, and she was doing him a favor by going. She walked swiftly down the hall to check on the mass spec, clean out her last sample and shoot in a new one. She would run six of the de-identified samples and see if there was anything of note, and if there was, she'd tell Will—but not before then.

Over the next couple of hours, Eve methodically ran

tests on six of the blood samples sent by WRAIR, and by dinnertime, she'd started to get back the analysis. Analysis showed five had a peak where one showed none. Something was different—she was onto something. Tomorrow, she'd test for cell death.

# CHAPTER 15

On Friday morning, Eve woke to the sound of water gushing through gutters half-clogged with leaves and debris while oversized drops of rain plopped and pelted the roof and windowsill. A frog-strangler would've been the appropriate Mississippi term to describe the uncharacteristic and unwavering deluge of November rain. Eve dug her rubber boots out of the closet. It was too cold for a rain jacket and too wet for her wool peacoat, so she opted for her golf umbrella. She walked at a brisk pace under the "good side" of her umbrella (at least one metal tine was detached from the vinyl canopy) and made her way toward campus. At the corner, a delivery truck plowed through a puddle, sending a wall of water in her direction. By the time she got to the lab, she was drenched despite her best efforts. She was the first to arrive and reveled in the morning solitude. At her feet, she turned a rogue space heater on to dry the bottoms of her pants. She fired up her computer and reviewed her lab notes on Larmentin while she waited on her email to load. Deep in thought, she didn't hear Amy step up behind her.

"Hey, what's up?"

Eve jumped in her chair. "Oh, hi. Nothing, just reviewing some lab notes."

Amy eyes shifted to the notebook. "What's Larmentin?" Amy's beady brown eyes appeared to double in size.

*Nothing quite that exciting*, Eve thought.

"It's a drug used to prevent leishmaniasis. Military personnel have to take it when they serve overseas in areas where they're at risk of infection."

"Ah. This is that big project that he had everyone scrambling on. I am used to dealing with the parasites; can't say I've ever done anything on the drug side."

"I think this was a first for Dr. St. John, too. He didn't apply for this grant. They must have looked at investigators with expertise on leishmaniasis, and voila—he was approached by the army to screen Larmentin for neurotoxicity. They've had some military experiencing side effects."

"And the verdict?"

"Well, the brain-on-a-chip units showed no sign of cell death."

"So an all-clear, huh?"

"Yeah, pretty much." Except for the $20,000 worth of neuro-chips in the incubator full of de-identified blood samples—blood samples that she was supposed to throw out.

Amy trailed back to her desk, her earbuds now in,

head bouncing. In the few minutes that followed, the students filed in one by one, and the hum of instruments in the lab, the freezers and the building's air exchange was accompanied by the chatter and laughter of the students as everyone mulled over their holiday plans, reminding Eve she'd need to make plans to fly home for Thanksgiving. She'd promised her dad. She looked at the calendar. Thanksgiving was on the 22nd, so she'd fly home the 21st and back the 23rd. She texted her dad.

Eve: See you on the 21st! I'll be home for 3 days!

As if he'd been waiting by his phone, the reply was immediate.

Dad: You just made my day! I'll tell your mom. She will be so happy.

Eve wasn't sure if a huge weight had just been lifted off her chest or lobbed onto it, but the idea of going home made her feel like she was doing the right thing. She'd be home in time to help her dad with cooking while her mother orchestrated everything from her chair, where she'd no doubt sit and drink for the duration of Eve's visit. Seeing her parents was a mixed blessing. Her mother was lucky to be living, and at the same time, her dad felt a sense of purpose in taking care of her, especially now that Eve was away—he couldn't exactly care for her anymore, and she no longer needed it. Eve was independent in every way, and while she was glad, sometimes she felt isolated and alone.

The day seemed to drag on in the way it does when

there is nothing to do but wait. Sit. Wait. Sit. Wait some more. Finally, Eve was ready for the moment of truth. She shot her final samples into the mass spec and stained the neuro-units with the live-dead staining kit. Putting them under the microscope, she felt a surge of something. Dread.

She leaned in and looked through the eyepiece to her answer. Red. She stood up straight and blinked. She leaned back in to be sure, and this time she was. Everything was red. Everything. Dead. The blood samples the colonel had sent killed the brain cells. *Something in the blood I was instructed to toss out with the trash is toxic. Now, I know the truth.* The pages of a story she didn't quite understand were beginning to unfold. She'd wait on the mass spec to see whether anything was off, but she already knew the answer.

On her way to get her morning espresso, she ran into Will in the hallway. A wave of guilt passed over her, and as a result, she tried consciously to appear innocent. Textbook style, she straightened her posture, shoulders back, opened her eyes a bit wide, and proceeded to make good eye contact, all of which resulted in Will eyeing her dubiously. He furrowed his brow slightly and sighed into his words.

"Hey, Amy is going over to see these diabetic mice—she actually managed to get five of them for our experiment. We're going to transfuse them with blood from our leish-infected mice and see what happens. Fingers crossed. Why don't you go with, since this will be your new project. You can check out the animal care unit. It's kind of hard to find, and she can show you how to get there since you'll be making regular trips."

"Sure, let me grab my coffee and stop by the restroom."

"Like last time?"

"I'll be quick." *I just need to get six more samples started. I'll be right back.*

Eve felt like she was in one of the movies where someone was being watched by a nefarious character. Will felt like a dark shadow lurking, stalking, but she knew it was just her guilty conscience. The brain-on-a-chip units weren't cheap, and she was blowing through them. She went down the back hallway to the BSL2 lab, started the incubation on six more samples and met Will back at the elevators, breathless and flushed.

The elevator opened, and Cindy Tan stepped off.

"Will, just the man I wanted to see." Cindy wore white corduroy pants and a white sweater, a monochromatic look that made her look even taller than she was.

"And here I am. Hey, I'd like you to meet my new post-doc." Will bowed slightly and gestured to Eve. "Eve whose last name I can't pronounce. Eve, this is Cindy Tan. She is responsible for all of our mass-spec analysis."

Cindy extended her hand. "Nice to meet you, Eve. You're working for one of the good guys, here." She slapped Will firmly on the back and winked.

"That's what I hear. Nice to meet you also."

"Amy and Eve are headed over to animal care, and I was just going for a bagel and coffee. Care to join me?"

"Sure." Cindy waved off as Amy and Eve got in the elevator, the silver doors closing into a vertical line.

"So how's your new person? Think she'll work out?"

"I think so. She's a little stiff. You know, uptight maybe. And maybe even a little strange in a way I can't pin down, but I think she's just getting settled in. The students seem to like her, and Paschal said she's a keeper. She's published thirteen papers in four years, so she's a fucking machine as far as that goes. If she works out and I have enough grant funding, I may keep her on and make her a research professor." *If I don't lose my job.*

"Enough grant funding?" Cindy faked a coughing fit. "You just got millions."

"I want more." Will chewed on a plastic straw. "Enough is never enough, Tan. I need to be funded out the ass."

"Tell me about it, moneybags."

Will threw his head back in laughter, his dark waves spilling around his twinkling eyes, the glimmer of discovery hidden from his good friend for now. They disappeared behind the door of the coffee shop. He thought about telling Cindy about his suspension, but it seemed like such a small matter, all things considered. When he put things in proper perspective, what seemed most important was the cure. The cure that would end the suffering of millions of people. The cure that would save millions of lives. The Title IX office would do well to back off and let Will do his job.

⚬⚬⚬

COLONEL SAVARRE SAT AT HER DESK, MASSAGING THE base of her neck with her hands, trying to elicit some feeling of relief, but her neck was stiff with tension, and she could feel a muscle knot forming at the top of her spine. If she was ever tempted to kick her feet up on her large mahogany desk, today would be the day. Or have a shot of whiskey before lunch, or go to the gun range and go a few rounds with her new Glock nine mil. But she wasn't the type to celebrate. She wasn't even the type to smile. That she was managing her moods without medication was good enough. These days, she was a fucking champion. What she really wanted, more than anything, was to string the secretary of the army up by his nutsack. Or better, snip them off and shove them down his fucking throat. His type of arrogance, the sound of his fucking voice and every last condescending, patronizing, bullshit threat was the kind of shit she'd choked on as a kid—the kind of shit boarding school beat out of you. And as she sat there musing about that fact, she wondered why she wasn't impervious to his brand of bullying. No one bullied her, ever. She'd left a wake of fear everywhere she'd ever gone. Boot camp, in the field, on the front lines of the battle zones and at WRAIR. She was a tour de force. She shut her eyes and stared at the floaters on the insides of her lids. She had the reports he wanted, just like he'd demanded. Now he could take it to the army's criminal investigation command, and they could cover it all up. Make it all go away. Let that poor bastard who shot Secretary of State Elizabeth Rhodes take all the blame in whatever way they'd decided to paint it.

She had to admit, even she was surprised with the results Will St. John had sent her. She had been confident

Larmentin was a problem, and yet his tests suggested otherwise. Momentarily she pondered his words: *We may have missed something important*. Too late for that now. She was going with what was behind door number one—Larmentin showed no signs of neurotoxicity. And while it was what she needed to hear, the answer they'd all been hoping for, she wasn't convinced. Serving in Iraq, it wasn't hard to notice the way everyone changed on the day they took the pill, how everyone was a little off, their personalities altered, some more noticeable and bizarre than others. Even her own had changed, causing a brain fog and wretched dreams that left her off her game the next day. At times, she was tempted not to take it, but then she'd seen the ghastly sores that leishmaniasis caused, not to mention the fact that it had potential to be fatal. Coupled with the fact that taking medication when serving abroad was a direct order, *not an ask*, that made skipping it an all-around bad idea. Soldiers didn't have a choice. One soldier in her platoon had lost his mind over a mangled corpse in a village after taking Larmentin. He had to be sedated for the flight back home and was later discharged from the army as a Section Eight. The entire platoon took the heat for that one. Section Eight was unacceptable. *Better that poor bastard died in Islamabad*, she thought. Her mind turned back to the Rusty Carver, and as if summoned telepathically, he appeared in her doorway.

He was a large man and a heavy breather, and it occurred to her that the stress of this latest situation could cause cardiac arrest. Today he wore brown pants with a yellow button-down shirt and a plaid tie that stopped just above the depression of his belly-button, where he'd once been connected to something larger than himself, hard as that was to imagine now, looking at him. His gut hung below his belt, and a small triangular window of hairy flesh was visible where the shirt buttons couldn't connect. He smelled like black coffee and bacon-fat fried eggs. Her mouth watered, and she swallowed down the urge to puke.

"Good morning, Susan."

"Morning," she replied curtly enough.

It was indeed morning, but he was here, and so there was nothing good about it. She stood and handed him an unmarked envelope, happy her part in all of this was over.

"The reports you requested."

"Thank you. Susan. This should satisfy the curiosity of the army's military investigative team. CID has been up my ass on this one." He paused while his heavy breathing built up to a coughing fit that could rival that of a two-pack-a-day-fifty-plus-year smoker. He wheezed and gurgled and pitched forward and back, fisting his chest while he wrestled an old-school kerchief from his polyester pants. A breakfast receipt from McDonald's floated like a feather to the floor. The sausage biscuit with gravy hadn't made it all the way to his small in-testine from the looks of things. His shirt now fully untucked, she watched as his face went red, then purple, until his eyes watered and he regained composure. She thought about offering him some water but in the end decided against it. He needed a doctor and a wardrobe consult. "Elizabeth Rhodes is still in a medicinally in-duced coma. Not sure when she'll come to, if she'll wake up. I appreciate your efforts on this, Susan. I knew I could count on you."

Susan fingered a pencil on her desk, rolling it as she listened, but she had to ask. "That soldier, Joseph Bishop. What did they tell his family?"

"He was high on cocaine at the time of the shooting. Why?" Rusty cleared his throat into his handkerchief and tugged at the waist of his pants until a full apron of flesh was showing.

A lump came into her throat. *Can't you feel a fucking draft?*

"No reason, really." She had checked, though. Joey Bishop was a sniper, a decorated soldier with an im-peccable record. There'd be talk among his fellows in combat. *You better pray to God one of them doesn't reach out to the family with the truth, or they'll come down on this thing with a billion-dollar hammer.*

"That's the story. I thank you and your team for help-ing craft the narrative—one the army can live with. I know your labs here at WRAIR developed Larmentin, and I know how much this drug means to the army… billions in revenue every year. Would've been a huge loss. Instead, what we have is a huge win, so pat yourself on the back. You saved our asses, our reputation and our bottom line. Thanks again for this." He tapped the envelope. "You may return to business as usual. Heard you guys are making some headway with the anthrax project. Good luck."

"Thanks."

She walked to her door and watched him lumber down the hall. She could hear Louis intermittently eating and typing. That might be the only usual thing about this place anymore.

# CHAPTER 16

EVE AND AMY STOOD AT THE CAGES AND WATCHED the mice—the ones that could still move—crawl slowly back and forth through the cedar shavings. Most of them were huge, their hind quarters puffed up and out, their scrawny feet pinched under the weight. They ate and drank voraciously, and Eve marveled at their girth. Some of them could barely move. Others were so large their feet stuck straight out from their bodies in a cartoonish manner.

"These are huge! I've never seen mice this big. They're like guinea pigs. My cat, Boris, would love to get his paws on one of these. Mice this big are slow like he is." Eve laughed. "He's not much of a mouser, but he could put the hurt on these guys. They wouldn't stand a chance."

Amy also laughed. "The first time I saw them, I wasn't sure they were mice. They were so enormous. To me they look like large furry hockey pucks."

Amy reached in and pulled out the first mouse. It

moved slowly in the palm of her hand, unsure of itself on the new surface. It wriggled its nose, using its whiskers to assess the new situation. She held it, gently stroking between the ears, whispering assurances as though it were a child frightened at its first doctor's visit. The Institutional Animal Care and Use Committee, IACUC for short, had strict protocols regarding research animals, and Amy felt a pang of guilt. She hoped this would help, not hurt. She looked at Eve, her eyes wide. "Ready?"

Eve nodded. She pulled a syringe from her bag filled with blood taken from the leish-infected mice and pushed it into the hindquarters of the diabetic mouse. The experiment, while crude, was just that simple. If Will's hypothesis was correct, the immune systems of the diabetic mice would be reset as a result of the of the leish parasite, and they would be cured of their diabetes. Methodically, Eve and Amy performed injections with the next four mice until all five had been inoculated.

"How long do you think this will take if it is going to work?" Eve asked.

"I think we'll see changes in as little as a week if Will's hypothesis is correct."

They placed the last mouse back in the cage and shut the door. Amy marked the bottom of the cage with a dot of red nail polish so that Joe would know which cage to avoid with his own set of experiments.

"Well, that's it." Amy beamed. "Let's hope this works!"

They left the animal care unit after checking on their own mice. Since the sun was now shining, they opted to walk outdoors to get back to the lab. It was at least a fifteen-minute walk, even at a brisk pace, but Eve was happy for the fresh air. The smell of leaves giving back to the ground filled the breeze. It was a favorite smell for Eve. It reminded her of the park in fall growing up when her dad would push her on the swings and help her up the slide. She and her best friend Audrey would run between trees and spy on the teenagers snuggled on park benches or collect leaves of red, orange and yellow for collage-making. Once she was back at the lab, she would need to check on her latest round of experiments.

—⁂—

SCIENCE IS NOTHING IF NOT AN EXERCISE IN PATIENCE. Eve was waiting on the incubator. Waiting to start more brain-on-a-chip units. Waiting on staining kits. Waiting on mice to be cured. Waiting on mass-spec analysis. Waiting to get caught. Waiting on Saturday. Here, she paused in her mind and let the nagging second thoughts set their tendrils in her mind. She could hardly have said no. The way Will described his grandfather and the rest of his family, she knew how brutal family gatherings could be. Despite his reputation, he seemed to be quite the gentleman and nothing like she'd heard. He had been respectful and kind since she'd started, and at least some of her initial apprehension about working for him was beginning to drain.

Back in the lab, she dropped her notebook at her desk, checked her email—one from Will regarding the group meeting, one from Amy about a birthday lunch for Devon, and two from her dad about the holiday breaks and a reminder to get the oil changed in her car. Eve looked around. The lab was mostly quiet without Amy, who was the loudest and most gregarious and had taken a break to run an errand. Sanjay sat quietly at his desk writing, while Shea had gone to grab something to eat. Now would be a great time to check on her experiments. Eve looked right, then left, before she walked across the hall to the BSL2 room, careful that no one saw her coming or going. She checked the timer; one hour and thirty minutes until her next sample collection. She decided to walk over to the rec center for a quick run. She grabbed her running gear from her desk drawer, stuffed it in her pack and walked out of the building feeling anxious. The cold damp air didn't help her anxiety, and her teeth chattered as she walked. In the air, the smell of burning leaves wafted from a nearby neighborhood, one of the many smells Eve loved about fall, her favorite being pumpkin spice lattes and muffins. She scanned the sky for some promise of sun but could see only a faint glow through a thinning patch of pale gray clouds.

The gym was almost empty, with the exception of a couple on the weight floor spotting each other on bench press and squatting between sets. Eve hopped on her favorite treadmill, put in her earbuds and warmed up walking quickly for five minutes before starting her run. Music filled her mind, energizing her in a way few things did, and she ran her first mile in 6.5 minutes. Her legs felt limber enough for a 5K, and she continued running at a fast pace until she reached her cooldown. The same girl—the one who'd checked on Will last week, sat at the desk with her head buried in her phone. Eve watched as she contorted her face, scrunching her nose, crossing her eyes and kissing the air, snapping selfies for an entire ten-minute cooldown period, and marveled at the carefree nature that was eighteen years old. Eve hadn't been so lucky. She'd never lived that life—the kind where her biggest problem was brows that needed waxing. Instead, she'd had to deal with a mom who showed up to school on parents' day drunk, who vomited out the car door in front of her friends after her senior prom, or who passed out on the floor at a neighborhood New Year's Eve bash and then peed on herself. Hers had been the kind of life that made you want to hide in a bag, and in many ways, she was still hiding. She'd plowed through grad school the way she plowed through life, so focused on her studies she left no time for anything that wasn't exercise or sleep. It was this tunnel vision, a life singularly focused, that freed those parts of her mind that might've caused her stress.

She had filled her life to the brim with her science. She loved pushing herself to her limits, she loved testing her mettle, and she loved the challenges that came with her education. When she earned her PhD and looked out into the sea of parents to see her mother half-slumped-over against her father's shoulder, she felt as though she'd conquered something behemothic—her own fear of failure. But leaving her childhood demons behind wasn't as easy as simply pulling out of the driveway and onto the highway. They trailed behind like cans rattling behind the car of a newlywed couple. Noisy and obnoxious and tethered to her, behind her down every road she traveled. The memories were never very far, nor the sting of humiliation, the side effect of which had become her obsession with perfection and her inability to trust anyone.

She had arranged her life very carefully. She had a cat, a fish and some plants—the only living things allowed to coexist with her. Her solitary existence felt very safe, and she often checked herself when she felt the stirrings of emotional attachment. The people in this lab would be colleagues, not buddies. Will was her boss, a mentor, but he was not her friend. The distance she kept from others allowed a nearly seamless transition between groups—like swapping apartments and waving casually to new neighbors without stopping to chat about anything deeper than the weather.

Back in the lab, Eve hovered over the inverted epifluorescence microscope. She leaned in close to the eyepiece. *Okay, let's see what we can see.* Just like the others, the brain cells were dead. *All of them. Dead.* Thus far, all but one had shown massive brain cell death. She took a deep breath and sat down on the stool. She had one outlier, but the rest confirmed what she now knew must be the truth—Larmentin was toxic to the brain. Larmentin was very clearly a neurotoxin.

Her ears were full with the hum of equipment, and her mind swirled. Millions of dollars. A shortened timeline. More money. Daily calls, Skypes, emails. Something didn't add up. The money and the race to an answer that wasn't even definitive. There'd been zero controls. Had the colonel known the tests on the Larmentin would come back clean? And why had she asked Will to dispose of the blood samples? None of it made any sense, and now she herself had used thousands of dollars in supplies on finding out the truth, but what to do next wasn't clear. Not yet.

⸺ ∞ ⸺

Louis sat at his desk, mulling over the information on his computer screen, a Cool Ranch Dorito flat on his tongue so he could enjoy the full flavor and ruin his breath all at the same time. Nothing was quite as bad as Dorito breath, a surefire way to make sure the colonel didn't lean in too close. The problem with being in a wheelchair, among many, was the inability to back away from someone who encroached your personal space. Doritos and corn chips kept Savarre at a full arm's length and then some. He pressed his tongue to the roof of his mouth until the spices dissolved while he scanned the results from the Larmentin studies. Other than the final FDA approval, there'd been no subsequent testing on Larmentin. Unless of course you counted military personnel as unwitting subjects of drug trials.

It was uncanny how fast a story could travel and how far. Even at WRAIR, far removed from the military posts of the middle east, Louis had heard the rumors about the anti-leish drug. It did things to people. Confusion, bad dreams and brain fog to start, but also psychosis, paranoia, auditory and visual hallucinations, fears and psychotic episodes that required sedation, but the worst part was that sometimes it never went away. Sometimes, a person got trapped in their psychosis forever.

The story of Joey Bishop, a highly skilled sniper and respected soldier, had made its way to WRAIR. On the day Bishop was supposed to ensure the safety and security of the secretary of state, he had taken his Larmentin as ordered. Before he'd even made it to his security post at the airport, his fellow soldiers were talking him down, telling him everything was okay, he was fine, he just needed to go and do his job. But he wasn't okay. He sobbed intermittently and said things to members of his platoon that made zero sense. He was frightened, convinced he was being followed, that someone was trying to kill him. Even his closest friends couldn't calm him down. He was tormented by the drug, and what should have been a routine operation had cost him his life. In the end, his best friend had gunned him down to protect the people on the tarmac—most notably, the secretary of state. Louis knew what it was like to serve and protect next to your closest friends, your best friend. He couldn't imagine what that day must have been like.

Louis repositioned what remained of his left leg, barely a nub. He winced as he heaved it over slightly to the center. The ghost pain was bad sometimes and today was one of those days. The wheelchair was the result of an explosion while serving in Afghanistan, not far from where Joey Bishop died. Louis was smart, a patriot who'd come from a large military family. His dad, a lifer in the army, his brother a Marine, and Louis's mother had also served in the army. He had a strong sense of country and loyalty to his commanding officers, and though the colonel treated him poorly at times, he knew his place just as he knew hers. That said, Louis had limits. He'd seen firsthand how poor decisions in the field led to injury or disasters that resulted in loss of life. Forcing a guy who was clearly buzzed on his meds to climb onto the roof with a sniper rifle was just shit-for-brains. He was surprised when he saw the reports—shocked to see the Larmentin was not to blame after all.

The phone at his desk rang just as the colonel was walking past. She stopped just in front of him.

"Webster."

"Louis, hi, it's Eve. Eve Konisken."

Louis did not respond immediately. The colonel searched his face for clues. He feigned listening carefully and nodded.

"Louis? Are you there?"

"Yes, uh-huh. Yes. My colostomy bag? Yes, I do have questions about how to properly change out the new bag."

The colonel wrinkled her nose and turned in a huff down the hall.

"I beg your pardon? Louis, this is Eve. Eeeeve. The researcher working on the Larmentin project."

Louis responded in a low voice.

"Yes, yes, I know. Sorry. You-know-who was standing right here. She makes me nervous, and I don't like to be nervous. I didn't want her hovering over me while I was on the phone, listening. She loves to listen and watch people. She should've been a spy for the CIA."

"Oh, right. Gotcha. Is she gone?"

Louis peered down the hallway toward her office. "She is now."

"Listen, I need your help, and I'd rather you-know-who didn't know that I've called either. Something's not right. I need to know who these de-identified samples belonged to—I need to know whether these soldiers suffered psychological side effects. After we got back the initial results on the Larmentin, Dr. St. John instructed me to toss the samples you sent. He said we were done as far as Colonel Savarre was concerned. But—I was curious. So I decided to run just a few of the blood samples, and you need to know what I found."

"Mmm. Go ahead, I'm listening." Louis sat up as straight as he could in his wheelchair and scanned the perimeter to be sure no one else was listening.

"The blood samples that you sent…I didn't throw them out like Dr. St. John asked. I tested them." Eve looked all around the room, including the ceiling corners, knowing full well she was in the BSL2 lab alone. "*Your* blood—the blood *you* sent—killed *my* brain cells— the brain-on-a-chip brain cells. Larmentin *is* toxic. The Larmentin itself is not toxic, which is why initial tests showed no adverse reactions. However, when it is broken down by the human body, it produces a toxin—something that makes it dangerous. Neurotoxic."

"Okay. I'm following you. You want to know whether

the soldiers—the ones whose samples you have"—Louis scanned his surroundings and lowered his voice further still—"you want to know whether or not they experienced psychological side effects?"

"I can barely hear you. Why are you whispering? Is she—?"

"Yes. She is down the hall, and she is suspicious all the time—it's the nature of her beast. She was born suspecting other people of things. She watches me like a hawk. The only way I can keep her away is to eat."

"I'm sorry. Eat? Did you say eat?"

"Yes. She hates—I mean loathes—the sound of others chewing. I noticed this some time ago at a lunch meeting, and since then, I've taken to eating at my desk. Loud foods. Chips mostly. She can't hack it, and so she leaves, and I get my privacy. It's a win-win. Plus, there's the issue of my Fritos breath. That helps."

"Ah. Well, aren't you the clever one. How should we do this? Should I read the serial numbers out and you look at the reports or…?"

"Why don't you read off the serial numbers, let me dig here on my end, and I'll get back to you with yeses and nos? Then you can match those results with your brain-cell death cards."

"Sounds so bleak when you put it that way, but okay. Sounds like a plan. Should I call you or will you—?

"I'll message you at this number with a list. They log our calls here. It will come from my cell, area code 301."

"Okay, I'll wait for your message."

"Sounds good."
"Louis?"
"Yes?"
"Be careful. Take care."
"You too, Eve."

# CHAPTER 17

Eve woke on Saturday morning satisfied that she had called Louis, inoculated the diabetic mice—poor fellows—and was now going to have a manicure, take care of her hair and makeup pre-Clemson fiftieth anniversary celebration at Martha's Vineyard. *Martha's. Vineyard.* She was a girl from smalltown Mississippi, born to immigrant parents who didn't understand American plutocrats, their couture or their extravagant lifestyles.

She walked into the salon and was immediately snagged by a man in full makeup who introduced himself as Francis. He had sparkly pink pout, peach-frosted lids, and eyelashes like a Hollywood starlet. He was, Eve thought, very beautiful. He promised her a face and hair to make the moon blush.

"Something to work with!" Francis whistled. "Honey, honey, don't you worry. Sit back and let Francis work his magic." Francis plucked at her hair and quickly selected what he promised were the best products. Eve sipped on champagne and nibbled on strawberries while she thumbed through fashion magazines—including a *Cosmopolitan* cover that touted "tight abs, sexy butts and 10 things he craves in bed." While one person painted her nails a glossy, classic red, another person shampooed her. Francis swore the red would stun with anything, which worked since her clothing was a mystery. He pulled her hair into a high French twist with long, flouncing tendrils that framed her face and swept over her neck. He spent over an hour on her makeup, lashes and lips, and when he turned her around to face the mirror, her mouth dropped open. She didn't even recognize the face staring back at her. Her lips were red, her face flawless and sculpted, her lashes a voluminous black. Any doubt she'd had, any cause to be concerned that she might not look the part, faded in that moment. The woman staring back was not the reserved classic persona she'd spent years perfecting. The woman in the mirror was stunning. Gorgeous. Francis had made some big promises, but she would never have guessed he could've transformed her like this. Not the kind of face that got lost in a crowd. She looked, and so felt, like a movie star. Her eyes watered with tears, and she hugged Francis's neck.

"Thank you, Francis. You've no idea. Thank you."

"You are welcome, darling!" He gently took her face in his hands. "You are a vision, but I had some help from mother nature, oui! This hair so platinum, your skin so beautiful! My sweet, you are radiant."

Eve could feel her face flushing.

"I love, love!" He kissed her forehead. "Your beau is going to love, love!"

*My beau. Ha!* If he only knew the charade she was playing with her boss, and at Martha's Vineyard, no less. Nevertheless, she was pleased with her appearance and hoped Will would approve. She gathered her things and headed for the private airport, a little tipsy with champagne and more relaxed than she'd been in a long time.

She pulled into the small lot, parked, and made her way into the concrete building to meet Will. The air outside was still and dry, and she was thankful, though Francis had used more than enough hairspray to keep it in place for perpetuity. *His words.* She set her quilted duffel on the ground and looked around for Will. After a few minutes of panicking that she might not be in the right place, she spotted him talking to the pilot. He wore a black, slim-fit, single-breasted tuxedo jacket with a shawl collar, a white shirt and black bow tie. In his dark sunglasses, he looked like a Hollywood star trying to avoid the paparazzi. He was as handsome as the rumors, perhaps even more when he laughed, Eve thought. They were laughing like old friends, and it occurred to her, it was Clemson's plane, and so the pilot must be a longtime friend of the family.

Will shook his head in hysterical laughter and suddenly stopped, something caught in his periphery, and turned toward her. He pulled his glasses down, his narrow eyes twinkling as always, and his countenance softened in a way that made him suddenly seem very human—touchable—in a way that embarrassed Eve, and she wished for the Will who was above it all, larger than life, to come roaring back. But he didn't. Like she'd cast a spell, he stood and stared for an uncomfortable period of time. He motioned her over and introduced her. He touched her lightly on the shoulder.

"Bill, this is my date for the evening, Eve whose last name I cannot pronounce—it's Finnish. Eve, this is my great-uncle Bill St. John, minus the saint part!"

Bill smiled, took Eve's hand in his and, with a gentle kiss, whispered, "Pleasure to meet you, Miss Eve."

"You as well, Bill."

He looked at Will. "I tell you I don't know how my grand-nephew managed a date with someone as fine as you, Miss Eve, but I think you will do a bit more than just fit in with tonight's crowd. You will set a new bar. A couple to behold indeed, my boy William!" He slapped Will on the back and took Eve's duffel. Walking across the tarmac, Will told Eve all about the plane, a Gulfstream IV, and assured her that the flight would be fairly smooth and that drinks and light hors d'oeuvres were waiting on the plane.

Eve stepped inside the cabin, and her heart fluttered. It was beautiful. Along one side of the plane, a long white leather sofa with large navy pillows, and on the other, a pair of matching chairs on either side of a table, a high-gloss polished mahogany. In the center of the table, a bottle of champagne on ice waited next to a pair of crystal flutes with tiny navy ribbons around the stems. Will motioned toward the back.

"Just behind that partition is your gown, shoes and something for your neck," Will said.

"Thanks." Eve smiled and disappeared behind the partition with a cold glass of champagne, and sometime later, reappeared, fully transformed. She stood nearly a half foot taller in her stiletto shoes. Will's eyes trailed up the slit in her dress, over her sculpted calf and ample thighs, to her small waist. The light fell across the velvet swell of her breasts accentuated by the V-neck of her gown where sequins, the tedious handiwork of the seamstress, reflected the light in varied iridescent hues. Around her neck, a pearl choker, three strands in all, came together in front, complemented by a round diamond clasp that glimmered in the light whenever she moved. Eve smiled sheepishly.

"Is this real?" She touched the choker with her fingertips.

Will straightened in his chair and gulped down his glass of Dom Pérignon. For a minute, he didn't speak. His eyes moved over her, and she was pleased and uncomfortable at the same time. He poured himself another champagne.

"You look stunning, Eve." His voice was throaty. "And yes. The choker is real."

"Thank you. And thank you for all of this." She waved her arms over the dress and touched her choker. "It's gorgeous. I'm not sure how you picked it out, but it is lovely, thank you." She wondered how much he'd spent but knew not to ask but to be gracious.

"You are most welcome. This is a huge favor you're

doing for me." Will glanced at her shoes. "I wasn't sure about the shoes. They look great, but uncomfortable."

Eve bobbled a bit.

"You might want to sit down for takeoff. I think we'll be leaving shortly now that you're changed."

Bill popped his head in and whistled. "You two are something else. Now, that's what I call a killer couple." He winked. "Ready for takeoff?"

Will nodded. "Yes. Let's do this."

Bill disappeared into the cockpit, and Will filled another champagne glass for Eve.

"So Clemson's a tough one, huh?"

"Yeah, he is. But my dad is a great guy. You'll get to meet him also. That'll take some of the sting out."

"And your brother?"

"Who, George? Probably not. It's a bit early in the season for him. He'll show up at Thanksgiving. Always does."

The plane engines roared, and the Gulfstream IV took off down the runway and into the deep blue November sky. To the west, Eve looked through the window and watched shafts of sun splinter the pink cumulus clouds. The night felt magical already, and it had only just begun.

Will ran his finger over the rim of his flute, piercing the air with a high-pitched tone. Eve flinched in her seat.

"Now that I have your full attention, I think we should get to know each other better. Before the party where we are expected to be nearly betrothed."

"Nearly betrothed?" Eve blushed.

"Well, significant others anyhow. What do ya say?"

"Okay, I guess."

"All right then. Let's cover some basics. Cats or dogs?"

"Cats."

"I knew it!" Will rolled his eyes.

"Milk chocolate or dark?"

"Dark."

Will nodded. "Hmmm, bitter rather than sweet. Also predictable. Romance or adventure?"

"Definitely adventure."

"Science fiction?"

"Of course. That's three. My turn now." Eve fingered her necklace. "People or alone?"

"Alone."

"Really? That surprises me. My preference as well. Television or music?"

"Music."

"Football or baseball?"

"Baseball—the Cubs. My turn again. Tell me something about you that might surprise me. Anything."

"Okay...let's see. I love boxing."

Will cocked a brow.

"Growing up, my father watched a lot of boxing—and he had DVDs of all the great fights. Ali, Foreman, Frazier. Ali was my favorite by far and, in my mind, the GOAT. Did you know he was afraid to fly? He almost didn't make it to the Olympics in Rome. But he did. And he dodged the Vietnam draft and was stripped of all of his medals and titles and then won them back in a supreme court battle. He stood on principle. I always loved that about him. And he was a kind person despite the giant that he was."

"Kind?"

"Yes, *kind*. He wrote a recipe for life that includes all these virtues he wanted to be known for—he was much more than a boxer to me. He was my inspiration."

"Jesus. Guess I missed that when I read you at your interview." Will laughed.

They sat for a minute in silence, watching the sky and listening to the sound of the Gulfstream IV cutting its way through the cool November air.

"Was your childhood sad?" Will asked. It was a brave question.

"To be honest, I don't think of it much, but I'd say yes, it was mostly sad. My mother was drunk for most of it. And angry or depressed. There were days I remember thinking, I hope she's pissed off today—at least then she'd seem alive and like she cared about something. Many days she'd just lie on the sofa with the television on even though she wasn't looking at it. She always had it turned to some trashy talk show. You know, the kind where some guy finds out he was the real dad of a kid he didn't want. That's what I listened to while I did my calculus homework. That's why I prefer music to television." Eve pursed her lips. "She'd ask me to bring her cigarettes or a piece of cheese with some bread for dinner, but she'd usually pass out before I'd even have the chance to slice the bread. But I had some good times. I had a friend in my neighborhood, Audrey. I'd go to her house, and we'd eat our weight in brownies—*not pot brownies*—and listen to music. She had all the CDs I loved, and her mom loved to cook. When I stayed for dinner, she would always ask Jesus to look over my mom when she said grace. And she was always checking to make sure I had everything I needed. When Audrey would get tired of her dresses or jeans, her mom always gave them to me. Audrey had great taste, so I was always excited to get them. Sometimes when my dad thought I was feeling low, he'd surprise me with a pint of mint chip. Honestly, I'm not sure how I wasn't a hippo, you know? Every fall, he'd take me to the county fair for hot dogs and funnel cakes. My mom never went—it was always just us, and I'd bring Audrey. We'd ride all of the rides until I thought I'd throw up." Eve smiled. "Those good times, though they were few, managed to push me through. Kind of like a spot of blue skies on a mostly cloudy day. You focus on that, and that's how you keep going." Eve stroked the silk fabric of her dress as she talked. She looked up at Will. "I'm guessing your childhood was very different from mine. Anyway, it's my turn. What about you? Secrets?" This time, it was Eve who cocked a brow.

"Who me? Not really."

"Okay, well, what about your ability to read people?"

"Definitely a secret."

"Okay…" Eve looked around the plane, tracing the LED lights that ran across the ceiling and along the floor. "Okay, why didn't you go into medicine? Like your father and grandfather?"

"That's easy. I don't like people enough."

"What?"

"Too much baggage, too much small talk. I could never do what my dad does—I could never have a serious conversation about a butt lift or breast implants. He can do that. He's empathetic in a way I've never been. And my grandfather, well, he cuts on people in one of the most vulnerable areas of the human body while he talks trading stocks and sailing. I'm not that detached, either. Make sense?"

"Yeah, that does make sense. My turn again."

"Nope. It's mine." Will chewed on a stirrer while he stared at Eve. "Tell me something else I don't know about you… Do you have a birthmark?"

"Yes."

"Flat, raised, dark, light?"

"It's flat. It's shaped like a heart." Eve chewed the inside of her bottom lip, and her face colored.

"Is it somewhere I can see?"

"No way! It's on my hip bone. High enough that you might see it in a bikini, but you'll never see me in a bikini." They both laughed. "Okay, my turn again. You have to answer this time. Tell me how you do it. How do you read people so well? I mean maybe you should have been an FBI profiler or something."

"Funny, you're not the first person to say so. As an undergrad I took a psychology class. Not really my cuppa, but I was fascinated by the study of body language and how outward signs are connected to what a person is thinking. I went to the library and checked out all kinds of books. I'd always had a knack for reading people, watching them, studying their habits. it became kind of a hobby, and eventually, well, I became known for it. It became that thing I do, I guess."

"Hmmm. Anyone ever read you?"

"Nope." Will rolled his eyes and grinned. "I'm too complex."

"Uh-huh!" Eve faked choked on her champagne and thumped her chest with her fist. "Sorry. Something in my throat. Let's see…" She eyed Will up and down. "Tell me about getting high. Why do you do that? You're so successful, so together. Even under pressure…like when the colonel visited. Why smoke? You don't seem to need it."

Will looked at her thoughtfully. He pulled the stirrer stick from his mouth.

"It's not your turn, so this one's a freebie." He pointed at her with the stirrer. "I might seem relaxed, but I'm wound pretty tight. Like a duck on a pond. Looks like it's gliding around on top of the water effortlessly, but underneath, it's paddling its webbed fucking feet off. I run and lift weights, and that helps some, but there are days I really need my brain to slow down and deep breathing doesn't cut it. So I smoke. It helps me turn down the noise in my mind. Sometimes I just wanna be…I don't want to think."

The plane shook as it passed through some turbulence, and Will grabbed the flutes so they didn't spill. His uncle apologized over the speaker.

"Whoa! Nice save!"

"Thanks." Will smiled. "Would hate to have to mop up the Dom Pérignon with a bev nap." Will handed Eve her champagne. "What does Eve whose last name I can't pronounce fear most? Will's eyes sparkled in the light of sunset.

"That despite all my efforts, I'll become my mother. That my melancholy will grab hold of me someday. That I won't get out of bed to feed the cat. I'll just lie there in the dark with a bottle on the bedside table. It's one of the reasons I don't drink alone. Ever."

"Really. Not *ever*? Just to wind down after a day in the lab?"

"Nope. Maybe a drink with some people at the bar, but not at home. Never."

"Wow. Well, you don't seem like the type to just lie in bed. You're a fighter."

"You read that, do you?"

"Yeah."

"What else do you read?"

Before Will could answer, his uncle announced the descent.

"Buckle up, people. It's gonna be a bit bumpy on our approach."

Will and Eve buckled their seatbelts.

"We have time for one more, and it's my turn now." Eve drained the remainder of her champagne. She felt warm, her tongue soft.

"Go ahead. Make this one count."

Before she spoke, she studied him. His hair was prettier than her own, his eyes undeniable, his smile mischievous. She wanted to ask about the chewing. At the foot of his crystal flute lay a pile of mangled stirrer straws. Apart from that, he was as polished as a royal bridegroom in his tux, gold cufflinks and Italian leather shoes. It was enough to make the best of the London haberdashers envious. She imagined that he could have anything he wanted in life. Anyone.

"Women," was all that came out of her mouth. At first.

"Is that a question?" His eyes narrowed, his mouth tipping ever so slightly toward a smile.

"Do you have one? A woman in your life?"

"No."

"Has there ever been one?"

"Yes."

"Tell me about her. What was her name, how did you meet, and why'd it end?" Eve leaned forward, her hands supporting her chin as if she were about to hear a fairy tale.

"Science."

"What?" Eve furrowed her brow. This was not what she had expected. Not what she had hoped.

"*Science* is the woman in my life. And science is the perfect woman. She is mysterious at first, full of intrigue. And you spend a long time getting to know all about her, and then one day it clicks, and your heart is on fire. You understand her. It hits you, and you know she is the one. She doesn't run scared. She is, quite literally, the sun, the moon and the stars. And once you get her, you're hers for life. No betrayal. She is truth and light and all that is good."

"But—"

"Oh, and did I mention, she doesn't talk back."

Will laughed at his own reply, but Eve sat a little bewildered if not disappointed. What she had hoped for was a deeper glimpse. The plane touched down, and both passengers pitched forward in their seats. This was it. Martha's Vineyard. Clemson. The party. Eve could feel her nerves pushing their way through her champagne.

"You ready for this? My family can be intense. But I got your six, okay?"

"Okay. I think I'm ready." She took a deep breath in.

"Good."

Will raised his glass and leaned in toward Eve. "To us."

"Nearly betrothed." Eve responded.

Will's face relaxed as they clinked glasses. "You look radiant, Eve. Thank you for this."

"Thank you. And you're welcome."

# CHAPTER 18

OUTSIDE, THE SKIES WERE OVERCAST, AND THE offices at WRAIR were unusually quiet, and for that reason, Louis felt especially conspicuous, and for that reason, he felt like he was wearing a sign advertising his secret data mission. Lucky for him, the colonel had stayed in her office stewing over something he didn't know about—but he knew she was stewing because she always ate guacamole when she was pissed off about something. Said it calmed her down to eat something green. Since Eve's phone call, Louis had collected all five hundred names that matched the de-identified samples they'd sent to the university. Why had he made the impulse decision to keep this from Colonel Savarre? Instinct. In the moment Eve had called, it was like he'd been caught in a seditious act. He felt nervous and didn't know why. People around him knew things he didn't know. It was a decision made not in haste but in a split moment of gut check. Something was rotten at WRAIR. He didn't know why the colonel was so secretive and uptight, and he didn't know why she'd asked Dr. St. John or Eve to throw out the samples. And he didn't understand the urgent nature of this research project. Something was amiss, and whatever that something was, was what had kept him from telling the colonel. Something was going on here, and his actions, while fully qualified as espionage, felt like a moral imperative.

"Louis!"

Louis flinched, and his papers slid off his desk and scattered to the floor like a trail of illegal reconnaissance breadcrumbs that led straight to him. He looked at her, to the floor and back to her, knowing he couldn't get them off the floor himself.

"What's this you're working on?" She collected the strewn papers from the floor and with her enormous hands tamped them horizontally, looked at and convicted him in a single glance, and tamped the papers again vertically until they were in a neat stack. She handed the stack to him, her coal eyes blank. *She knew.* She knew exactly what he was working on.

Louis cleared his throat. "I'm just closing out these files. You know, the files of the five hundred samples." He could hear the lie in his voice. "Making sure we log that each one was destroyed by the university." His tongue felt thick with deceit. "Making sure our research office here connects with theirs. No stone unturned." He licked his bottom lip.

She pinched her face into the perfect scowl. "No stone unturned." Her obsidian eyes bored into him, shifting left and right and back to his eyes again, shaking in their sockets like castanets. There was blood in the water. She was circling. Louis swallowed and waited, thankful he couldn't tap his foot or shake his leg nervously.

"I trust you, Louis, to make wise choices. Do you understand what I mean?"

Louis nodded.

"The army is about honor, Louis. It's about trust. This place—" She motioned with her hands. "This place is about what it means to serve our country with pride and duty and with confidence that we here know what is best for the citizens of this nation when they themselves do not. Protection from those who would seek to destroy us, from terrorists who despise us, from crazies who hate the way we live, hate what we have that they do not, hate our flag, our anthem, our people in uniform!" She pounded her fist on the desk, knocking over Louis's mini Han Solo figure. She smoothed her uniform with hands the size of dinner plates, lowering her voice. "These people at the university, Louis. These people are *not* our friends; they are our *responsibility*. We are here to provide them safety so that North Korea or some crazy-ass dictator doesn't blow us all to hell should they have the desire to fire off a nuclear missile the likes of which would rock this very planet off its goddamn axis, but most important, Louis, and this is *paramount*, we need to protect them from *themselves*. They've done their job, and they did it well, and now it is over. Am I clear?"

"Yes, ma'am."

She tapped the papers with her fingers and looked at him like she knew all of his secrets, then walked away down the hall and back into her office. She walked with a sense of purpose—something he could no longer do, and he felt a twinge of envy, the first in a while. Right now, he had business to attend to which involved something larger than the both of them even if it meant breaking the military code of conduct.

On his phone, he had screenshots of all of the names and their associated ID numbers, and as soon as he was off-site and off the network, he would send them all to Eve. He believed in honor. It was at the core of his military service, and even in his civilian service to WRAIR, he believed in doing the honorable thing. Finding the truth for the families, for the soldiers—for Joseph Bishop—that was the honorable thing to do.

⌘

THE PLANE TOUCHED DOWN EARLY, AND SO THE DRIVE out to West Tisbury was leisurely. Time allowing, Will had promised to walk Eve down to the beach. Will and Eve exited the private jet and climbed into a black Mercedes for the remainder of their journey. Will sensed Eve was nervous. Her décolletage was covered in deep pink splotches, the color rising in her cheeks as she downed another glass of Dom Pérignon.

"Feel some adrenaline pushing through that champagne buzz of yours?" His eyes were full of merriment at the thought.

"Yes, quite."

"Well, I've filled you in, and hopefully Dad will be here. It will all be good, you'll see. I promise I've got your back. We'll head over to the bar, get you something strong and then check out the ice sculptures draped with tiger shrimp and crab claws. They're always pretty spectacular at these events."

"Sounds good." Eve bit her bottom lip.

The drive to West Tisbury was idyllic, and Eve fell into a trance as her eyes followed the miles and miles of horse fence and large swaths of fields that dipped and rolled like the sea that surrounded the island. Horses donned with heavy blankets grazed under the fading sun, and occasionally cows joined them. A jogger passed by with a large shaggy dog on a leash, waving and calling hello to the driver, who waved back. They drove past the large agricultural center that was the town's pride, Will told her, and past the church with the famous clock tower, still wound by hand. A short time later they reached a drive, long and narrow and split with a perfectly manicured grass center. Turning in, they drove between two long fence rows lined with sycamores and oaks until it opened up onto a gracious lawn framed by large boxwoods and strewn with twinkle lights. It was unlike anything Eve had ever seen.

"Take a deep breath." He surprised her by taking her hand in his. He squeezed. "It will be okay, I promise. Clemson doesn't bite."

They stepped out of the Mercedes and into the cool November air, hand in hand. The act was on.

They strode up a long lit path toward a gray two-story frame house. Lights hung from the covered porch, and inside the yellow glow of the windows, a sea of people milled about, exchanging niceties with those they loathed, hugging the necks of those they loved. Eve and Will walked right in, immediately swarmed by people who introduced themselves as family friends. Eve shook hands with Carla and Frank, Bridget and Cleo, Jeanne and Nora and Miles…all who greeted her warmly and spoke fondly of Clemson and his time at Harvard Medical.

In the distance, Will could hear the sharp edge of Clemson's voice talking Harvard, politics and retirement. Clemson could wait a while longer, he thought. "Let's go grab a drink."

Speechless still, Eve nodded.

In the back of the house, off the veranda, was an enormous white tent strung with festive white lights and filled with round tables set with china plates and crystal flutes. In the center of each sat a nosegay of antique-pink English roses with trails of ivy that spilled from them, and tea lights at each place flickered like fireflies, giving the entire scene a strangely summer aura. Strategically placed heaters ensured the comfort of the guests who gathered at the bar, clinking glasses of amber-colored liquid set with fancy twists of limes and lemons, spiked olives and fruit. In the center, far from the destructive forces of heat, was a large ice sculpture comprised of a large round column that supported two square platforms draped with shrimp, and at the top, a large round piece of ice with "50 Years" etched into it alongside a likeness of Clemson.

At the bar, Will turned to Eve and gave her a knowing

look—she needed to help him out with a few details so it seemed as though they were a genuine couple.

"Honey, would you care for another champagne?" he asked.

"No thank you. Jameson, neat, please."

They left the bar, glasses in hand, and he turned to her, grinning. "Jameson? Neat? My God, you may have stolen my heart, woman."

"I grew up in Mississippi, remember? We cut our teeth on moonshine."

Will guffawed.

"Tough on the ole taste buds! No wonder you're vegan."

"I'm not strictly vegan. I'm vegan-leaning. And how the hell you knew that in an interview is still a mystery to me." She felt his arm go in firmly around her waist.

"See that ice sculpture?"

"Yes. That must be your grandfather's likeness etched in the center, right?"

"Yep. A perfect likeness, coldness and all." Will pulled her closer still and whispered into her ear, "See for yourself."

They turned, and there stood perhaps the most exquisite-looking elder gentleman Eve had ever seen. Will was the spitting image of his grandfather. They had the same narrow, twinkling eyes, the same thick wavy hair and the signature St. John grin that lit up even the darkest soul. He smiled at her, and she went warm all over.

"Eve, hello." No *You must be Eve* or *Eve, I presume.* This was a man certain of himself. He took her hand in his, raised it to his mouth and kissed it through his smile. He shook Will's hand in an affirming you-done-good kind of way.

"How is my grandson these days? Tenured yet? Endowed chair in your future?"

"Not yet."

Clemson frowned slightly at this.

"It's early yet. Tenure review won't happen for another year."

"Year? Here at Harvard, you'd be past that already."

"Maybe. Maybe not."

Clemson smirked, and Will already felt like he'd failed in some small way. Here he was on the verge of something huge—something that would change the course of autoimmune diseases the world over, and he suddenly felt small.

"I am on the verge of a scientific discovery. I think it's going to—"

"I'm sure it is, Will. I'm quite sure it's all that you say— your eureka moment. I'm proud for you. Truly I am. Your father's a fool, your brother a waste, your mother… my god where to begin with that woman. You've always been the St. John family's only hope. Our redemption." The skepticism wound tightly around every word.

No pressure.

Clemson turned and offered his arm to Eve. "May I introduce you around?" Like Will, his eyes were penetrating.

*Sure, Dr. Condescending A-hole. You can introduce me, the post doc who's running experiments behind Will's back, around. #nothisrealgirlfriend #you'reatotaldick* "That would be delightful."

Will followed closely behind, never leaving her side, and Eve felt safe from Clemson's snares. She looked and felt gorgeous, and every woman there stared and admired her, just like the men. Her gown was a standout, and she could see that Will had known exactly what it would take for her to feel like she did—like the most sought-after female there. She was exquisite, and she knew it. She also knew Clemson was more than proud to introduce her as Will's significant other. It was a win-win.

"Will!" a voice called out from a table. A man sat alone with a plate full of prawns.

"Dad!"

The man stood to receive a hug.

"Dad, this is Eve. Eve, my father, Charles St. John. Also my uncle's namesake."

"Nice to meet you, Eve." Will's father was handsome enough, but not with the same immediacy as Will or Clemson. His good looks were slower to reveal themselves, a kind of acquired tasted after studying his features. His face was friendly, and his casual manner forgiving. It was clear to Eve why Clemson and Charles did not get on well. Charles lacked an edge and the arrogance that was Clemson's hallmark and likely party to his success. A woman passing by snagged Clemson for a moment, and Charles took advantage of the momentary distraction. "Don't fret too much about Clemson." He nodded toward the elder gentleman. "He's not half as important or smart as he thinks. And poor Will here, with all of his success, still doesn't measure up, though he's miles ahead of the rest of the family." Then he looked at Will. "Ignore the remarks about tenure, Will. You'll get there and then some. We all know it, including Darth Vader. Oh, and your mother says hello and hopes you are well." Charles still talked to his ex. Another chink in his St. John armor. Eve knew she'd left him for another woman, and yet he spoke of her with reverence and tenderness.

No longer distracted, Clemson rolled his eyes.

"I'll call her soon." Will nodded.

After a short exchange regarding holiday plans, Clemson gave a slight tug to Eve's arm. "Stick with this crowd, my dear, and you'll grow soft. We wouldn't want that, now would we?" Clemson and Charles exchanged menacing glances.

Charles's eyes flickered, and he chuckled. "This from a man who thinks Sun Tzu's *The Art of War* is a romance novel."

Clemson's jaw went hard, his gaze fixed on his son. "If I'd known my son would grow up to be the Hollywood version of an ambulance chaser whose pinnacle included marrying a lesbian historian and his expert witness testimony in rhinoplasties gone wrong, I'd have read it every night at bedtime. Will, Eve, there are other guests I'd like you to meet."

Eve turned to Charles and smiled knowingly. "It was lovely meeting you."

"Likewise, Eve. And for the record, Marcus Aurelius makes for far better company than Machiavelli." But by that time, Eve was already ten feet from the table.

The trio stopped at a table near the dance floor, where a band was playing cover songs from the seventies. Two couples sat sipping champagne and chatting with the waiter about the crab dip, the weather and the significance of his tattoo, a phoenix whose wings splayed across the left side of his neck. One woman wore a pale pink silk gown that gathered in rosettes off her square shoulders. A large pear-shaped diamond hung around her neck, and her breastbone shimmered in the candlelight. Her brunette hair was pulled back into a French twist, setting off her high cheekbones. The gentleman with her had red hair, pale skin and wore a charcoal gray tux and Irish claddagh cufflinks. Across from him, a woman leaned in close to examine the cufflinks; she wore a red floor-length gown, also silk, wrapped tight around her tiny waistline. Large sapphires hung from her ears, neck and wrist, and her shiny black hair was pulled into a loose bun with spiral wisps that framed her round face. She smiled, exposing her teeth, perfect veneers, and her eyes twinkled with curiosity. The man next to her had a darker complexion with dark hair to match his countenance. He wore an Italian suit, Eve knew, because the waiter had asked about it just as they'd approached. Both were handsome couples and, for indefinable reasons, stood out from the crowd.

"Senator Wallace Kohnhorst and his wife, Madelaine." Clemson gestured toward the woman in pink and her spouse with the claddagh cufflinks. "And Senator James Brosnan and his wife, Chloe. May I present Eve

Konisken." He'd pronounced it perfectly. "My grandson Will's significant female."

*Significant female?* Single white female was how she was feeling right now.

"Pleased," they rang in together.

"Eve is working with Will on his latest projects."

"Oh?" This piqued Madelaine's interest. She was a biochemist at Harvard. "What projects?"

Will put his arm around her and pressed his thumb firmly into her kidney. Any harder and she might've winced. *Say nothing about the molecule or autoimmune diseases.* She knew.

"I'm currently screening a drug for neurotoxicity—one of the medicines given to soldiers to prevent leishmaniasis infection. It's a military project."

"Oh? How interesting! Senator Brosnan here serves on the Senate Committee on Armed Services. I believe I just read something about that drug in the *Post*, didn't I, darling?" She glanced at her husband for confirmation but continued. "There's speculation the soldier who shot the secretary of state had a breakdown after taking that drug."

Senator Brosnan eyed Eve carefully as he interrupted. "Madelaine, I think Clemson's party is not the time for shoptalk. Besides that, we've got bigger problems than some rumor about a grunt in the Corps. ISIS, Russia, North Korea and China to name a few. I am sure there is some explanation for that soldier's behavior that's got nothing to do with the medicines prescribed by our military." His smile was thin and disingenuous as he shook his head in dismissal. "I'm afraid you're wasting your time on that project." For a moment his eyes bored into Eve's. "Now, if you'll excuse us," he said as he took Chloe's hand in his own. "Dance?"

"It's much more than just some rumor. Larmentin is a dangerous drug with neurotoxic implications." It was Eve who spoke.

Will whispered in her ear, "Eve, this is not the time."

She ignored this.

"I believe the drug should be pulled from the shelves so a full evaluation can be performed."

The senator glowered. "Ms.— That is what FDA approvals are for. Larmentin went through the process and was approved for use as an anti-leish drug for our troops, who are in the best hands—my hands."

"Something I should know?" Clemson looked directly at the senator.

"Nothing we haven't already discussed, Clemson. This situation will blow over very soon, and this entire matter will be laid to rest." Senator Brosnan turned to Eve. "If you'll excuse us. My wife and I are here to enjoy this lovely celebration. You should endeavor to do the same."

The senator's wife, Chloe, stood, her magnificent gown falling in cascades of red to the ground.

Madelaine looked at Eve apologetically. "I recall from the paper that grunt was a trained sniper. Devil's in the details." Madelaine winked. "Nice meeting you, Eve. And good luck with your project. I'm sure you'll find your way to the truth of the matter." As she spoke, her own husband, Wallace, pulled her toward the dance floor.

Eve waved. "Thank you, we will. Nice meeting you all."

Suddenly everything was coming together. The rush, the pressure, the sudden request to just toss the blood samples. This had to be it. Eve had not seen the story in the *Post*, but she could imagine the buzz. Colonel Savarre hadn't wanted them to run the blood samples because she already knew what they would show. Larmentin, when broken down by the human body, produced something poisonous to the brain. She'd have to tell Will, now. She'd have to come clean about what she was doing with the samples.

"Well, that was a lively exchange. Seems the senator disagrees with your assessment of Larmentin. If you'll pardon my absence, I'm going to track down my assistant. I'll find you all in a while." Clemson left their side, and they were alone at the edge of the nearly empty dance floor. Will took her glass from her hand and led her out onto the portable dance floor. A soft melody played. He pulled her close and pressed his face to hers. In her ear he whispered, "Dance with me."

"Okay," was all she could muster as it dawned on her she liked this feeling. Pressed against his body felt good. She wanted to run, but she didn't—couldn't—not now. People stopped talking and turned to watch them. It felt like their eyes were watching, seeing, *waiting* for something. Please God, not a kiss. The tempo, soft and slow, lasted only a few minutes before suddenly switching from violins to guitar and drums to bongos. Eve thought she heard the sound of maracas and claves. The dance floor mostly cleared.

"Watch my feet. Follow my lead." Will's breath was warm against her ear.

They began instantly, stepping in time to the Latin beat, the split in Eve's dress opening and closing as she stepped and spun, faster and faster. She watched Will's body morph into something without bone as he accepted the music in waves, his body fluid. Her hips twisting and moving with his, he squeezed her hand as she went into the turns. A wide grin spilled across his face.

"Wow."

"Phys Ed class, salsa-style dancing. It was a required part of the curriculum. Who knew?" She winked.

"What else don't I know?"

This time it was Eve who grinned on each passing turn until he threw her into a dip. The applause was deafening. Whistles and hollers rose from the crowd. When the music ended, Eve felt light-headed and took a seat.

"You were incredible out there."

"Thanks." She pulled off her shoe and rubbed her foot. "I don't think I'll be running anywhere anytime soon."

# CHAPTER 19

CLEMSON STOOD AT THE EDGE OF THE DANCE floor, watching the senator and his wife sipping champagne and waxing poetic about the benefits of salt therapy and salt caves and the healing power of the Mediterranean. He shot Brosnan a look. The senator slipped away from his wife and made his way toward Clemson, swapping an empty flute for a full one and snagging a shrimp from the ice sculpture.

"What was that about? Do I need to be worried?" Clemson spoke softly through his clenched jaw.

"I'm handling it."

"Well, you'd better. The size of the check I write to your campaign is inextricably linked to the drug company that manufactures Larmentin. If the drug is pulled, there is *no* money, and that means *no* campaign contribution. So unless you're ready to retire and spend your days planting heirloom tomatoes in your greenhouse and listening to books about the benefits of yoga for aging men, I suggest you get this situation under control. I know my grandson. I watch my grandson. He's not as dumb as he seems. If there's something to these allegations…"

The senator placed his hand on Clemson's shoulder. "Look, if there was a reason to seriously worry, I'd let you know in plenty of time to sell. We've got this situation well in hand. You have my word."

Clemson nodded wordlessly as he watched Will and Eve making their way toward the edge of the tent. He'd been watching, reading and listening to Will for a week. Thus far, he'd found nothing to indicate Will had any damning evidence that threatened the continued use of Larmentin. So far, so good. Still, he'd call his broker in the morning. Might be a safe bet to sell some shares—maybe half—and cut any losses. Will was not one to give up easily. If there was something about Larmentin that made it dangerous for human consumption, he'd find it.

---

THE EAST EDGE OF THE DANCE FLOOR ENDED WITH A wide sandy trail that led to the beach. Will turned to Eve.

"Take a walk?"

"Sure."

Eve slipped off her stiletto heels and carried them by their straps as she stepped down the path toward the water. Will slipped his jacket over Eve's shoulders for warmth before they plopped down in a pair of Adirondacks.

Will pulled something from inside his French cuffs and cupped his hands over it while he lit it up.

"A joint at Clemson's big party doesn't seem like such a great idea." Eve laughed.

"It's the only way to do Clemson for very long." Will inhaled, and speaking through his exhale, he said, "He treats my father like shit. He's a surgeon, same as Clemson. Just not worthy of the same respect. He's not a Harvard man, not an academic. He's a plastic surgeon living in Hollywood Hills."

The final remnants of smoke, like Clemson's respect for his son, disappeared into the air. Will began to laugh maniacally.

"You know, before the divorce—before my mother decided she was gay—I wanted to be just like my dad. I practiced on a neighbor's doll once. Rhinoplasty. Had to buy her a new doll with my allowance money. Took me nearly all summer. My first and last rhinoplasty. Then Mom left, and Clemson swooped in like a vulture and took over parenting. My plastic-surgeon dad wasn't fit, and neither was my gay mother. I have some resentments about that, but more and more I realize how much of who I am is just like that guy—Clemson. I'm driven like him. I make my own rules like him. I'm outspoken and blunt without thinking. It's like he wanted his legacy to continue via a younger version of himself. But I'm different on the inside. And I'm not a Harvard physician, not part of his 'club'—I'm just a scientist at a university…" His voice went somewhere sad. "And George, Christ, he was practically disowned. He was such a rebel, always pushing back against something, usually Clemson. He had a strength I never did, true grit. That's how he played. He had guts. We're twins, but we've lived very different lives, and mine has been easier in many ways. I was the favorite child, the one who always did what Clemson wanted. More than anything, I wanted to make him proud of me. But George just didn't give a shit what Clemson thought. George always knew who he was, and he owned it. God, I admired him… Parts of me still do. I'm jealous of him, actually. Jealous that he's no longer tethered to a lifestyle that doesn't suit him." The end of the joint glowed bright red in the sea breeze. "And here I am, tux and all, smoking a joint just to get through the night with a man I'm not sure if I love or despise."

Eve took the joint from his hands and took a long drag, coughing a few times. She loved the sounds of the party in the distance. A place she was near but not part of, her favorite place to be—on the periphery of something bigger than herself. Music played, glasses clinked, people laughed and hollered at friends through the crowds and over each other's heads, clapping their hands at tales retold with new twists, the sound of stories growing over the years. And nearer to her, the sound of seagrass reeds moving in the wind, and closer still, that of Will breathing.

Despite Clemson, for the first time in her life, she felt like Cinderella at the ball. Beautiful, desired, and magical. She looked over at Will. He was handsome and smart—a gentleman, and nothing like the rumors she'd heard. Nor was he a lesser version of his grandfather. Will was thoughtful, considerate. She found him to be quite honorable, in fact. She chalked up the haters, including Clemson, to jealousy. She felt like she knew Will well enough to have an opinion different from some of the others. And she loved this night even though she'd regretted saying yes. She suddenly couldn't imagine not having been here, on Will's arm.

"Thank you for this. You've no idea." Will's sentiment was heartfelt.

"I think I do, actually. I think I get it."

His eyes had a glimmer even in the dark of the night.

"Besides, I should be thanking *you*. I got to ride in a Gulfstream IV, in a beautiful gown and shoes, and dance the salsa at a party in Martha's Vineyard. I mean, c'mon. What's a girl from small-town Mississippi doing here? Look at me." She laughed.

He was looking at her. Mainly her breasts threatening to spill out of her dress.

"I think we're drunk," Eve said, breaking his trance. Her eyes traced his lips, and she wondered what it would be like.

"I think we are."

"I think we're stoned." She giggled.

"I think you're right."

"I think I want—" Her desire slipped out in a way it could not be tucked back in. She wanted to touch him.

"Me too."

The thought lay there between them, though neither moved a finger. Then Will brushed a loose tendril of hair from her forehead, his hand trailing down her cheek and across her lips. Eve took a deep breath. Will leaned in, and she closed her eyes, his breath soft against her lips. She waited, but nothing happened. Will smiled. He'd been so close…he could've kissed her, but he didn't. And she knew he'd done it out of respect. If anything was going to happen, she'd have to make the first move. Will St. John was a perfect gentleman after all.

It was time to go back up and mingle. Will offered to help Eve up, and she took his hand as he pulled her out of the chair, Eve dizzied but relaxed. She grabbed her shoes as the couple stumbled up the path, swaying like a pair of cattails. Words filled her brain, but neither spoke. She wanted to tell him the truth about the experiments, and now was just as good a time as any. With the amount of liquid courage she'd taken in, this might just be the perfect time. She ran through options in her head. *Will, I need to tell you something. Will, don't be mad but… Will, I need to be honest… Hey, you know those Larmentin screens we did? Well, I decided to dig further, and I spent a lot of money… Isn't science about getting to the truth of a thing?* She rehearsed it all in her head, and as she was about to speak, just before they reached the tent, a man stumbled out onto the path in front of them. He was instantly familiar in an odd way, and he'd had way too much to drink.

"Will! Jesus Christ, bro! Stoned at Clemson's party! You dirty rotten son of a bitch! You rat-bastard brother! We're related after all!"

"George! You scared the fuck out of me! What are you doing here? Have you seen Clem?"

"Hell no, and I won't. But I knew there'd be some tiger shrimp and an open bar." His eyes ran over Eve, up and down, side to side. He pointed at Eve with his Budweiser bottle. "Who's this lucky lady with my twin?"

"This is Eve. Don't ask me to say her last name. I'd butcher it for sure right now. She's my 'significant other.'" Will mimed quotes in the air.

"Ah. A baby maker worthy of a St. John. Nice to meet you, Eve. Short for?"

"Eevaleena."

"How beautiful. Beautiful name for a beautiful lady."

"Thank you," Eve replied. She studied the male figure in front of her. His hair was long and unkempt, but Eve could see it was the same dark waves that Will had. His almond-shaped eyes were larger than Will's and his overall physique smaller, but he had the same grin as Will, inviting you in like a spell cast on the unwitting. His face drew lines when he smiled, and he appeared weathered, like he'd spent a lot of time outdoors. She knew from Will that George had no permanent residence. She could see this, the pack on his back, the worn loafers and ripped jeans. He looked like a homeless man about to crash the party.

"Where you headed, bro?"

"Oh, you know, everywhere. I'll be back for Turkey Day. You?"

"Yeah, I think I'll come up for the day. Work's busy."

"I bet. I think those shrimp are callin' my name. Gonna

go score me some. Love ya, bro." George hugged Will long and tight.

"Love you too, George."

Will and Eve walked one way down the path, George the other. Wordlessly, they made their way back toward the tent.

Going for broke, they stepped back up to the bar for another, stoned and laughing, when a huge crash caused everyone to stop. In the center of it all, George, in an attempt to scrape some shrimp into his bag, had fallen at the ice sculpture, taking everything with him with Clemson standing right there.

Clemson raised his hand and snapped at the band, who immediately resumed playing.

"Everything's okay. Please, everyone, enjoy your evening." He spoke with authority, and just like that, everyone turned and resumed their conversations, dancing and laughing while George lay on the ground, bloodied but smiling. Will took Eve's hand and made his way over.

"Well, look what the cat dragged in. Get your sorry ass up, right now, and get the hell away from here! You're pathetic, and you are not welcome here. Ever."

George glanced over the ice sculpture, and as he stood slowly, he spat on the glistening remains of Clemson's face, the sputum sliding down the aquiline nose and over the splintered smile.

"Fuck you, old man."

"George…" Will tried to help, but George snatched his arm away.

"It's okay, bro. We both know where I stand, where I stood and always have." George slurred his words, barely audible with the music and conversations. "I've always loved you, golden boy. What's not to love? You always had my back, always did right by me. You always remember me. Too bad we've got a sorry-ass fuck for a grandfather."

Clemson backhanded George, who bobbled before Will steadied him to keep him from falling. "Say it again, and I'll have you arrested for trespassing, among other things, and you won't get your drugs and liquor in jail."

Clemson massaged his right hand.

Will stepped between them. "Please, let me handle this." His eyes, no longer twinkling, pleaded with Clemson. Simultaneously, Will's phone buzzed with a message. He looked down and could not believe it. Colonel Savarre. Eve looked down at her phone at the same time. Louis.

⸙

WILL COULDN'T IMAGINE WHAT COLONEL SAVARRE would be calling about now. This was Saturday night, and he was done with her. He'd given her what she'd asked for, so why was she calling now? He couldn't even think right now. He had to take care of George first. He toweled off his brother's face, cleaning up the blood, and laid him gently in the back of the Mercedes that would soon return them to the airport.

"I wish I had half your fucking balls, you know that?" Will brushed George's hair from his face. "Sleep this off, okay? Here's a bottle of water, and there's Tylenol in my bag—and a protein bar. Eve and I are going back to say goodbye." He left George lying in the back of the car.

He looked at his phone again.

"Call. Now," was all it said.

He rolled his eyes and looked at Eve. "Can you believe this shit? While my grandfather is backhanding my twin brother, who calls me in the middle of the fight? Colonel Savarre. What the fuck?"

Eve's phone continued to vibrate too, as message after message with names and identification numbers sprang up one after the other.

"Your phone is blowing up, too," Will said flatly. His buzz was gone, but clarity was still elusive. He watched her face now, closely. He chewed a stirrer straw from his whiskey.

"What is it?" He pointed to her phone with his stirrer stick.

"Huh?"

"Who's blowing up your phone. Why aren't you look-ing at it? It is the colonel?"

"Oh, no, I don't think—" She looked down. "CNN. Earthquake or something, I guess." Her voice trailed helplessly behind the lie. She was a fish with a trouble hook in her mouth, and no matter how she tried to remove it, it was going to hurt.

"Where?"

"Huh? Where what?"

"Where's the earthquake?"

"Oh, Mexico, I think."

"What magnitude?"

"I don't know."

"Why don't you look?"

"Because."

"Look at your phone," Will said.

Eve stood, her stiletto heel sinking into the soft ground under the weight of her deceit.

"Eve."

"Yes."

"What is going on." It was a statement more than a question. "Are those messages from the colonel?"

"No."

"Who are they from?"

"Louis. Louis Webster." She shivered as tears streamed down her cheeks now, falling freely onto the gown he'd selected for her, rolling down her neck and over her choker, down her chest.

Will swallowed. "Tell me what you've done."

Eve slid down into a nearby chair. She watched the candles dance with flames while she gathered her thoughts. Will stood over her, waiting.

Finally she spoke, her voice catching. "I didn't throw out those samples…the de-identified ones. I didn't throw them out. I know you asked, I know I was supposed to, but something just didn't seem right, and as a scientist I am nothing if not curious. I'm a digger…above all, a truth teller. I ran the blood samples through the neuro-units…" She choked back her tears.

"How many? How many did you run, Eve?"

"A dozen, maybe…enough."

"Why didn't you tell me this?"

"Because, I don't know. I was afraid. I knew you wanted to spend the money on other things, your discovery. We needed instrumentation. I was afraid if you found out, you'd stop me…I know the neuro-units are expensive, and besides, I was supposed to be checking on your mice…the fat ones…I was supposed to be helping Amy. I'm so sorry…I wanted to see for myself. The Larmentin is toxic, Will. It killed all the brain cells."

"Okay." Will chewed until the stirrer stick was a mangled bead of plastic. "Why do you think the colonel is texting me to call her? I can't think straight right now." He ran his hands through his thick hair. "I need to know everything."

Eve dabbed the corner of her eyes with a bev nap. "I don't know why she would be calling you…I called Louis to get the names and medical histories of the de-identified samples. I wanted to know if there was a positive correlation between the blood samples and reported psychosis. I think this is our answer. I think my phone blowing up…is the answer."

Will ran his hands through his hair a few times and then over his face. "I need another drink." Will stood up and slipped off his tuxedo jacket. There was no sign of Clemson, and despite the minus-one ice sculpture, the party was still going strong. Will stepped up to the bar, loosening his tie.

"Make it a double please with four straws and a cherry."

"Yessir," was the one-word response. The bartender

handed Will his drink, filled to the rim, with two cherries floating on top.

"Thanks." Will plucked a straw from the glass and took down half the whiskey in a single gulp. He speared the cherries with his straw.

Back at the table, he looked at Eve, still beautiful despite the tears. "Let's take a walk." His voice was cool but even.

They trekked back down the same path where they'd seen George, back to the Adirondack chairs. Will offered Eve his jacket.

"Are you angry?"

"Angry? No. Disappointed. Paschal spoke very highly of you. I trusted her. My father used to say trust is a heavy burden but makes light work when two carry it."

The sand blowing across their feet felt like tiny needles, and the moonlight poured down onto a nearby tidal pool. Eve drew her bare feet up underneath the jacket.

"You're right. I wasn't honest…but I was *trying* to be. Just not in the right way. This is not who I am. I don't want you to think that I just go around spending other people's money and running experiments using their resources and their facilities. I don't. I promise you…I am better than that." Eve looked at Will, but he was looking out at the water, his face tense. "Say something. Say anything. Please. I know you must be angry, but I was going to tell you, I promise you that."

Will didn't respond. He looked at the message on his phone and dialed the number.

"Savarre."

He imagined her hulking hands twisted around the receiver like a thick snake.

"This is Will St. John returning your calls."

"Dr. St. John. Thank you for calling me back on a Saturday night. Hope you are having a nice weekend."

"What do you need?"

"I need you to do what I asked. I need you to throw away the samples I sent and anything related, including any testing your post-doctoral associate conducted despite the fact that our business was concluded in full."

"Well, I'm afraid it's a little too late for that. You see, turns out that while Larmentin in and of itself is not harmful to brain cells, the metabolites that are produced by the human liver when someone uses the medication… turns out, that *is* toxic. Very toxic."

"Mmm. That's a nice story, but I'm going with the first one. Get rid of the samples and the data she collected, or there will be consequences."

"Consequences? Like what happened to that soldier? What'd they tell the family? What did they say? Did they tell the family that he was strung out on a drug the army created, licensed, and is both selling and buying for billions of dollars each year?" Will was near screaming now.

"Feeling feisty, or is that the whiskey talking? You listen to me and you listen good. I know what your post-doc has been working on, but more than that, I know about your little drug habit. I know about your Title IX violations and the accusations and your suspension. And you know what else? You know what else I know about?

I know about your little molecule—you know, the one that's going to make those fat mice skinny. The one that's going to cure those diabetic mice. That little molecule of yours that could change the way we treat autoimmune diseases and possibly cure them. And if you make one wrong move, if you breathe wrong, if you blink and I don't like it, and trust me I'll know, I will take that discovery of yours and I will beat you down with it. I will give it and all the glorious details to Dr. Brian Louden—the immunologist at Columbia—who is waiting as we speak, ready to file a patent, and oddly enough, the lab notebooks you think you have, well, those are missing. So you have two choices, Dr. St. John. You can play it like I want, or you can kiss it all goodbye—your career, your discovery, your tenure promotion—and you can go live with granddaddy and suck it up at Harvard. I'm sure he'd be happy to let you lick your wounds under his watchful eye. So call off your dog. Now, Dr. St. John."

The line went dead, and Will's face lost all color.

# CHAPTER 20

"W ELL?"

Will sat silently running his index finger on the edge of the glass.

"What did she say? Are you okay?"

"No." He pulled another joint from his cuff.

"Are you sure that's a good idea?"

"You got something better?"

"No, I just…just please tell me what she said."

Will cupped his hands and lit the joint. He took a long drag and looked at the sky. He counted Jupiter, Mars, Polaris and Venus. It was a beautiful night in one of his favorite places in the world. When he was younger, he and George would race toward the water and back to the house until their feet were blistered. Those were the days. Summer lasted forever. Peanut butter and jelly with cherry cokes was what was for lunch, for dinner, for midnight snacks, then *she* left for a she, and *he* threw himself into his work, and there was just George and Will alone on the sand, in the water, on the boats and dock, smoking and drinking, counting the seconds between the lightning fingers and the sound of thunder, getting high and screwing girls between the dunes. Clemson blamed George. George was weak. A bad seed. Clemson sent Will to boarding school, cotillion and equestrian camps while George did whatever he wanted. Nobody cared. The only time Will saw George after that was November and Christmas. No more running on the sand or kicking each other's asses in the pounding surf. Just Thanksgiving—and Will looked forward to it every year. The month he saw his twin. His brother. Now it was November again, and some psycho bitch was threatening him. Threatening his discovery, his career, his independence. She was out of her goddamned mind if she thought for a second she would get away with this.

For a long time, they just sat smoking, passing the joint like you would pass a drink to a stranger on the plane next to you, and sipping whiskey in the cold silence, listening to the November wind blow and the water lapping the coastline. Will thought of all the possibilities, the consequences, the risks. He would not lose his discovery. He would not lose his molecule. He looked over at Eve still sniffling, her eyes pink with tears.

"I want you to throw it all away. *All of it.*"

"What?"

"I said, I want you to throw it all away. Whatever you've done, the blood samples, the neuro-units, whatever you have in the incubator. If you've touched it, I want it thrown out."

"What? No. Why? I've been— That soldier might be

innocent in all of this. He will take the fall for this, and you know it. We have to be sure. What if we can clear his name? I don't understand. This is wrong, and you know it."

Will held up his palm.

"Because, Eve, it's my lab, my work, and I'm not putting everything on the line because of a misunderstanding."

"Misunderstanding? What misunderstanding? I told you, Larmentin is toxic. The blood samples prove that. If I can correlate the names on this list with those whose blood shows the metabolite, then we have an answer. Larmentin is toxic when broken down the human liv—"

"I think we are experiencing a misunderstanding right now. I'll say it again." He turned and looked at her, speaking through clenched teeth. "Throw it away, or you know what? Don't you worry about it. I'll destroy it all when I get back."

"So that's how it's gonna be? Fine. You know what. You're just like him—a chip off the ole block! An arrogant elitist who loves pushing people around. He should be really fucking proud." Eve surprised even herself with her tone and words. This was not who she was, or was it? She stood up, smoothed her dress and staggered back toward the party.

"And you know what's funny?" Eve turned back to look at Will. "You're the one who's done something wrong here. Not me."

She didn't see Will again until it was time to leave for the airport.

Bill was waiting at the plane with a steaming cup of

coffee in his hand. He looked at Will and Eve solemnly. "Lover's quarrel?"

Neither answered. They climbed the steps and boarded the Gulfstream IV to head for home. When they touched down, Will spoke to Bill privately for a few moments while Eve waited alone in the car, awkward and feeling like she might be the only person in the world capable of pissing off Will St. John—Mr. Happy Go Lucky—like she had. Yes, she had broken his trust, but what about the results? What about the fact that she'd found out the truth? Didn't that count for anything?

She sat on the sofa across from Will, who was pouring himself another drink. She watched him massaging his temples, chewing on a stirrer straw, scanning his phone. She was not traveling all the way back without speaking. She would speak truth to power.

"You know, I find it ironic that a scientist such as your-self—smart, successful, driven—is willing to just sweep data—scientific evidence—under the rug while people suffer for it. You know it's true, and you don't care, and I don't get it. If science is your woman, as you say, you have fucked her royally." Eve's voice cracked with anger. "You have cheated on her, Will. And if you don't do the right thing by her, you risk losing her forever. That's what's on the table, and you just don't get it."

He turned, his jaw clenched. "You know what I find ironic? I find it ironic that five of my people were work-ing on a project about a drug *already* approved by the FDA, and only *one* of my people was working on the dis-covery of a lifetime—a molecule that could potentially cure autoimmune diseases. Why don't you focus your energy on that? You work for me, Eve, and you will do as I say, or you will not have a job in my lab. End of conversation. Got it?"

"Yes."

"Do you understand me, Eve? I need to hear you say you understand me."

"Yes. I understand you."

"Good. That's what I like to hear." *You listen to me and you listen good. I know what your post-doc has been working on, but more than that, I know about your little drug habit. I know about your Title IX violations and the accusations, and you know what else? You know what else I know about? I know about your little molecule—you know, the one that's going to make those fat mice skinny.*

Will was torn. As a scientist, he knew he had an obligation to society to tell the truth. He owed it to the soldier, to his family, to all of those serving in the military who were taking the drug. On the other hand, he had a discovery, his discovery that had so much potential, and he couldn't let that slip through his hands. He wanted to tell the truth, but he was not willing to risk his molecule over some cover-up scheme the colonel cooked up to save face. He was smart. If there was a way to do both, he'd figure out something, but in the interim, the colonel needed to believe they'd done as she asked and thrown out the de-identified samples and any data they'd collected. Will reached into his leather satchel where he'd stowed a few Larmentin samples for safekeeping. His hand searched the inside pocket, then the bottom of the bag… It wasn't there. Maybe it'd fallen out. Or maybe Eve had taken it. She was asleep now. He reached over and nudged her.

"Hey. Wake up."

Eve opened her eyes, just barely.

"Hey. Were you in my bag? Did you take the pills I had in there?"

"Huh? No, I didn't take any pills." Eve was mumbling.

"Eve. Speak up. Did you take the pills from my bag?"

"No, I didn't take your drugs, okay."

*Drugs.* Dammit. What if George had gotten into his bag and… He picked up his phone and called George. No answer. Then he texted and waited. Eve had rolled over. Despite his anger, Will thought how beautiful she looked, her pale blonde strands blown loose by the winds hung across her pink face. She was as Paschal had described. She had good instincts. He looked at his phone, willing George to call or text. He looked back to Eve. The sofa looked pretty comfortable, but he knew better. *I know about your Title IX violations and the accusations.* How did she know all of this? He'd been so high, it hadn't even occurred to him that she had spies or she'd hacked him somehow…but how?

Eve's phone was on the table. He glanced at it. Locked. He took her thumb and gently pressed it to the phone. Bam. There were eleven messages from Louis Webster. Names, rank, diagnoses. Everything he needed to corroborate the story. He copied all of them, but he would make Eve delete them. If the colonel was crazy enough for spies, she was certainly capable of more nefarious things. He refused to take part in her sedition, but he would not risk his discovery either. He just needed time to figure this one out. And time was working against him. The bottom of Louis's text had this:

Louis: Colonel Savarre will testify before a senate committee that the shooting of secretary of state had nothing to do with Larmentin. She will testify that he was high on cocaine at the time of the incident. This hearing is in one week.

Time was something Will didn't have. He really wanted to run this by Cindy, but he couldn't risk dragging someone else into this clusterfuck. He'd have to go it alone on this one.

They touched down at three a.m. Feeling the jolt, Eve rustled and sat up. What was left of her French twist was shoved to one side. She rubbed her eyes and looked at Will.

"I'll do it. I'll throw it all away. I'll destroy the evidence. I have some neuro-units around in other incubators. You wouldn't have found them all. I'll look for another job, and until I find one, I'll keep working on a cure for the fat mice."

Will looked up from his phone but not at her.

"For what it's worth, I'm sorry. I should have come to you first. I see that now."

Will held his breath while she talked, afraid to interrupt her, afraid she'd change her mind.

"Did you find your drugs?"

"No. They must've fallen out of my bag."

He didn't acknowledge her apology with words, but his face relaxed some, and the veins on his neck faded back underneath his skin.

Out on the tarmac, she thanked him again for the dress and shoes. "I'll have them cleaned before I return them. Thank you. It was lovely…mostly." She got in her car slowly, waiting for him to say something else, but he never did.

# CHAPTER 21

Colonel Savarre had a way of lording over people that got under Louis's skin. He couldn't stand, and because he couldn't stand, she was always looming. It was her way of intimidation, and this morning it was working.

"Louis, I need those reports on the Larmentin—the data that cleared the drug." She cleared her throat and glowered at the bag of Cheddar and Sour Cream Ruffles on his desk.

Louis subconsciously pulled the bag closer.

"You know, the reports from St. John." Her eyes bored into him, and the corners of her mouth turned up slightly.

Her mind's eye gave her away. He could see the gears turning, clicking into place. She was like a symphony conductor waving her baton, and he was first violin, responding immediately, and if he did not, well then, he might get clubbed in the head with the baton. She was sending him messages, pull the bow across the strings.

Watch my hands. I set the tempo, *not you*. And that was when it came to him. The realization washed over him like baptismal waters. She was going to be nominated for general. If she cleaned up this mess, she would no longer be a full-bird colonel. She would be *General* Savarre.

"Yes, ma'am. Sending them now, ma'am." The sound of the bow across the strings. Louis wondered if Eve had received his message and if she'd confirmed her suspicions.

"Thank you, Louis." She turned and marched back to her office.

She plopped down into her leather high-back and stirred her guac with the last remaining tortilla chip, and like the final detail that needed to be dealt with, she scooped it into her mouth and swallowed.

Without missing a beat, she dialed the number.

"Carver."

"We have a problem. I'm going to need a favor."

⸺ ❈ ⸺

WILL WOKE WITH HIS HEAD POUNDING. HE WALKED slowly to the bathroom, tossed back some aspirin and stepped into the shower. He needed a strategy. He needed to tap into that merciless way of dealing with others that was the hallmark of the St. John men. He couldn't just lie his way out of this one. She knew things, and he didn't know how. She was watching and listening to everything. He had one week to gather the truth and use it against her at the hearing. He would expose her and whoever else she'd roped into her scheme. He had one bullet, and he was going to save it. He was going to use it on her in front of a senate committee hearing and expose the truth about Larmentin—it's toxic, it kills brain cells, it causes psychosis, and it led to the shooting in Islamabad of the secretary of state, whose life now hung by a thread. But first, he'd have to figure out a way to gather the data in a clandestine manner so the colonel was none the wiser. That meant no emails, no phone calls, no talking at work or in the lab. And, above all, Eve could not know. It needed to look authentic. He would let her help gather everything and let her watch as he threw it out. He would go back later and collect it, put it somewhere safe, download the mass-spec data showing the metabolite and end this. One week.

He made it into work quickly. In his office, he guzzled scalding hot coffee while he ate a bagel thick with hazelnut cream cheese. The food and coffee brought clarity, and he suddenly felt better, felt like he was in charge. His phone buzzed.

Dad: Call me.

It was his dad. Will called immediately.
"Dad."
"Will." Something was very wrong. "It's your brother." His dad's voice cracked. "He, uh, he got into something bad, Will, I don't know…I don't know what. He spun out of control, and he's in the psychiatric ward at Tufts. Clemson wouldn't dare hear of him coming to Harvard. Will, I don't know if they can fix him. He's trapped in his own mind. They had him in a padded room, straitjacket

and everything. He sedated now. The doctors can't say when or if he'll come out of this."

"I don't understand." Will's eyes watered.

"He snorted something. Don't know what. Don't know—"

The pills in Will's bag. George must've taken them thinking they were something fun and crushed them up to snort them. *Jesus. No.*

"I need to know if you can come up here and handle this. I've got patients backed up until Thursday. I can come back then. I need to get back to California, and Clemson's no help. You know how that goes with him and George. I haven't called your mother yet. I just don't know how to break the news to her. I can barely keep it together myself." A sob escaped, followed by silence.

Will felt like he'd been kicked in the gut. There couldn't have been a worse time in his life for this kind of crisis, but what else could he do? He had one week to execute his plan for revealing the truth about Larmentin, and now this. But he had to go. This was George they were talking about. Will sighed into the phone as he held back his own tears.

"Sure thing, Dad. I'll be there." Will hung up. He could feel the guilt mounting, but he couldn't let that win. He needed to collect himself. He would leave, see Eve, then he'd catch the first commercial flight out to Boston. Clemson would not be sending his plane. Not for this.

Will needed to go back and talk to Eve about throwing out all of the samples and data—and he would have to make it look convincing. He could do this. He would do this. Then he had to get on a plane and go see George. The order of events did not marry with the priority necessarily, but that couldn't be helped. He walked into the lab, finding Eve hovered over her computer, reading literature.

"Monoclonal antibody treatment in diabetic mice."

Eve looked up from her computer. Her once pink face was colorless, and her eyes had dark circles around them. She wore a T-shirt and jeans, not her usual fare, and Will felt another pang of guilt. She looked as though she had cried all night long, but right now, she was expressionless. And despite it all, she was still stunning.

"Come with me."

Eve followed him back to his office.

"Shut the door. Have a seat."

Eve did as he asked. Will chewed on a stirrer stick and paused speaking while she wiggled in her seat.

"We, you and I"—he motioned with his mangled stirrer stick—"are going to toss out any evidence of those de-identified samples." He raised his eyebrows and looked at her. "You will help me do this, yes?" He nodded in the affirmative.

"Yes."

"Thank you. You may go." Eve furrowed her brows.

"That's it?"

"Yes. I need to leave town for a few days. Can I count on you to hold down the fort here?"

"Sure." Eve got up from the chair and turned to say something but instead only sucked in a bit of air.

Will set out to find a burger for lunch. When he returned, there was envelope on his desk. Inside, a note:

*I am so very sorry. I will help you however I can. The gown is at the cleaners—I will return it in two days. P.S. Not feeling well. Going home for the day.*

Maybe he'd been too hard on her, but she needed to know who was in charge. He decided he'd look her up and stop by on his way to the airport. Maybe there was something he could say that would make her understand the stakes better. His phone vibrated, and he glanced down momentarily. Five text messages from Eve.

"Keep your pants on. I'm coming."

She lived only blocks from campus, so he decided to walk. He put her address in his phone and walked down the mostly empty streets with only an occasional dog-walker or jogger. A woman passed with a corgi, who sniffed at his pants leg briefly. The owner, a stout man in track pants with facial hair, only mumbled hello and walked on. The colder weather was no doubt a deterrent. He turned left and spotted the apartments. Half a block down on the left, past a cluster of baroque-style brownstones, stood a quaint four-story brick building with old windows in need of painting, and doors that had recently been scraped of their finish but not yet refurbished. Ivy grew thick on either side of the broken sidewalk, and he stepped through an honest-to-God wrought iron gate into a small courtyard area. He had to admit, the place was charming in a very British kind of way. He'd bet that was what she thought when she first saw it. *This is a place I can live with my cat and eat dark chocolate at night by myself in my flannel nightgown while I watch* Golden Girls *reruns.* He felt bad for thinking it, but he did. That joint was probably good for her, he thought. She'd certainly loosened up and relaxed a little. How did someone so smart and beautiful ever end up wound so tight? And he wondered if it had to do with her alcoholic mother and the fact that Eve had had to depend on herself and the pressure of living without another to count on. He continued up the sidewalk lined with pansies in clusters of goldenrod and purple until he reached the main door. He stepped inside and took the stairs to the second floor. Probably best that she was on floor two. Ninnies never lived on the ground floor. He reached the landing on two and was greeted by a large orange tabby that rubbed against him, leaving a swath of orange-and-white cat hair on his pants.

"Watch it there." He looked at the tag. "Boris." He brushed off his pants leg and began to sneeze. Her apartment door was ajar, but Will knocked nonetheless. "Eve?"

He called out and listened. He thought he could hear movement but not the sound of footsteps or an audible response. "Eve, are you in there?" He thought he heard a moan. "Eve, I'm coming in, okay? It's Will." He stepped inside and looked around. The air inside smelled odd—familiar but still something Will couldn't place. Her place was much more modern than he would have suspected. Clean lines, two small sofas facing each other set on a geometric rug with a thick glass table between and stacks of oversized gardening books. On the wall, an enormous poster of Muhammad Ali in an active boxing stance read, "Float like a butterfly, sting like a bee." Will smiled. "Nice poster of Ali, Boris, wouldn't you agree? Much better than a cat poster." Boris hissed. "Truth hurts, buddy." So she wasn't a fuddy-duddy after all, still OCD from the looks of the place, with books in neat little clusters or rows, her mail in a sorting tray, and placemats perfectly spaced for guests who never came. Boris meowed loudly.

"I don't speak cat, Boris. Sorry. Dog. I speak dog. You?" Will called again, "Eve? You here? I just wanted to apologize for everything. I wanted to say I was sorry. Sorry about the party… That was a huge favor you did and then to get dragged into the drama with my brother…I should thank you. So thank you. And I am sorry." He started down the hall, but something caught his eye. A foot. A human foot near the sofa. Eve was on the ground, curled up into a ball, her knees drawn in to her chest.

# CHAPTER 22

"Eve! Hey, hey. What happened?" Will bent down and brushed her hair from her face. "Eve, it's me. Will. What happened?" But he could see something was very wrong. Her body was stiff and her skin hot to the touch. "Jesus. Eve, you need a doctor. I'm going to get you some help, okay? What happened? Shit! Eve, talk to me. Can you tell me what happened?" Will was pulling his phone from his jacket pocket. "No, don't talk. Just don't talk." Tears sprang from his eyes.

She looked at him, her eyes pleading as blood trickled from her nose and ears. She mouthed the words, "I'm sorry. My fault."

Will shook his head no. "Shhh…This is nobody's fault. I'm calling nine-one-one. Just hang on. Stay with me, Eve." Will dialed 911.

"Nine-one-one. What is your emergency?"

"I—my friend…" Though his eyes never left her, he was at a loss for words. He had no idea what was going on, and the panic had tied his thoughts in knots. He watched her struggle for breath as he spoke. "She's, uh… she's burning, I think…" Will wasn't sure what else to say, how to describe it.

"Sir, is there a fire?"

"No, no fire. Just please hurry. My friend is burning…I think she's…" He couldn't say the rest. Eve's pellucid blue eyes pleaded.

"Your friend is burning but there is *no* fire?"

"That's what I said, dammit! Are you listening? My friend needs help *right now*!" Will was screaming at the top of his lungs now. Boris jumped, and Eve flinched slightly.

"Sir, I'm gonna need you to calm down. Help is on the way, but I need you to remain calm. Can you do that for me?"

"Yes."

"Okay. Now, can you tell me what happened to your friend?" The voice on the phone was reassuring and experienced.

"I don't know. She is burning from the inside out. And she's bleeding from her nose and ears." His voice caught on the finality of his words, and that was all he could say before he broke down again.

"Sir? Sir? Help is coming. I need you to stay on the line."

Will hung up. That help was coming was all he needed to know. His phone buzzed back from the 911 dispatcher, but he didn't answer. He watched helplessly as Eve twitched. He wanted so badly to touch her, but he couldn't. Eve made a few odd noises, but no words were audible. Will watched as a small flame came from her mouth followed by puffs of smoke. Will watched helplessly as the sockets of her beautiful blue eyes turned black and the jeans she was wearing began to melt. Blood now ran from every orifice of her body.

"What the—Jesus! Eve! What—who did this?" His heart pounded as he looked around her apartment for evidence of something else. *Someone else.* "The ambulance is coming. I called for help. Jesus, Eve, they're coming."

She looked up at him, her eyes drenched in red. Will tried to swallow his concern, but he could tell something horrible was happening. He wanted to comfort her, but he just didn't know how. He looked around her apartment and back to her face, digging deep for an idea, but there was none.

"Wanna know a secret? I didn't tell you while we were at the party. I wanted to kiss you on the beach. I wanted to kiss you so badly, Eve. True story. But I'm in some trouble with the Title IX office, and I was afraid of what you'd think…but then I guess you told me what you think anyway. Funny, huh?"

Eve's lids were heavy; she blinked and opened them only halfway.

Will's tears fell like rain. "So that's it…yeah. I am so sorry, Eve. I was an asshole…" Tears streamed down his cheeks. "Chip off the old block, isn't that what you said? Guess I have been lately and, Eve, I am so sorry… so sorry. God knows…" Will choked out his words. Eve was looking at him now, but he couldn't tell if she could see him. "Listen to me." He stroked her hair as gently as he could, but in his hands, clumps of blonde strands fell from their roots. "I am going to tell the truth about Larmentin. I wasn't going to tell you; I was just going to do it. I am going to expose the truth, sacrifice my discovery…put it all on the line…and…" Tears fell onto her skin, steam rising, and Will backed away a little, frightened he might bring more pain. "I am so sorry, Eve. I am going to find out what happened here. I am going to find out who did this, and I am going to be that asshole—that St. John trademark prick who makes them wish they'd chosen someone else to fuck with." Eve was fading, he knew. "Stay with me, Eve. You have to. I've been practicing your name, you know. I was going to surprise you by pronouncing it correctly, like, on your birthday or something. Eevaleena Konisken. See? Hear that? Eevaleena Konisken. Perfect, huh? Stay with me… stay, please stay, Eve." Suddenly, Will could hear the sirens. "The paramedics are here, Eve, just hang on…hang on." He ran into the stairwell to meet the paramedics. "Up here! I think my friend's on fire!"

Paramedics rushed up the stairs as Will pointed.

"I just got here and found her like this."

The paramedics rushed over and bent down over her body to begin inspecting, but her skin was hot to the touch. The paramedic pulled his hand back in shock and looked at Will.

"What's her name?"

"Eve. Eve K-o-n-i-s-k-e-n."

"What happened? How long's she been like this?"

"I don't know. I just got here a few minutes ago."

Will's voice was strained as another paramedic prepped IV fluids.

"Did she say anything?"

"No. She couldn't—can't talk." His voice fell to a whisper.

The paramedic put the stethoscope to her neck for as long as he could grasp the metal without burning his hands. He turned to Will.

"I'm sorry. She's gone." Then looking at his partner, he said, "Not going to need IV fluids."

Will slumped over in a fit of uncontrollable sobs.

"Sir. You want to try to tell us what happened here?"

Will's phone buzzed with a text:

Unknown number: Say nothing.

He was still processing. How could he possibly say something at this point when he didn't know *anything*.

"I don't know. I just got here, and she was curled up in a ball, bleeding from her…eyes, and she was hot an—" He couldn't finish. The convulsing sobs came back.

"Take your time, sir."

The paramedics sat with Will for a long time, until he could speak, but there was nothing he could say. Nothing he would say. No one had ever seen or heard of something like this. She had suffered was all anyone knew. They waited for Eve's lifeless body to cool before putting her onto the gurney.

"You her boyfriend?"

"No." *I was her boss. Maybe her friend. Not a very good one. Maybe a lousy one.* "A friend."

"All right, sir. Well, the police will need a statement from you."

"Okay."

"Sorry we couldn't do more for your friend. I can't say I've ever seen anything like this before in my life."

Will knew he meant it. The paramedic looked as downtrodden as Will felt. They were all still in shock.

Boris mewed and rubbed up against Will's legs. Will looked around for the first time. The apartment was classy, sparse, but not in a manner lacking personality. And it occurred to him this was a true reflection of Eve. Classy, and more than meets the eye in many ways. There were a few nicely framed photos and postcards of Rome and Florence on a corkboard in the kitchen. In the living area, there was a nice Samsung flat-screen TV and a small teak wine rack full of expensive wines. Two beautiful crystal goblets sat on top. This was where she had lived. And where she had died. Eevaleena Konisken. He whispered her name perfectly. He had barely known her, but he might've loved her. Now he sat wondering if her death was somehow his fault. Still, he knew who had done this. Of this, he was certain. Say nothing.

⋙

"What in the hell were you thinking? Were you thinking?" Rusty Carver roared his way into a coughing fit. His pear-shaped face turned purple, his pores bubbling with perspiration.

The colonel rose and slammed her door shut. "Lower your voice. Louis is sitting right down the hall, and he is not innocent in all of this! He sent them the names and medical histories."

But Louis would hear it all. He adjusted his hearing piece. Through the door, it was muffled, but he powered down his computer and turned up the volume in his ear. Perfect.

Rusty Carver was re-tucking his shirt in his pants, giving the colonel a temporary reprieve from the sight of his bearded gut. "Well, I can't worry about that now, can I? Now, because of you, we need to find a way to make that girl's death records disappear. That and everyone who saw her die. What in the fuck were you thinking? What was wrong with good old-fashioned anthrax? That drug you used was top secret. It was top secret, and it was *never, ever* going to see the light of day. You can't hide a death like that. It's too horrible. People remember when they see things like that. This is the kind of shit that goes viral, and this is on your head, Susan!" He was so close that he spit in her face as he said the words.

"You watch your filthy mouth. I called and said there was a problem when I realized what that girl was doing. I was only doing what *you* asked, staying on top of it. I was 'handling' the situation. If you don't like the way I handled it, then perhaps you should've chosen more wisely when asking someone to clean up the mess. I'd no idea they were going to kill her. I thought they'd scare her a little, shake her up some. I'm no dumbass, Rusty. In the end, this was not my call to make. I didn't choose this method. That came from the top. You got a problem,

I suggest you look up, not down! This is not all on me. This is not my circus, not my monkeys!"

"Fix it? Really? That ship has sailed, hasn't it, Susan? Now what are *you* going to do to solve it? I need to know."

"I've got people on him watching his every move. The police scanner confirms he said nothing. Exactly as I instructed him. They're following him as we speak. If he makes one wrong move, I'll know about it."

Louis had stopped crunching ten minutes ago. Somebody, who was not the colonel, had used the latest drug developed by the anti-terrorism unit inside the Defense Threat Reduction Agency aka DTRA. Had to be somebody high up. The drug, aptly named "dragon's breath" for the smoky breath and signature flame emitted from the victim's mouth, was classified and had also been decommissioned, though there was still some around WRAIR somewhere. Disposal had proven to be difficult if not impossible. They'd had a scientist at WRAIR helping out with safe administration standards before it got axed. It was simply too horrible. But it was here, and *someone* had gotten it out of the building and into the hands of *someone* who had administered it to *that girl*…Eve. Louis trembled in his chair. He had sent the names to her…and the medical histories. This was his fault. But maybe he could make this right. Maybe, he could fix this *and* the Larmentin lies all at once.

# CHAPTER 23

THE PARAMEDICS STOOD TALKING INTO THEIR PHONES with a supervisor who was asking a ton of questions. At the same time, Will was fielding questions from a lone detective who stood six-foot-six and likely weighed 250 pounds—all of which was muscle—and whose bald head along with his physique reminded Will of Mr. Clean on the household cleanser. It didn't help matters that he sounded like Rocky Balboa when he spoke. He looked around the room, his eyes settling on the poster of Ali. He nodded as if paying reverence of some kind. He also seemed distressed by the spectacle of Eve's deteriorated figure lying on the gurney. It was bizarre and frightening. Even Will, in all his years of studying infectious diseases, traveling to countries and visiting clinics where people died horrible deaths in negative pressure isolation chambers, had never seen anything like this. Will politely responded to all but answered none of the detective's questions. The truth was he didn't know much. Only one thing for sure, and he wasn't about to give that up. He and he alone would handle that. He would tell the truth. He would do this for Eve. *Fuck the colonel.* If it meant losing his discovery, then that was the price he would pay. Maybe he could go back to the cape and teach sailing to spoiled little rich brats. Whatever his plan was, truth was on the table. He pushed back against the urge to cry. It wasn't hard. He was in shock, and a strange numbness took hold of him, resulting in an odd cycle of detachment and mania that would define his behavior for the coming days.

The detective spoke in a low Balboa baritone that allowed Will's mind to drift. He would leave here, go to Tufts Medical Center to be with George, and then he would find Louis. In that order.

"Mr. St. John, I'm going to need you to stick around until we get this thing settled. I've got a few more questions for you, so don't wander off, but first I've got to talk to my crime scene guys over here, see if they've got any ideas on what may have caused all of this. You stay put until I say you can leave. Understood?" The detective held out his hand with a tissue, which Will accepted graciously.

"Yes, sir. Will do." *Over my dead fucking body. Just as soon as I check on my twin brother and make sure he's okay and then find out how the fuck this happened and do what I should've done in the beginning—reveal the goddamned truth.*

The detective shook his hand and went to talk with the paramedics and others who'd just arrived on scene. Will looked around. There was nothing else he could do here. The detective and a few forensics guys were talking amongst themselves and seemingly uninterested in Will or what he was doing for the time being. He heard them talking about Eve's condition, and one of the paramedics suggested spontaneous combustion. But Will knew better. He needed to leave, but he couldn't just walk out the front door past the detective. He decided to slip out the back. Down the hall, he spotted a pair of French doors. He made his way toward them with a mind to leave quickly and walked right into Eve's bedroom. Suddenly, he felt like an intruder—like he was somewhere forbidden—a place he would not have seen under any other circumstances. He looked around. A modern-style bed was covered in a deep gray velvet blanket with white satin pillows in a neat row. The bed, a combination of wood and metal, was flanked by two small nightstands. Lights mounted on the wall provided reading light, and Will spotted a stack of magazines on the table. A full inch of *Cosmopolitan*, probably an entire year's worth of issues, was clearly visible beneath a few issues of *Vanity Fair* and *National Geographic*—almost as if she knew someone might be coming and it was best to hide the Cosmos like they were hidden at the checkout—the kind of magazine they cover with a brown paper bag.

Through her closet door, he could see her shoes, just as he described them in their initial meeting—in their original boxes and ordered by style and color. But what struck him most was the number of pairs of house slippers she owned. A lump came in his throat. *Why am I looking at these things now? Move.* She was gone. *Gone.*

The girl whose home never saw a friend and who read *Cosmopolitan* magazine at night in her fuzzy bed slippers had just died in the most horrible manner one could imagine. And here he stood in her bedroom, under very different circumstances than he might've hoped. The room was like her. Tidy bordering on austere but with some surprises and maybe a few secrets—just like she'd been at the lab. And now…now she was dead. He almost felt a nervous laugh coming on. He wanted to step into her closet and bury himself into one of her sweaters and cry, but he had to pull himself together. He couldn't fall apart. Not now. He owed her that much. He was going to make this right. He needed to leave before the detective thought of more questions.

Will stepped out onto the small deck off her bedroom and walked quietly down the metal stairs of the fire escape. Across the street, an engine came to life. Will failed to notice the black sedan but turned to find that Boris had followed him outside.

"Back inside, Boris! Shoo! Now!" Will shooed at the cat, but Boris was determined. "Get. Back. Inside." Will hissed. Boris hissed back. "I don't have time for this shit. You can't come with me. They hate cats in Boston. Hell, I hate cats."

Boris rubbed up against him. "Goddammit, Boris, get back inside!" Will shout-whispered.

Boris replied with a mewing that seemed to cut right through Will, and fresh tears sprang from his eyes.

"Fuck. Fuck. Fuck."

Will walked down a back alley, turned up the side

street a block over from his earlier route, and headed toward the university. Boris padded beside him like they were old pals, neither aware of the low rumble of the sedan that followed from a distance. Will walked inside his building with the twenty-five-pound orange tabby in tow, grabbed his pack from his office, careful not to be seen by anyone, and walked out to his car. Next stop, home for a change of clothes and a few personal items, then straight to Boston to see George.

At the airport, he purchased a TSA-approved pet carrier, which set him back $150. He shoved a resistant Boris in, threw in half of a Twix bar, and said, "I'm sharing," before zipping it closed. He ambled through security with an occasional cooing over his new feline companion, but Will couldn't respond. He was numb and angry and heartbroken all at the same time. His eyes were still swollen and red from his crying jags, and simultaneously he felt helpless and determined; he would claw his way through this one. Boris was heavy, and Will set him down every few feet as the line through TSA moved slowly. Unlike the charter jet experience, he stood in a long line full of people who forgot about the metal on their belts or in their hips, their liquids, or to take off shoes, which added an hour to his wait.

He might've felt his anger building if he wasn't so shocked at everything that had transpired, but he had to focus. He knew these were the kind of situations where he rose to the occasion. As soon as he arrived in Boston, he would check on George to see what was going on, then he would figure out a way to contact Louis. Since Louis had sent Eve the information on the de-identified samples, he felt like that was a good starting place to figure out what had happened. Then he would hunt those who did this and make them wish they'd never been born. He blinked back tears and centered himself.

On the flight, his mind was full. He watched Boris out of the corner of his eye while he ordered a bloody mary and got to work. First, he googled spontaneous human combustion and read everything he could find. He wondered if the paramedics or medical examiner knew what they were seeing. He thought about how hot Eve had been to touch…how he would've liked to touch her tenderly under different circumstances. He thought of the flame that came from her mouth, the bleeding, her eyes hollow and gray with smoke. He couldn't get those images out of his mind. That was what drugs did for him. It was how he turned down the noise in his mind. But this. This ran through his mind like a siren. He would never be able to turn this off. He would never forget. This would haunt him. Eevaleena Konisken. He wondered if her parents had been notified yet, what her dad and mother must be experiencing, and he hoped that whoever had delivered the news had done so with a modicum of tenderness. He swallowed down his grief. The lump in his throat had been persistent. *Focus, Will. What would Clemson do?* He knew.

He switched gears to Larmentin and began making notes. The flight attendant delivered his drink and some nuts. He got three packs of peanuts instead of the standard issue of one. She winked and also slipped him and extra bottle of vodka "just in case this one's weak." She nodded in the direction of her coworker. "Sometimes he goes a little light, saves the extra for himself."

"Thanks." Will muttered his response. He did not feel like chatting up the crew. He needed answers. At his feet, Boris shifted in his carrier, looking for the perfect sleeping spot. Will found this futile exercise distracting and tapped the side of the zippered bag with his foot. "There's only one choice, Boris. The carrier is small. Now, be still and lie down."

Boris gave him an eat-shit-and-die look like only a cat could. Will ignored this unspoken challenge and returned to his online research. If George had crushed it and snorted it, he needed to know all he could. This search yielded hundreds of results. Larmentin had been in the news off and on for years. Reports of civilians losing their minds on African safari and soldiers in the field suffering from mental breakdowns. It wasn't until the secretary of state had been shot that a true investigation into the effects of Larmentin drew real media attention.

Will looked at the calendar. In four days, the Senate committee hearing on the incident would take place in Washington, DC. He would need to move quickly, and it occurred to him that, given recent events, public transportation was a poor idea. He'd have to call his uncle and see about taking the private jet. That was the only way possible for him to move about undetected. Then, in four days, he would travel to DC himself and put it all on the line. He was going to tell the truth.

The 747 touched down in Boston, and Will grabbed his pack and Boris and exited the aircraft. He was on a mission. He glanced in the carrier to check on Boris. The Twix bar hadn't been touched.

"If there's one thing I can't stand, it's the smell of fish, so whatever kind of snobby-ass diet you're accustomed to eating, it's gonna have to change. Just eat the fucking Twix bar."

"Excuse me, sir?"

Will turned around to see an older lady with several cats in an XL carrier. She, too, was XL. A knotted scarf around her head failed to hold in her big frizzy hair, and her neck jangled with plastic beads the size of golf balls—the same variety which hung from her ears, her ear holes stretching under the weight. She was clad in head-to-toe navy and hot pink polyester. *This is new,* Will thought. *I usually get hit on by younger women.* This woman had to be in her early sixties.

"Yes?" Will was abrupt; he didn't have time for interruptions.

"Chocolate is poisonous to cats. If you insist on feeding your cat a Twix bar, I'm going to have to report you."

Just what he needed; some crazy-ass bitch to report him for feeding an animal something she didn't approve of.

"He's not even my cat. I'm just taking care of him for a few days."

"Mmmm. Uh-huh. Whose cat is he, then? Does he by chance belong to her?" She pointed at the television, which had a photo of Will next to a photo of Eve with a caption that read: "Man wanted in connection with mysterious death of researcher."

Electric shockwaves ran down his arms and spine.

"Nope. Nope, and that is not me, lady. You're crazy."

That was when she began screaming for security. Without missing a beat, Will sprinted for the door, and outside waiting for him, as if heaven-sent, was his uncle Bill.

Bill threw open the sedan door. "Will, get in!"

Will hopped in with Boris and slammed the door. In the rearview mirror, no sign they'd been spotted or followed.

"Will, wanna tell me what's going on? Your photo is all over the news. The authorities are looking for you. What happened to your friend? Are you okay? Why do you have a cat? I thought you hated cats."

"Long story. Yes, I hate cats…" He looked at Boris lying next to the untouched Twix bar, regretting he'd taken him. "This is Eve's cat. Eve is…" Will's voice broke.

"Hey, Will, listen. If you're in some sort of trouble, tell me. Maybe I can help."

"Not this time. Thanks."

"I saw the news, Will. What in the hell is going on? What happened to that girl? The news isn't saying much, only that she died a suspicious death. I am so sorry. I also know you, and I know you had nothing to do with it. Shoot me straight."

"I can't." Will sniffed. He would not lose another person he cared about—not the way he'd lost Eve. "The less you know, the safer you are. Believe me when I say they have ways of getting it out of you, and if they don't, well, they have ways of gutting you… You don't want any part of that, trust me. There is one thing you can do for me, though. I'm going to need help getting around the country under the radar. Think you can help me with that?"

"Consider it done."

On the way out to Tufts Medical Center, they made a plan to meet after Will had seen George and figured out what to do. Will needed a drink or something to smoke. Or both. But he knew his adrenaline would push through it all. His entire world felt like it was coming apart. And in his mind, images of Eve at the party and on the floor of her apartment ran together and apart over and over again. He remembered dancing with her one day, watching her burn to death the next. He felt sick. He wanted to cry. He pulled himself together. *Focus, Will. She would want you to tell the truth.* He could still do something for her. He could still right a wrong.

Will checked into the treatment center, removing his laces from his shoes and locking his personal items in a locker before a hospital worker keyed him up on the elevator, Boris in hand. They typically did not allow animals, but Will sweet-talked the female security officer, and she obliged. Boris could go. She even offered to share some cat food she'd been feeding to a stray outside their building. Will thanked her and let Boris eat for a minute.

"You're keeping that Twix bar, too. It's fiber. Good for you."

Boris didn't look up from his Meow Mix, but Will could hear him purring.

"I think he likes you," the security lady said. Evidently, so did she.

"Yeah? You want a cat?"

"Oh no! The way he's purring, it's obvious. He's in love with his owner." *Was. Was in love with his owner. Maybe I was, too.*

Boris in tow, Will stepped out into a concrete block corridor covered with a 1960s-era green paint that was only just now beginning to peel. Probably lead. There was nothing on the walls, and the few sleeping quarters they passed looked like something from a World War II prison camp. The hallway led to a small common area with nothing but plastic tables and chairs, an empty bookcase and a nurse's station enclosed with thick glass but with a pass-through large enough for a hand to pass a small paper cup full of medicine.

A nurse directed Will to a small table near the window. The entire place reminded Will of *One Flew Over the Cuckoo's Nest*, and Will imagined depression was hard to beat in a place as dismal as this. The skies were overcast and gray, which suited Will just fine. The sunshine would've been too much for him today. He was thankful to be on the ground and below the thick clouds.

George appeared from around a corner, shuffling slowly, arm in arm with a nurse. He wore blue scrubs and foot covers, and his usual five o'clock shadow was now a full beard. Despite everything, he looked okay, Will thought.

Will surveyed the nurse, who wore scrubs with stick-figure cats and dogs like she worked in a children's ward. George was like a big child. Her hair was solid white, parted to one side in a low ponytail that was braided and tied with a rhinestone barrette. She was medium height and carried her extra weight in funny places, her scrubs stretched tightly over her arms. Her hips were narrow, but her ass was a dimpled bubble, and her stomach pooched despite attempts to suck it in when she saw Will. She wore a thin line of blue glitter across the top of her lids and bright pink gloss on her lips that made her look like a teenager trying colors for the first time.

She helped George into a chair. "The sedation is only just wearing off, so he's not steady on his feet just yet." She smiled. "You must be the twin. You sure have got an entertaining one here." She smacked her cinnamon gum and drew out her words in an unmistakable thick New York accent. "He's had me in stitches since he's been awake. Haven't you?" She looked at him, her glossy pink lips spread, exposing her white teeth.

George smiled back. "I try."

"Well, I'll let you two talk. I'll be back for ya later." She winked at George.

The twins watched as she turned, her pants taut across her large dimpled bubble-ass.

"Did you sleep with her?" Will was incredulous.

"No, hell no. The meds aren't worn off yet. Give me some time to get my third leg in gear."

"Dad told me you were in a padded room, unresponsive.

Now, I get here, only to find out you're hooking up with the staff." Will was shouting.

"Dude, take a pill."

"Poor choice of words, George." Will couldn't believe he'd dropped everything he was doing, only to find out George was on holiday making nice with the nurses. Will's sense of urgency about other matters now threatened his sanity. He was happy, truly, to see George was okay, but Will was not okay. Eve had died in a manner so horrific it sent a shudder down Will's spine to think of it. And while she couldn't speak in the end, Will felt certain she would have cried out with pain if she could have. His eyes watered, threatening to spill over into tears.

George looked at him with genuine pity. "Look, I'm sorry, okay? You saw how I was treated *and* by my own flesh and blood."

"Speaking of, where is Dad?"

"He's assisting on a rhinoplasty here. Some celebrity hotshot's in town. Somehow knew Dad was here in town and called. What's with the cat? We hate cats." Boris hissed.

"Not important. Christ, George, I thought you'd finally done yourself in. What happened? What'd you do? Did you take my pills, crush them and snort them?"

"Hell no, bro. Just a little too much of the downers, I guess. Didn't mix right with the alcohol. I don't know. Nothing a spot of epinephrine couldn't fix."

"Goddamnit, George. My life is upside down right

now, and I just traveled—on a commercial flight—to make sure your ass was safe."

"Shit. Cool down, brother. I said I'm sorry, okay? It's not like I asked you to come. But I'm glad you're here, and okay, I'm sorry that your life is upside down right now. Mine too."

"Yes, but…dammit, George." A mix of relief washed over his anger. "Look, when are they letting you leave this place?" It occurred to Will that anyone who knew him or was close to him might be in some sort of danger…possibly.

"I think in two days. Got to make sure I'm not a danger to myself or others. Right?" George smirked and rolled his eyes.

"Sure, sure. Same drill as before. Don't you ever get tired of this, George?" Will waved his hands around at the dismal surroundings that was the common area for visitors and patients. "Don't you ever want something more?"

"What do you mean, golden boy? You mean like you? A PhD, PhDick, Prick-h-d… Think I have what it takes to be some fancy scientist at some swanky university like you? Like Clemson? C'mon. We both know the answer to that."

"This isn't about me or Clemson, George. This is about you. You're smart, George, I know you are. But this? This is just stupid. You just—"

"Don't apply myself. Right. Yeah, I just need to apply myself is all."

"I don't feel sorry for you, George." This was a lie. Will had just vowed to be truthful, and now he was already lying to his brother. "I didn't get where I'm at—and Dad didn't either, by the way—because of Clemson. So you can bitch all you want and cling to your fantasies about how you think we got where we are, but it's not so, George. How Clemson treated you was not fair, but he didn't blaze your trail in life. You did that, brother. That was all you."

"Well, look who's defensive now. Why don't you get back on that high horse of yours and ride on outta here. How 'bout that, *brother*. Go back to that pretty little blonde of yours and make babies and join a country club." George sneered.

And that was it. This was the thing that broke Will. The proverbial last straw. He dropped Boris on the table and grabbed George by the collar and shook him, and looking him in the eye, Will screamed at the top of his lungs, "Watch your fucking mouth!" *She's dead. Eve's dead.* He couldn't say it, he just couldn't say it. He wouldn't have to. It was already national news. People would be looking for him, he knew. He didn't have time for his brother's bullshit.

The nurse with the bubble ass came running down the hall. "You guys all right? I heard screaming."

Will let go, and George smoothed his scrubs.

"We're good," George answered. But they weren't.

Will turned to the nurse, his anger all-consuming. "Let me guess—"

"Oh goodie, here we go." George rolled his eyes and

looked at the nurse. "Just ignore him—he can be a real prick."

But Will, unfazed, continued. "You were born to a single mom—dad left before you were even born—in an Upstate New York hick town full of Yankee rednecks and white trash. You still drink Coke at breakfast just like when you were five before you walked to the bus stop by yourself where you were bullied about your weight, which it appears is still a challenge to this day. Your hair's not real, your teeth aren't real, and your breasts aren't either, but then George knew that. You skim pills here and sell them on the side to finance your vanity vacations to the fat farms and trips to the fly-by-night plastic surgeons, and now you're saving for a tummy tuck, but here's a piece of advice. Lay off the Taco Bell after Sunday church and the late-night Skittles you eat while watching soap operas on demand. Make adult choices at the cosmetic counters, join a gym, stop stealing pills, and leave my brother the fuck alone. He's got his own drama—doesn't need yours."

"Shut the fuck up, Will!" George's bellow echoed through the hallways, and nurses and patients all stopped and stared.

"Don't worry. I'm done here. I'm going to check in to my hotel. I'll come by again tomorrow morning."

George looked down at the floor apologetically, though it wasn't the floor that needed an apology. Will could see it. The regret was there, and that counted for something. Had to.

Will cocked his head goodbye, picked up Boris and

left. Downstairs, he collected his things, including his shoelaces, and walked outside where Bill was waiting. He got back in the car, and they drove in silence to the hotel. Will needed a whiskey and a bed.

They pulled up in front of the hotel, but Will could tell Bill was hesitant.

"I don't know about this. You got an army looking for you."

"Yeah, I know." *Literally. Really, literally*. "I'll be fine. I'll call you tomorrow."

THE RESTAURANT AT THE RITZ CARLTON WAS NEARLY empty. The walls were lined with polished mahogany, and tea lights flickered at each table. Will was thankful for the darkness and quiet. He sat at the bar alone, chewing on his third straw between sips of Jameson. Things were still surreal to him. The image of the flame from her mouth played over and over again in his head. How could he ever forget that? And how would he ever forgive himself? Whatever it was, he knew it was only a matter of time before the other shoe dropped. Besides the "say nothing" text, he'd heard nothing. Not a peep from the colonel or anyone else.

He looked at his phone. He had the names, the medical histories and diagnoses. He had everything he needed to tell the truth at that Senate hearing, but he also knew security would be tight and that he wouldn't just be able to bust in the meeting and interrupt with an "I interrupt this meeting for an important message. I have the truth."

He'd be thrown out before he ever got started, and the colonel was going to lie through her fucking teeth. His mind kept going back to Eve. How had she been poisoned? And with what? And who had given it to her? The colonel or an accomplice? Whatever had happened to Eve was the result of a cover-up…because she had wanted to tell the truth. Now she was gone. But there was still the truth. Will would do this thing for her even if it cost him his discovery. And he would begin with the truth of what happened to her.

# CHAPTER 24

WILL SAT AT THE BAR UNTIL HIS PSYCHE WAS soft with whiskey. He took his phone from his pocket and dialed the number where truth lived. It went to voicemail. He didn't leave a message. He decided he'd wait thirty minutes and call back.

He felt someone slide into the bar chair next to him. The entire place was empty and yet…he turned slightly in his chair and caught in his periphery a woman digging through her purse for something. Her head down inside a large bag, he could only see her hair, blonde, pulled into a tight bun.

"Eve." He didn't realize he'd said it out loud.

"Pardon?" She raised her head. She was beautiful, and from a distance, she could've passed for Eve. Her eyes were round and amber-colored, and her high cheekbones disappeared slightly when she smiled. She had nice teeth and full lips, and he decided she resembled Angelina Jolie more than Eve.

"Sorry. I—you looked like someone else."

"Mmm." She glanced at his hands in an obvious way. "Someone else who is here, or someone else who is not?"

"She's not." His eyes fell.

"I'm sorry. It seems that makes you sad. It's something to miss someone, don't you think?"

"I guess. Not thinking much right now."

She continued to fumble through her purse, and Will couldn't help but wonder what she was looking for that was so important.

"Lose something?"

"Just my room key. And my mind."

"Ah." Will stirred his Jameson. "You know, there are a ton of empty seats in this bar. Did you sit down next to me intentionally?"

She smiled at this, but she didn't blush. "Obvious?"

"Yes. Let me guess. You're in real estate, commercial not residential, and you're in Boston on an interview, looking to make a move from the DC area. No kids, no pets, no plants—nothing living in your fancy condo in Chevy Chase but you. You're reserved, introverted almost, but you enjoy talking to strangers in bars because it fills a void in your life—meaningful conversations with people sans attachment. You remember their stories, learn from them, cherish some, even. You are not big on holidays, and you spend most of them abroad, alone. You love expensive champagne, London and hiking. And sex. Lots of it."

"Wow, Mr.?"

"Dr. Will St. John."

"Well, Dr. St. John, you're good. I am impressed.

Except for the sex part." This was a lie, and he knew it. In fact, it was all a lie.

"I'm Sam. Pleased to make your acquaintance." She extended her long cool fingers. "Can I get you a drink?" It was Sam who asked Will.

"Sure." He raised his glass to the bartender. "I'll have another and—"

"Prosecco, please. And the check please, thanks." Then she returned her attention to Will. "Come here often?"

"First time." Will took the Jameson down in a single shot.

"You won't mind if I sip mine like a proper lady, will you?"

"Not at all."

For a few minutes, they chatted about the markets, her interest in trading in the Asian markets and her love for Thai food—in Thailand. Will talked about science and his study of diseases.

Sam was genuinely impressed. "Your work sounds much more interesting than mine. Mine involves mostly money while yours is built upon principles and virtues. There's nothing virtuous about money."

Will pondered this. Science was virtuous but also expensive. Without the money, virtues didn't matter much, and science didn't happen. Sam agreed but suggested that she had a soft spot for those who tilted at windmills. She was smart—Will liked smart women and especially those who challenged him. She was also stunning.

Sam wore a simple red satin spaghetti-strap dress, nearly floor length, with a mink wrap. Her bag was

Italian leather—black and filled with papers spilling out of the interior pockets.

"I suppose I'm not very organized. I'll need to ask for another room key. Mine's been eaten by my purse." She blinked at him. She was waiting, he could tell.

"Or we could just go back to my room."

"We could…I suppose…" She pulled some cash from her purse and stood, the red satin falling in over her curves. "Shall we?" She offered her delicate white arm, and they made their way back to Will's hotel room, where inside, he tried to blank out his mind, her soft kisses between his legs, and for a time, he was free.

When they were spent, she excused herself and went into the bathroom. When she returned, she found Will gone, along with her gun, and a note: *You're on the wrong side.*

He'd read her well, and it'd probably saved his life, and for now, the truth. He was truth walking and breathing, and he couldn't afford any more close calls. Whoever she was, he'd been a mark. He stepped out into the stairwell, Boris in one hand and her Walther PPK in the other. He slouched against it to rest, noting that his mouth felt hot and dry. He touched his lips in panic that she'd somehow slipped something in his drink. She hadn't. Will took a deep breath and looked at Boris, who sat quietly purring.

Will could think only of Eve. The argument they'd had, the apology he never got to make, her death and how horrible it'd been. He didn't know how yet, but he was going to make this right. He needed to get back home and make a plan. Now that he'd put eyes on his brother, alive and well and with female company to boot, he could get back early. George seemed perfectly fine, and if he'd know his brother was shagging the nurse before he left, he wouldn't have come at all. Whatever the drugs had done, his libido was perfectly intact, and their father was already back in LA and probably in the middle of a breast lift as he sat there thinking.

He dialed Louis again. No answer. He wouldn't risk leaving a message, and he didn't want to text either. He would keep trying until Louis answered. One way or another, he would get to the truth of what happened to Eve, and he would tell the truth about Larmentin. He had two days.

Will called Bill.

"I've got company—not sure who or how, but I'll need to be picked up a few blocks from here."

"Tell me where."

"Northeast corner of the Freedom Trail."

"I'll be waiting. Be careful, Will. I'm getting too old for this shit."

"Don't worry. I'll be there." *I have to be.*

Before leaving, he checked the street and spotted a black Audi with no plates. Boris hissed.

"I agree. Those people, whoever they are, are not our friends."

He'd take the back fire exit to avoid detection and trade the pet carrier for his backpack.

"Sorry, Boris, this is your new ride. I've got to run, and that XL carrier won't work." He stuffed the twenty-five-pound tabby down into his backpack and left to meet Bill near the Freedom Trail. By the time they realized he was gone, he'd be halfway to DC.

Will ran as fast as his feet would carry him until he spotted Bill's car.

When he was sure he had not been followed, he approached the car and hopped in. Boris's head popped out of the North Face pack, and Will grabbed the last of the Meow Mix from a baggie and fed him.

"Boy am I glad to see you."

"Likewise. Had a close call last night."

"You know you can tell me anything, right?"

"Yeah, I know. But the less you know about this, the better off you are."

"You're the boss. If you change your mind, I'm here to listen."

"Thanks, Bill. I already feel I've put you at risk just having you drive me around."

"Anytime. You just say the word. I'm always happy to help you out."

"Good to know. I'm gonna need it."

Will figured after he checked on George, he'd be in DC before dinner to begin tracking down Louis, even if it meant a trip out to WRAIR.

Bill pulled up in front of the Psychiatric Care building.

"Don't forget the cat." Bill sneezed.

"I won't. Sorry. You allergic?"

"I'll be fine. I got some Claritin with me."

Will arrived upstairs, shoeless, with Boris in his arms to find the nurse checking George's vital signs while she giggled at a joke he'd made that Will couldn't hear. Turned out, George would be leaving a day early *with* the nurse, who looked sheepishly at Will after the previous day's exchange. She gave a weak smile.

"Don't you worry. I'm gonna take good care of that twin brother of yours." Turning to George, she pointed a finger in his face. "No drugs, mister! I'm gonna make you some chicken and biscuits with white gravy that will change your life. You'll wonder what all the hoopla was ever even about with all those drugs you did. I'm going to go and get your last dose of meds before you leave, and those are the *only* drugs you'll be gettin'."

They watched her leave the room. She wore scrubs with miniature palm trees and martini glasses with umbrellas.

"Whose ass looks good in scrubs?" George was beaming, and his cheeks were a deep rosy tone.

"Are you blushing?"

"I don't know, am I?"

"Brother, are you in there? Aliens abduct the real you? Where's my crass co-partner who's always out for himself?"

"I don't know."

"Jesus. You *like* her…"

"Some, yeah."

"Unbelievable."

They laughed, and Will said his goodbyes, and George gave him the nurse's cell just in case. As he was leaving, she reappeared with a small paper cup containing three pills—one peach, one blue and one translucent yellow.

George tossed them back with zero resistance and

gave Will a wink. Will didn't even make it to the elevator before his phone buzzed. It was Louis.

—⚬⚬⚬—

"Hello? Louis?"

"Yes, Dr. St. John, hello. It's me, but I guess you saw that. Sorry I hadn't gotten back to you before now. Her army anniversary was yesterday, and I was at the party when you called. Things went late, and I didn't want to call you back in the middle of the night. I'm at home now about to head in to the office. I think the colonel's watching me. I think she knows I sent Eve the names and medical history of the soldiers to match the samples that showed cell death with those who suffered adverse side effects. Was Eve able correlate the samples to the soldiers who had psychoses?"

*She's dead. Eve died. She's gone.* Will tried to think how to say it. He ran his palm over his face, his eyes stinging as he swallowed. "I—Louis, I'm not sure I can say this… how to say this. Eve passed away. She's gone." *She was swallowed by a fire from the inside of her body.* Will gulped at the recollection.

"What? How? I'm sorry, I don't mean to ask so many questions. I liked her—Eve. She was tenacious. Smart. Exquisite. What happened, if you don't mind my asking?"

"I take it you haven't seen the news. I was hoping you could tell me. I think Eve was murdered." *Eevaleena Konisken.*

"Murdered? How? Why?"

"I was hoping you could help with that. I think the

colonel had something to do with her death. I got a text from an untraceable number just moments after Eve's death, while I was being questioned by the paramedics and police. The text read 'say nothing.' I think it was meant to be instructive and also a threat. I think she sent it." Will was clenching his teeth.

"Whoa, hold on just a second, Dr. St. John. The colonel's a lot of things, but a murderer? I don't know about that. I can see why you would think that, but I don't see her ever killing someone."

"No? What about that soldier who shot the secretary of state? Joseph Bishop. And what about Larmentin, the drug you developed and that is sold all over the world, earning billions each year. What would happen if people discovered he freaked out on Larmentin—a drug developed by the army? That sounds like motive for a cover-up to me." Will's voice got louder as rage washed over him. "I watched her die, Louis. I watched her burn—she was on fire on the inside of her body! Christ, a flame came from her mouth! What the fuck is that, Louis? Who dies like that? It was fucking horrible, and nothing I do can erase that memory. It keeps playing over and over again in my fucking head. She suffered, Louis. She suffered badly, and if you want to help Eve now, help me find out who did this and help me tell the truth about Larmentin at that Senate hearing in two days. Say nothing, my ass. She doesn't know who she's dealing with. To hell with it all. I am telling the truth." Will bellowed into the phone.

All he could hear on the other end was the uneven breath of Louis, clearly shaken by the news. The breath continued for a minute until Louis was able to speak.

"Wait. You say she burned from the inside…that a flame emitted from her mouth?"

"Yes. Goddamned worst thing I've ever seen. Ever. And I've seen a lot."

"She was hot to the touch?"

"Yes. Very."

"Her clothes…did they—"

"Melt? Yes, her jeans. And her eyes bled, before they smoked and turned black. I can't…I can't stop seeing it."

Louis didn't respond for another minute.

"Louis?"

"Yes. I'm here."

"Well?"

"I think I might know what happened."

"You have to tell me. I need to know what, and more than that, who."

"I can help with the what. Are you sitting down?"

# CHAPTER 25

"Scientists at WRAIR in conjunction with DTRA developed an anti-terrorism product. It's called liquid smoke, and when it's ingested, well, you saw. It was originally intended to be used as an interrogation incentive against ISIS, the Taliban and others, but in the end, it was just too horrible to use and clearly a violation of the Geneva Convention. The project was top secret, but the program was eventually canceled. It was just too awful." Louis shuddered at the thought. "The research was conducted here, right down the hall, actually. I thought they'd terminated the project, but I did overhear the colonel speaking with one of our scientists just last week about it. I remember I thought it was odd that they were talking about dragon's breath when the program had been shut down. I guess they're still working on it."

"And how do I get my hands on this dragon's breath stuff?"

Louis was quiet for a moment. "What? Why?"

"I need it. I need to prove how Eve really died."

"Do you know what you're asking? That's espionage. I could be sent to prison for life, or worse. Look, however horrible it seems to you, in the field, when you're up against the enemy and your friends are getting blown to bits all around you, I guarantee you something like that could be very useful."

"I saw it, Louis. Firsthand. I watched her… She didn't deserve that, and when you helped her out with the list you sent her, you sealed her fate, and now, like it or not, you're going to help make this right to the extent it can be made right. This is on you, too, Louis."

Will waited. He listened to Louis sigh heavily into the phone.

"Well? Say something."

"Give me a second. I'm thinking. This place is like Alcatraz. Nobody and *nothing* gets in *or* out that doesn't belong."

"There must be a way, Louis. Someone has obviously already figured it out." Will was practically foaming at the mouth.

"Maybe…"

"Maybe what? Maybe what, Louis?"

"Maybe…okay…thinking out loud here… Sometimes I'm catheterized to be sure my kidneys are functioning properly. They collect my urine over a seventy-two-hour period. Dragon's breath is a pale yellow color. I could sneak it out in my urine bag—not the real bag, of course, but a second bag… That could work. The colonel has no idea what my schedule is for catheterization. I've got a friend who works in the lab down there. He gave me the door code a while back so I could check an experiment while he went to the dentist. I still have it, and it hasn't been long enough for them to change it, which they do periodically. There's only two people on assignment in there anymore. Both have long commutes, so the lab empties out around four p.m. I can get it today after everyone is gone and bring it home to my apartment…" His voice trailed. "I am so sorry, Dr. St. John. I don't know what to say. Poor Eve, I can't imagine. I didn't think the colonel had it in her, but I guess that explains the nasty fights she's had with the secretary of the army lately. He's been up her ass."

"Where do you live? Give me the address, and I'll be there before dinner."

Louis gave Will the information he needed. Will hung up and immediately dialed another number.

"Bill. It's Will. I'm going to need the plane. I'll catch an Uber and meet you at the airport to save time."

"You sure? I can come get you. I didn't wander far— afraid your friends might be hanging around."

"I've been careful. No sign of anyone suspicious or that car outside. I'm going to grab something to eat and call an Uber. I'll see you at the airport."

"Roger that. Be careful."

Will would fly direct from Boston to meet Louis, get the dragon's breath and fly home. Cindy could do the analysis, and he'd be on a plane in time for the Senate committee hearing on the incident involving the secretary of state.

He walked across the street to a bar-and-grille type restaurant and took a seat at the bar. He set Boris on the stool next to him.

"Be good and maybe you'll score some sushi. If you're bad, you get another Twix."

Boris mewed and proceeded to clean himself.

"Stow the tongue. Not here."

The bartender was mixing a margarita, listening to Will talk to the cat. She was a dark beauty with dreads down to her ass and long, thick lashes. Her T-shirt was tight and her jeans even tighter. She smiled a toothy smile at Will.

"I hope it's okay he's here." Will gestured to Boris. "I don't have anywhere else to store him."

She replied with a thick islander accent. "He's fine, but we don't sell sushi here. We have a grouper sandwich if he likes."

"That sounds great, hold the bun." Will looked over the menu. He didn't feel much like eating, but he needed the energy for what he was about to do.

"I'll have the bacon cheeseburger with fries and an IPA."

"And a grouper sandwich, no bun, for the kitty. On the house." She collected the menus and poured a glass full of beer for Will.

He watched her moving behind the bar. She was tall and reedy and moved like a dancer, filling drinks and mixing and washing mugs and glasses.

The food came almost instantly. Boris hopped up on the bar and buried his face in the grouper, purring loudly. The bartender, Brenda, stroked Boris while he ate.

"He is a fat one, this one is. You must take good care of heem." *She did. Eve took very good care of him.*

Will ate slowly, remembering the dance with Eve, how big she'd smiled, her body turning toward him and back away. Indeed, she'd been exquisite. Eevaleena Konisken. He'd only just gotten to know her a little. He felt guilt creeping in—guilt about the way he'd treated her during the interview, about the wisecracks at the gym, about the argument…about not being there—not getting there sooner, about not knowing what he'd been up against, the depth of it all. He felt like a narcissistic asshole. Maybe he could've prevented it somehow. He would never know what happened. Not really. He would never know if someone was there, standing over her while she drank the poison. If they kicked Boris. If they slapped her, threatened her. If they hurt her some other way. Whatever the cost, no matter what happened to him now, if it was the last thing he ever did, he would tell the story she wanted to tell. Eve's death would not be in vain. He would do what she'd set out to do. Expose the truth.

---

LOUIS SAT AT HIS DESK, FLICKING THE HAN SOLO bobblehead and eating Doritos. He thought about the situation at hand and wondered how things had come to this. Sending Eve the list of soldiers' names to match with the blood samples had been his way of making sure the truth got out, and in the process, he realized he'd committed treason. He felt like Edward Snowden must've felt. It had been the right thing to do but also a violation of a host of federal laws. And now Snowden was living large in Moscow, if there was such a thing. He imagined a life in Moscow in a wheelchair, drinking vodka neat and eating perogies with cabbage underneath a perpetually gray sky. He played out the worst-case scenarios in his mind, none of which involved Moscow but at least one of which involved a short stint at Guantanamo Bay and perhaps his own experience with the very drug he was stealing. *Jesus*. He was about to steal a top-secret drug manufactured for the express purpose of making the most evil humans in the world shudder just before spilling everything they knew. That was what dragon's breath did. It scared people fuckless. And now here he was, ass on the floor in a classified lab doing everything he swore he'd never do. He let the seditious pall fall over him while waves of guilt bubbled up inside until his sense of patriotism was wiped out. *No, no, no, Louis! Will is right. You sent her the names. You got involved. You are responsible. You have an opportunity to make this right—to help avenge Eve while also preventing more soldiers from suffering the side effects of what he now knew was a neurotoxin.* He took a swig of water and swallowed hard. *This is on you, too, Louis.* Will's words hammered it home. It was too late now. He knew what he had to do.

It was his lucky day. Not only had the guys in the lab

down the hall left early, but so had Colonel Savarre. She was being debriefed prior to the hearing and wouldn't be back.

As soon as the coast was clear, Louis shut down his computer, tossed his chips and wheeled down the hall. The lab was dark and the hallway empty. He punched in the code, knowing full well it would be recorded but also knowing he could erase it, and wheeled into the room. The lab was a tight fit for his chair—something he thought might happen, and no sooner had the thought occurred than he bumped into a small end table full of lab notebooks, sending books and papers flying everywhere.

"Shit. Shit! Louis, you dumb shit!"

Now he had multiple problems—a mess on the floor, an obstacle since the books and papers lay between him and the refrigerator full of the liquid smoke, and evidence that things had been disturbed. He would have to clean this up perfectly, or his ass would end up behind bars. There was only one way. He would need to lift himself out of his chair and onto the floor to retrieve the books. Thank god for his upper-body strength. He locked his wheels in place, scooted to the edge of his chair and, leaning forward, placed one fist on the ground while guiding himself with the other. Carefully and without so much as a grunt, he lifted himself down to the floor.

One by one, he gathered up the notebooks and papers, careful to keep them in the order they'd fallen in. Luckily, it had fallen in a clump, and he was able to maintain the integrity of the stack. He slid the books and papers back up onto the end table. He was nearly done when he heard *her*. *Oh God, she's back.* He hadn't turned on any lights. There was only ambient light that flowed through the glass front of the refrigerator, but he was mostly in the dark. She would be looking for him, and he'd shut everything down—his computer was off, his lights out, his desk tidied.

He listened as she clacked right past the lab he was in, still on the floor. He pressed his head close to the floor and watched her dark shadow pass under the bottom crack of the door. He breathed in and out, taking shallow breaths, afraid she might hear him the way an eagle hears its prey deep in the ground. He waited and listened. She was pacing the hallway and stopped right next to the door. His heart raced. *Calm, Louis, stay calm. It's not like she can see through doors.*

"Margaret!" the colonel bellowed down the hall to their secretary. "Where is Louis? I saw his car in the parking lot."

"Ma'am, I think he left."

"Sneaky bastard. I must've passed him. His computer's still warm. He couldn't have been gone long."

"Actually, I think it's been a while."

*Damnit, Margaret, shut it!*

"I'll try to catch him at his car. He's got something I need for the briefing."

Louis sighed his relief at the same time the beeping started. A shrill beeping cut through the lab and out into the hallway. What the—? Louis's foot had caught the edge of the refrigerator door, and it had remained open long enough to trigger the sensor. He shut it immediately but not fast enough. She turned on her heel, clacked back over and peered in through the window. He felt his heart stop. If she came in, it was all over. He dared not breathe. He didn't even shift his weight, but his eyes remained fixed on the light that came underneath the door, and he could see clearly the edge of her shoes pointed directly at him.

She paused, and then he heard her mutter, "I don't have time for this shit. Margaret!" she screamed. "If you see Louis, tell him I am looking for him, and he needs to see me immediately!"

*Fuck!* He placed one hand on his chair and one on the floor and hoisted himself up into his chair. He opened the fridge and grabbed the bottle of dragon's breath aka liquid smoke. He held his breath, careful not to inhale any of it. With trembling hands, he poured it, transferring some but not all of the contents into his urine bag. He closed everything up and exited the lab as quickly and quietly as he'd come.

As he suspected, she was waiting by his car in the lot.

"Louis! I was just upstairs. Where were you? Where have you been all this time?" It was an accusation.

"I had to stop by the restroom on my way down."

"The bathroom? The bathroom. The bathroom took that long?"

Something inside Louis snapped. Maybe it was the pressure of having just stolen a classified toxin developed by the military and the likelihood he might end up in prison for it—in a wheelchair, in prison. Maybe it was the guilt over Eve's death—he should never have shared that information with her. Maybe it was the accumulation of years of verbal abuse and the suggestion by the colonel that potato chips were the reason he was still in a wheelchair—that poor lifestyle choices rather than a fucking IED was what landed him in the chair to begin with.

His eyes bored into her. "I'm a T1 paraplegic. That means I am paralyzed from here"—he gestured to his chest—"to here." He pointed to his feet. "When you don't move from here"—he gestured again—"to here, your organs don't always function properly. Hence the bag full of piss dangling from my side, if you catch me."

She eyed him suspiciously, but he knew he'd shut her down.

"You know, I don't know what it is with you lately. I don't need to know about your toileting habits, Louis. I just need the data from St. John for the briefing so I can get the army's ass out of a sling."

"It's in a folder on my desk in the vertical organizer—third slot."

"Thank you. I'll get it myself." She stood, staring him down for a minute, but he didn't care. Not anymore. She no longer frightened him.

⸺⸎⸺

WILL MET BILL AT THE AIRPORT, THANKFUL TO BE LEAVing Boston and hoping he'd lost whoever had been following him. Bill was standing by the plane, smoking a cigarette and playing solitaire on his phone. Bill had lanky limbs with a rounding middle, and his XL Polartec jacket draped off his belly. He'd never married, and so he'd devoted all of his time to George and Will when they were growing up. Taught them to fish, waterski, and sail. He was a handsome enough guy, but a broken heart in his early twenties had resulted in a life of solitude. He didn't seem to mind, and his life was full enough, it seemed. As Will approached, he noticed his uncle was sporting a Van Dyke style beard.

"You made it. I was beginning to worry!"

"Yes. I was extra careful leaving the grille and waiting on the Uber. Had to be sure I wasn't being watched. What's this here?" Will patted his uncle on the scruff.

"Oh, you know, getting lazy in my old age. Trying something new. Truth be told, I'm tired of shaving. Think I'd rather just trim once a week." He grinned that St. John grin. "That young lady with you the other night…she was as elegant a lady as I've ever seen, and you know I've been around some. Head turner, that one was. I know you'd rather not say, but I hope that whatever's going on, you get the bastards."

Before Will could think, he said, "Thanks. I will." *And then some.*

"Where to, chief?"

"DC, then back home for a quick visit, and then if you don't mind, back to DC for a meeting."

"Sounds like a plan to me. Will, I just want to say that with all this going on, I know Clemson's proud. He may not show it, but I know he is. And if you need his help—"

"I don't, Bill."

"I figured you'd say that. I just thought…"

"You haven't said anything to him, have you?"

"Nah." Bill stamped his cigarette out on the ground and collected the butt to toss it in the trash.

"If you have, it's okay, but going forward, I'd rather you didn't."

"Your wish is my command, sir."

"Thanks, Bill."

Will walked up the stairs with Boris and into the cabin of the Gulfstream IV. He sat down and emptied Boris out of his pack.

"Gotcha a treat." Will pulled a thermos from his pack. "The lady at the grille thought you might enjoy this." Will opened the thermos and poured a four-count of half-and-half into a small plastic saucer he'd pilfered from the grille. He set it down and looked at Boris. "There. This one's on the house. The next one'll cost you. Oh, and this pairs well with Twix. Just sayin'."

Boris purred loudly, and Will almost smiled. Almost.

He poured himself a shot of Jameson and fastened his seat belt just as the plane engines cranked up. Across from where he sat, something glinted in the sun. There, in the cushion of the sofa, was an earring. A talisman, he thought. A sign he was doing the right thing. Eve must've lost it while she slept on the way home. Fresh emotion welled up inside Will as he took the pearl surrounded in tiny diamonds from the sofa and pocketed it. A lucky charm.

An hour later, Will stepped off the plane into the cool

sunshine. Brown oak leaves rustled across the tarmac, a reminder that things change and renew. Whether or not people did was another matter. Will turned his face to the cutting wind. Despite having witnessed a horrible death, he felt very much alive. The plan was to meet Louis at his home, get the drug and meet Bill back at the airport to fly home. There, he'd contact Cindy Tan to coordinate the analysis. He wanted to know exactly what this liquid smoke dragon drug was. Then he would fly back in time for the Senate committee hearing on the incident in Islamabad *after* he spoke with the colonel. He was coming for her.

# CHAPTER 26

THE CAB RIDE TO SEE LOUIS TOOK LONGER THAN expected. Traffic was heavy, and the cab driver was a talker. He talked to Will about his kids, how spoiled they were and how they constantly had their heads in their phones and computers and how he'd grown up differently, in a developing country without clean water, electricity or health care. After a while, his voice became white noise, and Will focused on the bare tree limbs against the blue November sky.

Soon it would be Thanksgiving, and he would be expected home for the family dinner and then again weeks later for Christmas. In recent years, he'd worked some over the holidays with only a quick day trip home. But right now, he felt lost and needed something to anchor to.

A text photo popped up on his phone. It was from Amy. It was a before and after photo that showed an obese mouse next to a thin one and was captioned, "Guess what? I'm cured!"

So that was it. He was right. The leish parasites were producing a molecule that reset the immune system. This could be the answer to many other autoimmune diseases. And despite his somber mood, he smiled and fingered the talisman in his pocket. Maybe the tide was turning.

Will paid the cab driver to wait and tipped him extra and handed him a card with his cell number. "If you see anyone around, driving up and down the street or just hanging around, text me immediately."

"Yes, sir."

Will walked up the short brick sidewalk to a bungalow with a ramp outside. He rang the doorbell, and a friendly dog answered. Boris's tail blossomed, but he didn't hiss.

"Calm down. You'll lose your grouper and your half-and-half cocktail if you get all excited."

Louis called from the other room, "Be right there."

Will looked around at Louis's home, amazed at all of the modifications for a person in a wheelchair. The entire place was designed for someone at chair height, including what he could see of the kitchen. The furnishings were low slung, and the countertops in the kitchen were also low. In the other room, he could hear Louis struggling over something.

"Do you need help?" Will called.

"No thank you, I'm okay. Give Rocco a pat—he likes the attention."

"I can see that." Will scratched the German shepard between his ears. "Gentle for a shepard."

Louis wheeled into the living room.

"Yes, he is a gentle giant, nearly ten years old now. He's slowing down a bit. I see you brought your pet."

"You mean Boris. He's Eve's, was…was her cat."

Louis wheeled closer, contemplating. "I'm very sorry about Eve. I still can't believe…" He shook his head. "I have been listening to the colonel argue for weeks now. The secretary of the army, Rusty Carver, comes in and they go at each other. She doesn't know I can hear, but I can hear everything." Louis tapped his hearing aid. "In addition to my spinal injury, my ears were damaged in the war…explosives…and I have a supersonic hearing aid. I heard them in an argument about Eve…about using the dragon's breath. What you said. What you said was right—I share the responsibility. I should have never given Eve the names of those soldiers. I should've found another way. I was just so angry. I wasn't thinking straight. I was just so focused on the soldiers—that soldier, Joey Bishop, and how he lost his mind on the Larmentin. How in the field you have to do what your commanding officer says. It's an order. Taking meds is an order; it's not optional. Taking orders from someone who doesn't give a shit whether you flip out or not, that's just not right. The reason I'm in this chair is because I followed an order—an order I knew was asinine. My platoon leader had a hard-on to get down into this valley. Only one road in, one road out, but he suspected the Taliban had a hideout where some of the pricks we'd been chasing for years were. It was a suicide mission. We all knew it, but what could we do? We walked right into a shitstorm with no place to hide. Only thing missing was targets painted on our flak jackets. Tracers, bullets, bombs and…only two of us made it out alive. I have a lot of respect for the uniform, for my commanding officers—for the colonel, even. But if she's trying to cover up what happened so they can continue to prescribe a drug they know is dangerous to soldiers, well then, I'm in. I hope…I hope that doesn't make me a traitor."

He paused and scratched Boris's head.

"Anyway, I did what you asked. I got it. They monitor everything we do at WRAIR. Louis held out a urine bag containing a straw-colored liquid. "Here it is. Dragon's breath. It was most certainly the drug that was used to kill Eve. Don't worry, it's only harmful if you ingest it, so…just don't drink it, or inhale it, for that matter."

Will took the bag from Louis.

"How will you get on the plane with that?"

"I'm traveling on a private jet."

Louis raised his brows and whistled. "Fancy."

"I guess."

"Well, in that case I have something else. Wait here."

Louis wheeled himself into the other room. Will noted how his white T-shirt stretched tight over his biceps and chest. Years of wheeling himself around and upper-body strength workouts had kept him in good shape. Will glanced up at the pull-up bar hooked to the doorframe. This explained a lot. Louis was a fighter. He fought back against his disabled body. He'd fight this battle, too. He reappeared with something in his lap that Will couldn't make out until he held it out.

A gun.

"What is that?" Will didn't reach for it.

"It's a gun."

"Yeah, I can see that."

"Take it," Louis said.

"Hell no, I'm not taking that. I got what I came for right here." Will held up the urine bag.

"You might need it."

"Fuck, Louis. I don't need a gun."

"Really? They've already killed Eve. What makes you think they won't kill you? You think they're not coming for you? I can promise you they are. Larmentin is worth billions to the army, and they're not about to give it up. The soldier who shot the secretary of state is gone, and with him, his story. Any side effects or psychosis testimonials died with him. Unless you want to join the growing list of recently deceased, I suggest you take some protection. I think you'll need it." He held up the gun by the barrel, butt end toward Will, and motioned for Will to take it. "This is a Glock 26 9mm. It's small, you can hide it anywhere on your person. It weighs only 3.5 pounds, and it's made to *stop* someone. You might not think so, Dr. St. John, but you should be watching your back. They came for her; they'll be coming for you. I would avoid your home, your lab, airports, bus stations—avoid public places. If you want to make it to the hearing, make it back here to tell your story, you need to stay alive. Eve's gone. You need to stay alive for her so you can report your findings. I'm not saying you have to use the gun, but I think you should take it. Just in case."

Will looked down at the floor. This was all too surreal.

"They already have, whoever they are. Some woman at the hotel in Boston. She had a gun on her—a Walther PPK—which I quickly tossed after I confiscated it. I'm a scientist, Louis. I start with a hypothesis and work my way through the problem to the answer. The scientific method is my guidepost in life. It's what I do. I don't know about dragon's breath, what kind of people murder others, government cover-ups that go all the way to the top… This is all foreign territory to me. Three weeks ago, I was running a lab studying parasites in mice. Now I have millions in grant funding that fell into my lap and a dead colleague. You know how this makes *me* look? I also have a discovery…something big I've been working on, and Savarre has her hands all in it. She has threatened to *scoop* me. To take my discovery and give it to someone else at Columbia University. It's a cure, Louis. A cure for autoimmune diseases. I have the key. And she threatened to share it with another scientist, and when she does, the discovery and everything that goes along with it will be his. Like taking candy from a baby, only it's not. It's my hard fucking work and some dumb luck, but it's *my* hard work and *my* dumb luck! No one will ever believe a word I say. She will exploit me and make it look like child's play. She knows every stumble I've had at the university, all about my Title IX problems… She knows *everything* about me. I feel trapped. And for the first time, I feel scared. For God's sake, my picture is all over the fucking news in connection with what happened to Eve. I'm suspended from my university, and my career is probably over. All I've got left is the truth. But I can't deliver if I'm dead, can I? I want people to know about Larmentin. I want them to know what happened to Eve when she tried to find out the truth. And I want them to know who was behind it all. This was never about the soldiers. This was about the money. I'm already terrified, and now you're telling me that they're coming for me. Fuck. What the fuck." Will chewed on the inside of his cheeks. Even Clemson couldn't fix this.

"Okay, okay. Look, I get it. I'm scared too, but these aren't people with superpowers. They just happen to be well connected and well trained is all. They have limits. Do as I tell you, and we can pull this off. You have to trust me." Louis motioned for Will to take the Glock.

"Okay." Will took the gun and palmed it. It was cold in his hands, but light.

"Follow me." Louis wheeled himself through the kitchen and into his garage. To the left side of the garage was a long narrow room with a standard door. Louis opened the door, revealing a target at the far end.

"You have an indoor firing range?"

"Yes. Soundproofed, air cleaned and recirculated. I'm going to teach you how to fire that Glock, but first, we're going to field strip it and clean it. It's been a while since I fired that one."

Will sat across from Louis in his garage and watched while Louis methodically disassembled the small hand-gun, reviewing the various parts of the gun with Will.

"Ironically this is an Austrian weapon first used by their military. I chose it because it's compact and less intimidating than other choices, but if you have to use it, it'll get the job done." Louis was careful. Professional. It was clear he'd been a soldier once—a good one. "I've outfitted this with a grip extension. That'll help stabilize it during shooting."

Louis looked up from the table.

"Now, you won't have to do this because I am doing this right now, but it's useful to know the parts of the gun. The reason I want you to fire it a few times is to be sure it's not jamming—Glocks don't, usually—and so that you can get used to the feel and the occasional cas-ing coming back toward you." He reassembled the gun and handed it, loaded, to Will. "I hope you don't have to use this…but I want you to know how. Remember, if you need to shoot at someone, aim small, miss small."

"Aim small, miss small?" Will furrowed his brow.

"Yes. Aim for the person, miss the person. Aim for the button on their shirt and miss, you still hit the person. Make sense?"

"Yeah."

Will stepped up to the line just inside the long nar-row range, holding the gun for maximum control just as Louis had shown him. He squeezed the trigger. After he emptied the first magazine, he loaded another, firing until he was used to the feeling of it, the power of it. He thought about Eve, about how she'd suffered and how he wanted the people responsible to suffer like she had. He looked at the head on the target and imagined the colonel's face. He fired. Right between the eyes.

"Wow." Louis sounded impressed. "Pretty good for a first-timer."

"Thanks. I'm motivated." Something dark was growing inside him. Layers upon layers of anger. Anger over his discovery on the back burner. Anger over the colonel's threats. Anger over how Clemson treated George, how George didn't care, how his parents gave up trying and let Clemson fill in. Anger over Eve's death. Anger at himself for not being there for her…for not protecting her.

"It's not your fault. You can do right by Eve. Make it to the hearing."

Will turned and looked at Louis. He saw him differently now. He was tough and smart. And what he'd done had taken courage.

"I know it was a huge risk, you taking this dragon's breath out like you did. You should be careful, too. I don't know how you did it, but thank you. And for the lesson—and for this, too." Will held up the Glock.

"Good luck, Dr. St. John. I'll see you at the hearing."

"Yes, you will. Until then, thanks."

Outside, the cab driver was waiting. Will got in the cab

with three things he hadn't had the day before. A twenty-five-pound orange tabby named Boris, a Glock 26, and a urine bag full of a deadly toxin. He was traveling in style. He sank back into the leather seat and returned to the white noise of the driver's stream-of-consciousness chatter all the way to the airport, periodically checking the mirror for signs of someone following him, but he saw nothing.

The driver dropped Will off at Dulles airport, where Bill was waiting. As Will approached the plane, his uncle couldn't help but notice the odd baggage.

"Well, I'm not even gonna ask. A urine bag full of piss and a gun and a cat. Don't worry. Whatever it is, Clemson'll never hear about this."

Will gave a thin smile. "Thanks, Bill."

The plane engines roared to life, and Will poured himself a double shot. He flipped through the news, reading all he could about the shooting incident and the soldier who'd died. Then he read about the secretary of the army, Rusty Carver, who he thought very closely resembled the fat mice, only Rusty Carver was human. A human with lousy taste in clothing and lousy decision-making skills, Will thought. He'd fucked around in the wrong backyard. Next, he got online to check and see what the local news was saying about him. He was pleased to find the story had not made national news and that local news stations had very little to say about the incident. A photograph taken of him the previous fall appeared with the following text:

Police are searching for this man, Will St.
John, wanted for questioning in the mysterious death of a colleague. St. John was at
the scene when Ms. Eevaleena Konisken died
mysteriously but, according to police, fled the
scene. Police only want to question St. John.
It is not clear whether he had anything to do
with the death itself.

The photo looked like an inside cover ad for Ralph
Lauren in *Vanity Fair* magazine. At least something was
going his way.

After they landed, Will gave his uncle instructions to
wait for his call.

"I won't be long. Just need to grab some things from
the house." *Unless it's being watched.* "And a quick visit
with a colleague." *To ask her to analyze this horrible sub-
stance that killed Eve that Louis stole that was top-secret
classified, and now we've all touched sedition with our
bare hands.*

"I'm a little uneasy about all this. You be careful, Will.
And you call if there's trouble."

"I'll call, but I'm not expecting any, thanks."

"Well, your face on the news…I just…lay low, fly
under the radar, no pun intended."

"Don't worry. I will."

"Want me to take care of the cat?"

"No thanks. I got him." Boris seemed happy enough
in Will's pack.

They agreed on a plan and left in separate taxis, one to a bar to wait, the other on a mission.

Will needed to meet Cindy Tan somewhere off the beaten path. He opted for his favorite Italian dive and sat in the back room away from windows and the public eye. He couldn't be caught talking with Amy or Cindy—not in the lab or on campus. He didn't want to jeopardize the safety of anyone else. Louis had made it very clear that would be the first place *they*, whoever *they* were, would look. Using the burner phone he'd purchased, he dialed Cindy.

# CHAPTER 27

Rusty Carver sat at a corner restaurant in Georgetown, drumming his fingers on the red-and-white checked tablecloth while he waited on his scotch and soda. By the time Susan Savarre appeared in the doorway, he was two drinks deep.

"You're late." A piece of oiled baguette fell out of his mouth and onto his shirt, but he paid it no mind.

"Well, you can take it up with your pals in the Senate. I had to run back to the lab for some papers and couldn't find Louis and the briefing just ended."

"Mmm. Couldn't find a staff member who can't even walk. Can't say I'm surprised to hear it. The way you run your shop needs to change, or you can kiss that nomination goodbye."

Susan Savarre said nothing to this. She would not be baited into an argument that could cost her an appointment as general. She'd earned that appointment, every bit of it, and no soul-sucking pig was going to take that away from her. It was her life. All she had.

"Why did you call me here?" She pressed her lips together and held back the words she wanted to say.

"The scientist. He needs to go."

"What? He's not gonna talk, Rusty. He's not a threat to us anymore. You think he's got a death wish? He's sitting on top of a huge discovery he's not about to risk. This isn't necessary. Besides, we're watching him. He's not a viable threat. I'm trained to know about threats. Will St. John is no threat. This will all be done soon."

Rusty ran a piece of baguette across a plate of olive oil and spices. He shoved it into his mouth before answering, and when he did respond, bread fell from his lips as he spoke. Susan felt sick.

The waitress approached. "Ma'am, something to drink?"

*Something for nausea.* "Wine, please. Nine ounce white. Something dry."

"Let me put it to you like this, Susan. It was you who chose this guy out of a hundred scientists. You hand-picked him to handle this shitstorm with Larmentin. You chose poorly. He obviously cannot control the whims of the people he works with, and so now we have a dead girl. Blood on our hands, Susan. Blood you spilled. Now you can spill some more. You will take care of this, and you will do it before the hearing. Is that clear, Susan?"

Susan Savarre's anger was everywhere. On the bread plate, in her glass, in the metal knife she held in her hand. Her fury was palpable, and the skin on her face tingled from it. The waitress delivered the wine to Susan and dropped off a large bowl Bolognese sauce over linguine for Rusty.

"I think you're making a mistake. I don't think St. John is going to risk losing his discovery over a lousy cover-up. I think—"

"I want you to stop thinking, Susan. I want you to act. He knows too much—he watched that girl die. He's a scientist. Do you know what the defining characteristic of a scientist is?" A long noodle dangled from his mouth.

*Why the fuck doesn't he swallow his food before he opens his mouth to talk?*

"I am the lead scientist at WRAIR, and yes, I think I know. It is curiosity."

"That's right, Susan. Curiosity. What do you think Will St. John is doing right now? Do you think he's sitting around eating Froot Loops and watching football on television? No. He is not, Susan. He's busy figuring out what happened to his colleague. Why she died such a horrible death. How she died in such a wretched way. That is what Will St. John is doing right now. I had him tailed in Boston, and they lost him. He's on the move, and he's a step ahead. He is coming for us, Susan. We have to get to him first. This time, however, we aren't going to use dragon's breath. We're going to use a good old-fashioned gun. A gun, Susan, with a silencer and an assassin. Make it happen, Susan. I want to believe you can handle the tough situations. Make me a believer."

His jowls were full of linguini, and the sound of his eating reminded Susan of Louis. It was the Y chromosome. And right now, it disgusted her.

"I'll take care of it," she replied. She gulped down her wine and ordered another. It was going to be a long night.

---

Cindy answered her phone with a breathless hello.

"Cindy?"

"*Will!*"

"You okay?" he said in a panicked voice.

"Yes, *I'm* fine. Just in the middle of my run. The question is are *you* okay? Where are you? The university is going crazy. There's rumors you were suspended…rumors about shutting down your lab. What's going on, Will?"

"Cin, take a breath. It's a long story. You running outside today?"

"Yeah, outside. This weather is killer." *Killer. It means something entirely different now.*

"Have you seen the news?"

"News? No. I haven't watched. But I've heard. That researcher of yours…they found her in her apartment… murdered. Are you in some sort of trouble? What have you done, Will?"

"I'm calling you from a burner. How far are you from Luigi's?"

"Jesus, Will. Luigi's? The Italian joint?"

*And he needed a joint.* "Yes."

"Maybe a mile, mile and a half. Why?"

"Can you meet me here?"

"Now?"

"Yes, now."

"Order me a wine spritzer."

"I'm in the back room."

Will hung up. He didn't know what he would tell her about what was going on—how much he could say without putting her in danger. It wasn't like him to be cagey. He'd always been an open book. He was quick, though, he'd think of something.

He ordered a Caesar salad, a whiskey neat and a wine spritzer. In his jacket, he had a small vial of dragon's breath. Maybe it didn't matter, but he wanted to know what was in it. Seven minutes later, Cindy sat across from him in her spandex running pants and red running jacket. Her cheeks were red from the cool wind, and she smelled like burning leaves.

"All right, out with it, Mr. Cloak and Dagger. Spill it." Cindy, as tall as Will, slid into the booth across from him. "You're blowing up the university. Everyone is looking for you, and your poor students, Will. Where have you been, and what in the hell are you doing? And, Will, I want the truth, so don't fuck with me. Besides, you plucked me off my run game. Remember that time I called you in the middle of your run? You hung up on me when you realized it was work related. You just interrupted my best running time ever."

She laughed, and Will smiled a real smile for the first time in two days.

"Yeah, but I was running a marathon. I wasn't on my daily jog around the park."

"Daily jog? Daily jog?" She swiped at Will's grin. "I was putting down a six-minute mile, bruh!" She swished down some of her wine spritzer and straightened up. She looked Will straight in the eye. "Tell me what's going on. First, the students in the lab said Eve hadn't been in and she wasn't answering her phone. Then someone said they saw her on the news. She's *dead?* But I'm guessing you knew that. What? Why? How? Allegations of research misconduct? Suspension? And now you're wanted for questioning according to our chair, and she's not your biggest fan, you know. This isn't the Title IX council. It's not like you dropped an f-bomb in class. This is serious shit, Will."

"It's a long story. I had my grandfather's big I've-been-at-Harvard-for-fifty-years party, so I was gone over the weekend, and when I returned, I found out Eve had passed." *Maintain your composure. This is your story.* "Died. Evidently, she had some issues with seizures and died after a fall. Grand mal seizure. She hit her head on the way down." *And she had fire coming from her mouth, and there was blood from her eyes and nose and smoke...* Will winced.

"Oh my God, Will." Cindy shook her head. "Have you talked with Paschal?"

Will spoke softly. "No." He hadn't thought of that. Christ. What else hadn't he considered? "She's on my list, though. I'll call her." Things were still too fresh. Too surreal.

"You're back now, though, right? You're going to come to campus, and you're going to set the record straight. Face this thing head-on. I know you. I know you didn't do any of these things they've accused you of. I want to help."

"Well, since you asked…" Will pulled the vial from his pocket. "This was near her medicine cabinet. I was hoping you could tell me what it is." *How it's made. Who might've thought this shit up. What sick fuck is behind it.*

"Umm, okay. A liquid medicine. It wasn't labeled?"

"Nope."

"Then what makes you think it was a medication?"

"It was on her bathroom counter next to a measuring spoon—the kind you use for liquid meds."

"Ah." Cindy opened the cap and was about to smell it.

"No!" Will yelled, nearly scaring it out of her hands.

"Will, calm down! I was only smelling it. I almost spilled it."

"Sorry, Cin. Just please, just please do not smell it."

"Want to tell me why the hell not?" She put the cap back on. "What do you know about this stuff?"

"I think it could be poisonous, okay?" *It's some truly horrible shit.* "I just don't want to take any chances, and if you don't mind running the analysis personally. No students on this one."

"Wait just a minute, Will St. John. I thought you said you thought this was a prescription medicine. Want to tell me what you're not telling me? Is this something dangerous? And if it is, why am I taking it into *my* lab, Will? Why not *your* lab?" She was studying him closely, he could tell.

"Honestly, I don't know. I just found it at her apartment,

and it seemed out of place. Suspicious. I've been so busy with this leish molecule and the mice…and I feel kinda odd going through her stuff, and I just think it'd be better if someone not as close to the situation analyzed it."

Her eyes narrowed at this. She wasn't buying it. "I thought you said she had a seizure and fell down the stairs."

"Just please. You're gonna have to trust me on this one. Please. Do it for me."

"Okay. I'll do it. You're a charmer, you know that? You belong in front of a basket full of cobra snakes, not across the table from a female. But you're going to have to tell me the whole truth, and soon."

Will sighed in relief. "Thanks, Cindy. Text me what you find to this number." Will slid a scrap of paper across the table.

"I'll get right on it."

"Thanks, Cindy. This means a lot. You've no idea… just thank you."

"Thank me later when I have an answer."

"Cindy?"

"Yeah?"

"You trust me, right?"

Cindy looked at him with her large brown eyes twinkling.

"Yeah, I trust you."

"Just making sure."

"Should I be worried? Are you going to be okay, Will?"

"I will be."

"If you're not, you can tell me."

*Sure, you're now in possession of a dangerous military-grade toxic weapon meant to assuage terrorists in the field, and technically you're now party to treason, but let's not go there.*

"Everything's good, I promise. Just in a tight spot for a minute, that's all."

"All right, St. John. I'll contact you as soon as I have something." She winked and walked out.

Will sat for a long time wondering if it was too risky to go home. What if someone was waiting there for him…like they'd waited for Eve. It didn't seem like the best idea, but a trip to his car might be worth it if he had any weed left in the glovebox. He gathered up Boris from under the table, thankful Boris refrained from making any noise.

"You're a champ, Boris. He checked his holster to make sure the gun was in place. In his pocket, he felt for the pearl earring.

He walked from the restaurant to a neighborhood bar for a drink where he remembered the usual bartender was quite the marijuana connoisseur. Later, out back in the alley behind the bar, he smoked the joint alone, recalling the last joint he'd smoked, he'd smoked with Eve. *Eevaleena Konisken.* He whispered her name. A harvest moon large and yellow appeared in the dimming twilight of the fall sky. Will searched it for signs of life, but a light rain began to fall, with only an occasional car passing by on the cross street. *Stay alive.* Louis had urged him to be careful. Careful was not in his nature, but he would do it this time. He'd do it for her. For Eve.

Boris lay sleeping in the pack, and Will texted Bill, "On my way." But as he was about to walk down the alley, he spotted a black sedan. *Shit!*

Will stepped back inside the bar, where the bartender was batching margaritas.

"Looks like someone is feeling better." He wiped his hands on a towel and walked toward Will.

"Yeah, thanks, I am."

"How was the—?" He nodded and smiled, revealing a gold tooth Will hadn't noticed before.

"Excellent, thank you. Wondering if you can do me one more. Is there another way out of here, maybe up the stairs to the roof and down another stairway? I've got this ex-girlfriend who's a crazy stalker, and I think she's out front—"

"Say no more, pal. Follow me."

The bartender led him to the kitchen and through the freezer to the other side where a narrow flight of stairs led to the roof.

"When you reach the roof, you can walk down the entire block if you want."

"Thanks." Will walked up the stairs to the roof and peered over the parapet, his heart beating out of his chest.

The two men got out of the sedan, their weapons in the open, and converged on the bar. They didn't look like the types that would fare well with a bartender with a gold tooth. But Will also knew they were motivated, which made them dangerous. He ran with Boris on his back, down the entire block and down a back stairwell, and kept running until he was a safe distance away. At a corner several blocks from the bar, he caught a taxi and made his way to the private airstrip to meet his uncle. Bill was waiting, hovered over the *Washington Post* and eating a meatball sub.

"You're back. I was worr—well, never mind. I see you still have the bag of piss, the cat, and the gun, too." Bill sighed and shook his head. "I'm not even gonna ask. You scientists are strange folk."

Will nodded. "It's for a good cause."

"A gun, a cat and a bag o' piss for a good cause, huh? There's a shitstorm where you're headed." Bill held up the paper. The headline read: "The Bishops Go to Washington." There was a photo of Joseph Bishop, and two smaller pics. One of Rusty Carver, the secretary of the army, and a photo of the secretary of state. "These democratic senators are out for blood. They think that boy who shot the SOS was hopped up on some meds the army gave him. The Senate committee convenes tomorrow, and sounds like it's going to be a huge battle."

Will nodded.

"Hey, you all right, Will?"

"Yeah, I'm fine. Just ready for a nap." *After running three miles with a twenty-five-pound cat on my back.*

"I'll do my best. Wind's picking up. Might be a few bumps on the way."

"Thanks for the warning."

A few bumps in Bill's book was something else in Will's entirely. Bill had been flying long enough that he no longer got reasonably concerned about turbulence. Will would be better off popping some Dramamine and throwing back a drink, which was precisely what he did. The skies were clear, but the wind was fierce, and the Gulfstream IV blew all over the place. Will nearly lost his glass a few times, and the remaining contents of the "bag of piss" was getting swished around in a way that made him feel like a pussy. He wanted to put it somewhere he knew it couldn't spill or be accidentally inhaled or ingested or anything.

His thoughts went immediately to Eve. It had only been two days, but his mind could think of nothing else. Horror fueled his nightmares and filled his waking thoughts. He needed to push those thoughts out of his brain and focus on the task at hand.

Somehow, he had to get into that hearing. Louis had sent all of the pertinent info—the locale, time, security setup, etcetera. The doors would be guarded, and if Will was going to get in, he would need to walk in with her. And in order to walk in with her, he would need to intercept her somehow. Louis had sent the exact route that her car would take, and he knew exactly where to wait. Problem was, they would be waiting for him also. Louis had made that much clear. The colonel hadn't said anything to him specifically, but he'd overheard bits and pieces of conversations and knew enough. They were coming for Will.

So the police were after him, these black ops guys were on his tail, his face was all over the news, and now he had a cat, a gun and a bag of piss in tow. He needed to get rid of the bag for sure. He looked around the plane. He finally decided that an empty liquor bottle would suffice. He'd transfer the contents of the urine bag to a bottle—specifically to a miniature Absolut bottle, the irony—and he would leave Bill at the airport, Uber into the city and wait along the route her car would take. And when he saw her, he would walk over, knock on her window, and invite himself in.

He closed his eyes for the remainder of the flight. They landed at the airport smoothly enough.

Bill walked out onto the tarmac. He frowned with concern as he lit a cigarette.

"Thought you quit."

"I did. A hundred times. But stress sometimes calls for a smoke."

"Are you stressed over something?"

Bill stared at him a minute as he exhaled through a sigh. Then he looked Will straight in the eye.

"Will, what are you doing?"

"What do you mean?"

Bill threw the cigarette to the ground and shook his head.

"I mean, you call me in the middle of the day needing the plane, and I pick you up with a bag of piss and a gun and a cat, and then I fly you all over the countryside. I don't want to know everything, but I want to know you're going to be okay. Tell me you're gonna be okay."

Will thought about his answer for a minute. About how ridiculous it sounded.

"Well, if I avoid getting shot by black ops snipers, burned alive from the inside, treason, charges of research misconduct, sexual harassment and fighting the good

fight against the military industrial complex, then…
well…I'll be okay."

Bill rolled his eyes. "Boy I always knew you were full
of it! What a load of horse shit! Whatever you're into,
just be safe."

"I will, Uncle Bill. I will."

"Should I wait here?"

"If you can, that would be great. I might be a while."

"Gotcha. I'll be here."

# CHAPTER 28

WILL CAUGHT A TAXI INTO THE CITY. IN HIS pack, in the compartment next to Boris, was a miniature vodka bottle containing the dragon's breath. The Glock 26 was in a cross-draw holster on his left side with the grip facing right; Louis had suggested this particular holster in case Will needed to draw it in an emergency. In his right pocket, he fingered the pearl earring that had belonged to Eve. Louis had given him the precise path the colonel would take from WRAIR to the Senate investigative hearing. The plan was to catch her car just before she pulled around to Capitol Hill. It wouldn't be easy, but then nothing had been. Will wasn't doing this for himself. He was doing this for Eve. And for Joseph Bishop and the others who'd suffered the adverse side effects of Larmentin. And, perhaps most important, for the sake of scientific integrity.

Public confidence in scientists was tenuous, and if he was party to falsifying data, he was part of the problem—not the solution. He wouldn't be another nail in the coffin for scientists. He would set the record straight, even if it meant losing everything, including a cure for autoimmune diseases.

He waited at the light as patiently as his nerves allowed. He was punchy, to say the least. Traffic moved at a crawl, and Boris hung his head out watching the cars moving along the street like lava. Will looked at him. "If you see something, say something."

Boris mewed.

"Good."

Boris mewed again, followed by a hiss.

Will looked over, and a cop eyed him suspiciously. Or maybe he was just being paranoid. Or maybe the cop had seen his face on the nightly news. The cop pulled up past the light and over to the side of the road.

Will decided it was best to wait on another corner. He doubled back down the block, occasionally turning around. The cop was following him. He pushed the crosswalk signal to cross the street, when a black sedan pulled in his path. Will took off at a full sprint, his mind racing and his thighs burning. Boris hissed in his ear, and he could feel the bottle in his pack jostling. His adrenaline was full on as he darted in and out of spaces between cars. The traffic jam was a welcome situation. Will was fast and felt sure the thugs from the sedan would never catch him. The cop was plump but, despite his girth, seemed to have an edge—people were stopping, making a path for the police officer.

A citizen on the sidewalk who was taking it all in tried to tackle Will as he passed, but Will took it like a hurdle. No way he was losing this race. He'd come so far, risked so much. He wasn't about to fumble at the finish line. He pulled the Glock and turned on the cop, who was no more than thirty feet away. The cop fumbled for his gun.

*Aim small, miss small.* Will aimed for the taillight of a nearby vehicle and fired. The cop took cover at the sound of the shot, but the thugs weren't far behind, and their weapons were already pulled. One of them was screaming, and they split up, aiming to flank Will and trap him, and that was precisely what they did.

Will was surrounded on both sides. But he was not alone. Trapped with him was a black Yukon, and through the window he saw *her*. *Fuck all you bitches.* Her tight blonde bun and sharklike eyes were immediately recognizable. He walked over two lanes to the Yukon and pounded his fist on the window. Nothing. He pulled the miniature Absolut bottle of dragon's breath from his pocket and held it up. The window came down.

"Let me in right now, or I'll have a goddamn motherfucking field day with the media."

The door opened, and he got in.

"What in the hell do you think you're doing? You already five deep? It's a little early, St. John. Even for you." She tapped on the security glass and instructed the driver to pull over.

"I'm not drunk, but I'm sure you know that. You

recognize this?" He held the bottle of pale golden liquid up to her face.

"I don't know what that is. Lemonade? Your mother's cologne? Piss?"

"I think you call it dragon's breath."

Her face fell, colorless, and her black eyes tossed around in their sockets as if the answer were a flying insect. "I have no idea what you're talking about." But he knew she did.

"You killed my friend!" Will's voice, fierce and full of vitriol, filled the car and more. The time following Eve's death and all he had witnessed had crystalized into a rage like he'd never known, and it poured out of him. He pounded the protective glass between the colonel and her driver. "You killed her! And for what! Why?" His voice cracked, and he sucked in his breath and pushed back against the sting of tears. "What you did…" His voice fell to a whisper. "What you did to her was horrible. Nobody deserves that. Nobody. Not even the worst among us! Not even a terrorist deserves this shit! And Eve? For what? For telling the fucking truth?" His eyes locked on hers, his breathing heavy.

She blinked rapidly for a minute before responding. Her voice was even and assured. "I didn't kill her. I—"

"That's a lie. You know what this does? You know what happens if you ingest this? Let me tell you. Your insides burn. You bleed out your eyes before they begin to smoke. Your clothes melt on your body it's so hot, and flames come from your mouth."

"I just told you I didn't kill anyone. And I am not intimidated in the least by some cockamamie story you're telling. Who do you think is going to believe you? When they find out you smoke dope and drink and sleep around with young colleagues and coeds? Who do you think they'll believe, Dr. St. John? You, or a decorated general?"

He glanced at her uniform. "You're not a general."

"Not yet, St. John. But I will be after today. I suggest you keep things to yourself. I wouldn't want the news of a cure for autoimmune disease to come from anyone but you. Do this, and your discovery will go up in a puff of smoke. Quick as it came." She snapped her fingers in the air. "Now get out of my car and take your bottle of piss with you."

Will began to laugh maniacally. This was all so surreal. After all of the planning and running around, after watching Eve die, after meeting with Louis and finding out the truth, this was not how it was going to end. He pulled the Glock 26 from its holster in a single deft movement and shoved the gun into her ribs.

"Fuck you to hell and back. I don't give a shit anymore. Now, let me tell you how this is gonna go. You are going to give me the reports you have and replace them with the truth, the reports I have in my pack. You are going to go into the committee hearing, and you are going to tell them that Larmentin is in fact a neurotoxin, that the secretary of state's condition, while unfortunate, is the direct result of side effects suffered by a soldier taking Larmentin, Joseph Bishop, and you are going to recommend suspension of the use of Larmentin until further notice."

"Crazy talk. I will say no such things."

He shoved the gun in further and shook the bottle with his other hand.

"Unless you want to open wide for a swig of this, you will do as I say." Will stuck the bottle in her face, close to her lips.

She flinched. "You wouldn't fucking dare."

"So you do know what this is, then? You know what it does." With his thumb and index finger, he started to unscrew the cap.

"Stop!" she shrieked.

"Tell me the truth!" Will continued unscrewing.

"Stop! Yes! Yes! Okay? I know what it is! Just stop… seal it back up please!"

"Start talking. Now!"

"I know what dragon's breath is. It's the horrible brain-child of DTRA intended to deter only the worst humans imaginable. It was never meant for anything other than enhanced interrogation. I've no idea who murdered your friend, but it wasn't me. I swear it!"

"If it wasn't you, who then?"

"I don't know. I don't. But it shouldn't be hard to figure out. The list of people who have access to it is very short."

"Yeah well, I'm gonna need that list. Today."

"Fine. I'll get you your list."

"Now, instruct your driver to move along."

"Where do you think you're going?"

"I'm your date to the party on Capitol Hill. I'm sure you can explain my presence there today. After all, I conducted the research."

⸺∗⸺

OUTSIDE OF THE CAPITOL BUILDING, THE MEDIA swarmed. As Colonel Savarre exited her car, they were mobbed with questions about military drug testing and accusations from others of a cover-up, demanding justice for Joey, everyone talking and screaming over one another and shoving microphones in their faces. The colonel's officer deflected by pushing his way through, cutting a path for Colonel Savarre and Will to get to the building. They walked through the doors of Capitol Hill.

The cavernous lobby was bustling with people. Security was everywhere. Will had left the gun in the car but carried Boris in his pack along with the dragon's breath, which he assured her he would use if needed. If needed, he would expose the fact that she continued to conduct research on the enhanced interrogation potion after the operation was supposed to have been shut down. Outside, he'd set fire to the false reports, and all that remained was the truth.

Once inside the hearing, Will took a spectator seat, confident that Savarre would do exactly as he'd told her, or she and her dragon's breath would appear on the front page of every newspaper and magazine, not to mention they had violated terms of the Geneva Convention by manufacturing such a horrible biological weapon. She would take her lumps and enjoy every glorious second she still got to breathe. That was more than Eve had gotten. Or Joey.

This was the one thing Will could do. He could set the record straight and feel good about having told the truth in the end. He would never recover from not having told it soon enough. He would have to guard against believing all the horrible things the colonel had said about him. He was not Clemson; he would give up his discovery to do the right thing, if that's what it took. He was not George; he was not led around on the whim of his passions, and he would not allow his shortcomings to rob him of his integrity—it was all he had left.

Will sat down near the back with the reporters and the family of Joseph Bishop. He fingered the earring in his pocket as the hearing came to order. Fifteen senators—mostly white men, with one black woman, two white women, and an Asian man—sat at microphones, adjusting and tilting, sending the occasional pop of loud static over the speakers. Behind them, their assistants sat ready with a full copy of the briefing in hand. The air in the two-story paneled room was stale, and nearby, someone was wearing musky cologne—maybe patchouli or possibly the result of close contact with incense cones. Will couldn't quite make it out, but it was reminiscent of being in Mass during the advent season.

A gavel came down with an obnoxious bang.

"This meeting will come to order." Senator McNally would lead the questioning.

An elderly gentleman, he welcomed fellow senators and announced that the Armed Services Committee would be listening to testimony from Colonel Susan Savarre of Walter Reed Army Institute of Research and one officer from the Army Criminal Investigation Command. Behind Colonel Savarre, next to Louis, sat an enormous man whose mass spilled over the chair on either side. Will recalled Louis's description of Rusty Carver, the secretary of the army.

Carver leaned in and whispered in the colonel's ear. She leaned away, expressionless. She wasn't listening. She knew what to say. Nothing was as effortless as the truth.

"Eevaleena Konisken." Will whispered her name. *I hope you're watching this wherever you are.* A sadness washed over him as he thought it.

And so it began. Senator McNally announced, "We are here today to discuss the matter of the shooting of the secretary of state in Islamabad by USMC sniper Joseph Bishop. It has been alleged by some that Sgt. Bishop suffered psychosis due to medication prescribed by the army to prevent leishmaniasis infection. Since that time, Colonel Savarre and her assembled team have delved into the allegations that Larmentin, the drug prescribed to deployed troops to prevent this disease, is dangerous and should be discontinued. It is my understanding, Colonel Savarre, based on the briefing materials, that the drug has been cleared—the research conducted resulted in no findings of neurotoxicity. Is that true?"

Rusty Carver was sweating profusely. He dabbed his forehead with a monogramed handkerchief and shifted his weight in his chair. Under his arms, two large wet spots indicated how he was feeling.

Will sat very still, listening to the drone of handwritten notes and silent vibrations of the sea of cell phones behind him. He switched to breathing through his mouth until it was dry.

Colonel Savarre sat erect and cleared her throat. "First, I'd like to thank the members of the Armed Services Committee for allowing the scientists at WRAIR to assist in this investigation. Since the time of the briefing you have in your possession, new facts have come to light. I have an updated report that reveals a different result from the one found in the report you have. If I may." Savarre passed the folder to the stenographer, who passed it to Senator McNally.

"Thank you, Colonel Savarre." McNally opened the report. He read quickly until he reached what was undoubtedly the truth, the skin on his face tightening and relaxing as his eyes trailed slowly down the page. "Have you shared this information with anyone else, Colonel Savarre?"

"No, sir. I only just received it today."

"Today?"

"Yes. Our collaborators continued to look into the matter until they discovered the truth. Larmentin is a neurotoxic drug which causes psychosis in the overwhelming majority of those who take it."

Someone in the back of the room cried out—no doubt a relative of Joey Bishop. Sobs followed and the quiet hush of reporters whispering amongst themselves.

The gavel came down.

"In light of this recent development, the Armed Services Committee will take a short recess so that copies of the updated report may be disseminated to all of the senators on our committee. Thank you."

A staffer disappeared behind the hidden door in back to make copies for distribution.

Will St. John sat up straight in his chair because he could. He'd done it. His phone lit up with a message from Amy.

> Amy: Our mice are missing and our computers have been hacked.

So that was it. He'd won one battle and lost another. Even as he sat in a chair on Capitol Hill to ensure that the truth about Larmentin was told and that Colonel Savarre was the one to do it, he lost all he'd worked for—a cure for all autoimmune diseases. He had already disclosed his findings to the patent office at the university, so they had copies and data in their files, but his research was lost. All that remained of it was on paper in files in the university technology transfer office. He would have to start all over again.

He stepped outside to make the call. Amy answered, sounding sullen.

"I'm sorry, Dr. St. John. I don't know what or who

could have done this. Our data is erased, our mice all gone. Not dead—just gone."

Will thought he heard her sniffling.

"Okay, it's okay. We know what to do, right? We know what was happening. We know what we're looking for. We can reproduce it. I know it will take time and effort, but all is not lost. Okay?"

"Okay."

"I will fix this as soon as I return."

"You don't seem as upset as I thought you would be. I had braced myself for screaming and yelling, and you just seem so calm about it all."

"I'm not happy about it, Amy, but there are worse things than this. We'll get through this. I'm in DC in a meeting. I'll call you back when it's over. Go ahead and order up some mice."

"Will do."

Will hung up and went back inside. Science had lost one and won one all in the same day.

*We did it, Eevaleena Konisken. You are not forgotten. You live on in the truth.* It happened here today, and now Joey Bishop's family knows what really happened.

Will walked outside when it was over. The day had grown cold, and pink clouds scattered an odd light across the sky as the sun was setting. The cold felt right. Everything stripped away bare, leaving only what truly was. Nothing more to hide. Will walked across the street to a pub and ordered an Irish whiskey. The bartender poured the shot glass to the rim.

"Special occasion?" The bartender wiped down the bar with an old towel and watched Will throw it back in a single gulp.

"Celebrating for a friend."

"Ah. She's not here, then?"

"No, she's not here. But she would have wanted to be."

THE END

# ACKNOWLEDGMENTS

Writing a novel is a group effort, and I couldn't have written *The November Molecule* without the help and support of so many. I would like to thank my father, to whom this novel is dedicated, for his lifelong guidance on writing and wisdom at every turn. I'd also like to thank my family for their support—Mark, Chase, Isabella, and Josie—you inspire me every day. I'd also like to thank everyone who read early versions of this manuscript and offered advice, with special thanks to my sister Anne for her careful reading, suggestions, and encouragement; and David Wright, PhD, who shared his expert knowledge of chemistry and infectious disease and assisted with the scientific details through several readings. I took creative license with the scientific details, and any technical errors are mine alone. Lastly, I'd like to thank my editor, Lisa Gilliam, for her incredible work on this project.

# ABOUT THE AUTHOR

S.F. Richards is the author of numerous short stories, essays, and nonfiction. She is a professor of writing with 20+ years of experience editing scientific research. She lives in Nashville, Tennessee, with her family and beloved dogs.